Magic

of

Mirstone

EDITED BY RICHARD FIERCE

Dragonfire Press

Print ISBN: 978-1-947329-71-3

E-Book ISBN: 978-1-947329-70-6

First Edition: 2021

CONTENTS

Introduction   i

The Darklord and the God Machine   1

My Wish, Your Cage   42

Once Upon a Crossroads   62

Hinter Wizard   82

Us Gnomes Stick Together   103

The Armor of Dusan   129

The Ring of the Feywilds   194

INTRODUCTION

Welcome back to the world of Mirstone!

This time around, we're exploring magic and magical items. From rings to god machines, there's plenty of creative stories packed into one book. I hope you enjoy reading them as much we enjoyed writing them.

Happy reading!

-Richard

The Darklord and the God Machine
A.R. Cook

"This is the part where we die, isn't it?"

Galvanius Domhnall, Dark Lord of the Violet Flame, could have done without the goblin's remark, but the two-story tall magma golem that rose from the lava pool before them did make the situation look bleak. If this was something the group could have witnessed from a safe mile away, they might have considered the golem an impressive sight, a colossus of blazing amber and imperial topaz, dotted with glistening black crystals and topped with a crown of crimson fire. Its radiance was lost on the Dark lord, goblin, swarm elemental and its summoner, as they had to crane their heads back to look up at the monstrosity that was within spitting distance. The heat alone could have melted armor and weapon, and Galvanius now understood why his tutor had instructed him to procure heat-resistance charms for himself and his band before heading into the Ash Mountains.

Galvanius glanced at his party. "Any thoughts?"

"Running away," Greez replied, which was not surprising since goblins tend to not fight things that melt the skin off their bones.

"I don't know," Millie said, eying the molten monster. She wiped a lock of her sweat-drenched auburn hair out of her face. "Maybe we can ask him where the god machine is? I bet he'd know."

"Oh, sure, he looks like the talkative type," Greez sneered. "Why don't we just ask him for the full tour?"

Swarmdog buzzed nervously, inching back from the golem. Despite being a sentient insect swarm, a black mass of fluttering wings in the vague shape of a hound, its hive mind was aware it was no match for this burning beast. Millie cooed to her elemental, reassuring it that she would not let it come to harm.

Galvanius narrowed his eyes on the golem. "We didn't come this far just to be chased all the way back down the mountain. And

Dissandra said we'd have to come up against a guardian at some point. Just wish she had said it would be a magma golem."

"What's that hag know anyway?" Greez snarled. "She probably led us up here to get a good laugh when we all die screaming in agony!"

Before either Galvanius or Greez could make a move, Millie stepped forward and waved up at the golem. "Excuse us! Mister Lava Monster, sir?"

The magma golem looked down at the small dwarf maiden below.

"Millie! What are you doing?" Galvanius snapped.

"Come on, Jimmy, it's rude to not introduce ourselves," Millie said.

Galvanius gritted his teeth. "Galvanius of the Violet Flame. Not Jimmy, not Jimbo, and definitely not—"

"Our Mighty Purple Pookums," Greez snickered. "I always liked that one."

Galvanius sighed. "I swear, if anyone else in Mirstone could control that swarm elemental…"

Millie turned her attention back to the golem. "Yes, hi! I'm Millie Merrybrew of the Caskpike, this is Dark Lord Jimmy, Greezelsnag, and my faithful Swarmdog. We're looking for a god machine? Really old, hasn't been seen since the Dawn of the Gods. Have you seen anything like that around here?" She beamed a big, friendly smile.

The golem opened its mouth and spewed forth a stream of lava directly at Millie.

Millie darted back, narrowly dodging the downpour, and Swarmdog rushed to her in a swirling horde of buzzing, sweeping her off her feet and whisking her to safety behind a tall stalagmite farther back in the cavern. Galvanius and Greez also retreated for cover behind a cluster of rock formations, as the golem spat a glob of scorching ooze in their direction.

"That wasn't very nice of him," Millie huffed. "Thank you, Swarmy."

The swarm elemental, reforming its canine shape, gave her a whirring sort of bark.

"Greez, we could use frost orbs right about now," Galvanius said.

The goblin snorted, his two porcine ears twitching. "I'd need about fifty of those to even slow down that thing, and I'm a bit short." He quickly cast a glare at Galvanius. "On alchemy orbs. No height jokes."

"Joking isn't on my mind." Galvanius rummaged through his pack and withdrew a canteen, a small marble bowl and a birchwood spoon.

Greez curled his lip. "You really think this is a good time to consult the soup witch?"

The Dark lord glanced over at the golem, who had not left the confines of its lava pool. It simply stared in their direction menacingly. "It looks like it can't advance any further. As long as we're out of range of its attacks, we should be fine."

"Maybe we could just—" Millie started.

"You tried diplomacy, Millie. We need a more robust way to handle this thing, and Dissandra knows her magical monsters." He uncorked the canteen and poured a small amount of its contents—tomato bisque—into the bowl. He murmured the words "Ab imo tenebris" while stirring the soup and tapped the spoon on the edge of the bowl three times. After a beat, the soup began to gurgle and bubble, and a milky mist blossomed the surface, forming the vague impression of a female face.

An exasperated sigh came from the summoned visage. "Good gods, Galvanius, can you go an hour without needing to call me?"

"I could, Dissandra, if you'd tell me how we're supposed to deal with this golem!"

"Oh, that." The face, pale and gaunt as a week-old corpse, smirked. "I thought you could at the very least handle *that*. Any

Dark lord worth his caliber—"

Galvanius clenched his teeth. "Before we all roast to death, please!"

Dissandra rolled her eyes. "Fine. Golems are created with one sole purpose by their masters—in this case, a guardian. However, if a golem's master is long gone—and in this case, I'm betting his creator's been dead for quite some time—the golem's resolve to its purpose gradually weakens. Appeal to its baser instincts. Greed, desires, you get the idea."

"Of course!" Millie said cheerfully. "Poor guy's been stuck in these awful mountains for so long. And does anyone ask him how he's been doing? What his dreams and aspirations are? Of course not." She climbed up the stalagmite until she was near the top, which put her closer to the golem's eye level. "Hey Mr. Golem! We'd like to help you, if you'll let us!"

The golem tilted its head to the side.

"This must be a horrible way to live, stuck in that lava pool with nowhere to go. If you show us where the god machine is, then we could use it to free you!"

"We can?" Galvanius asked in a low voice.

"You said the god machine can make you a god, right?" Millie said. "So, once you're a god, you can do anything."

Galvanius peaked out from his cover, noting that the golem had not attacked again, and it looked docile for the moment. He took a deep breath and stepped out into view. "That's right! By my word as a Dark lord, my first act as a new god will be to grant you any wish you desire, as reward for your sworn allegiance to me."

The golem's eyes narrowed. It opened its glowing, hellfire maw again and said, "That's a rather magnanimous proposition, although how feasible your avowal may be is a matter of contention."

Everyone silently gawked.

The golem eyed the group. "What? Did you postulate because I am an amorphous automaton, that I am incapable of judicious repartee?"

Galvanius raised his eyebrows. "I…what?"

The golem let out a long, steamy sigh. "You thought that because I'm a golem, I'm stupid?"

"What? No!" Galvanius chuckled nervously. "After all, if I thought you were stupid, I wouldn't have made you my offer. We're rational men, you and I. Speaking of which, could I reason with you to turn down the heat? It's difficult to breathe in here for mere mortals, you know."

The golem lumbered out of the lava pool, but as he walked, the magma receded from his body, causing him to shrink until he was about six feet tall. A casing of ashen stone solidified over him, with hints of veins glowing through his igneous skin. The top of the pool also solidified into stone, causing the heat of the cavern to cool substantially.

"Dark lords consider themselves reasonable nowadays, do they?" The golem snickered. "You are unlike any lord I've ever seen, but I suppose time changes things. I'm Krag." He extended a huge stone hand towards Galvanius. The Dark lord shook his hand but winced as the golem's skin was hot enough for him to feel through his glove.

"And I'm Millie!" the dwarf announced as she slid down from her stalagmite and offered her tiny hand to shake. Whether or not Krag's touch was hot to her, Millie did not let on as she shook his finger with a genuine, warm smile.

Krag couldn't help but smile back at the dwarf's gregariousness. "It's been some time since I've seen treasure hunters come through here. Most don't get through the mountains."

"It helps to have a goblin who knows how to avoid the thickest hordes of monsters. And I have a swarm elemental that can scout ahead in many directions, undetected." Galvanius paused, wondering how much he should tell this golem. Just because this monster was eloquent did not mean it was trustworthy.

Krag scratched his chin, eying the group. "Hmm…a goblin, a

dwarf, a swarm elemental, and a…" He leaned closer to Galvanius, trying to see into the Dark lord's ornate helmet. All of Galvanius's armor was tinged royal purple, trimmed in bronze, and his helmet had a visor designed in a skeletal visage, only allowing his pale gray eyes to be seen. The golem murmured, puzzling. "The technique of flame-bluing on your armor is atypical for the humans of this region. And the build of it is too rudimentary to have been smithed by elven hand. You are…an exile? From the outskirts of Mirstone?"

"That's one way of putting it. Let's leave it at that." Galvanius crossed his arms. "I take it my proposition appeals to you? You can show us where the god machine is?"

"Ah, the god machine, so you mentioned," Krag said. He tapped his finger on his lower lip in thought. "I recall there being various oddities in the treasury, but my memories of them are vague."

Greez's beady eyes glistened with child-like intrigue. His voice dripped with honey sweetness. "Treasury, you say? And where would this treasury be, hmm hmm hmmmmmm?"

Krag turned towards the stone pool. He lifted a hand, which glowed a deep, blood red. The pool responded, heating with the same crimson red, and the stone slowly receded, molding like clay into a set of stairs leading down to the floor of the pool. At the base of the stairs, the molten stone formed an arched doorway, beyond it leading into a dark tunnel.

"If you'd like, you can see if your machine is in there," Krag said. "Follow me."

"Well," Millie mused as she and the others followed the golem down the stone steps. "You're awfully polite for a guardian."

"I confess, no one who has faced me has ever attempted to engage me in conversation, so this is refreshing," Krag replied. "And the thought of being able to ask a god for my one true wish is enticing."

"Oooooh, what's your one true wish?" Millie asked.

"Let's see if your device is even here. I'd rather not get my hopes up," said Krag.

Greez snorted. "You and me both, buddy."

As they entered the tunnel, the walls ignited with orange veins, lighting the way. Now the troupe could see that the tunnel led deep into the mountain, far enough that they could not see the end. Galvanius understood why no one had ever located the god machine before; if it was indeed here, it was a passageway no mortal could have feasibly accessed without Krag's permission. Previous seekers could have been exploring every crevice, crag and cranny of the Ash Mountains for ages, for naught.

"How does a goblin find himself in the company of a dwarf and a…an outlander?" Krag inquired.

Greez chuckled. "You probably only know about the goblins who stay here in the mountains all their lives. Bloody dumb lot, if you ask me. We smart goblins know there's a lot more to be gained if you join the union."

"The union?"

"The Underlings Union. The U.U. finds you work, matches you up with overlords, wizards, lich kings, those types. When Jimmy here was looking for a goblin scout—"

"Galvanius! Not Jimmy!"

"—I got matched up with his Imperial Purple-ness," Greez said with a snicker.

"Ah." Krag turned his glance to Mille. "And you and your swarm elemental? How did you come to be here?"

Millie giggled. "Are you kidding? Jimmy and I go way back. We've known each other since we were kids. He's a hoot!"

Galvanius tightened his lips and let out a long exhale through his nose. "All right, enough. How deep does this tunnel go? If we need to move the god machine from the treasury, we need to figure out how we're going to lug it out of here."

"It's not far," Krag said. "But tell me what this 'god machine' is. I don't recall anyone else searching for it here—they usually just want the Treasure of Dirge."

Greez's eyes glistened at the word "treasure." He chuckled to himself, his imagination already teasing him with the prospect of gold, jewels and priceless artifacts.

"Oh, it's an amazing story! Tell him, Ji—I mean, Gal," Millie said, catching herself.

Galvanius glared at her— "Gal" was arguably worse than Jim. "Fine. Some ancient texts from the archives in Laewaes described a mechanism from the Dawn of the Gods, a device that brought them from the celestial realm to our world. Most historians described it as a gods' chariot of sorts, a heavenly transport. But there are those who say the gods didn't come from another realm to our world—they came *from* our world. The god machine was a device that had the power to make a mortal a god. Naturally, such a device was deemed too dangerous by the elders of all clans and houses, and it was thrown into the Mouth of CharMaw."

"Ah, yes, CharMaw…the Magma Blood-Mother," Krag sighed, whether in fondness or sadness, it was difficult to tell. "Anything thrown into that volcano would surely be destroyed."

Galvanius held up an index finger. "Or so the elders would have us believe. But you mentioned the Treasure of Dirge. Would the name Tyranimus Dirge mean anything to you?"

Krag's eyes widened in recognition. "I was summoned from the lava at his behest."

"I figured as much," Galvanius said smugly. "It just so happens that our good friend Dirge was the same bloke commissioned by the Dwarven King to stash away a part of his royal treasure here in the Ash Mountains during the war between the dwarves and the elves, in case things went awry and the elves invaded Anghor. While excavating, Dirge stumbled upon an ancient machine unlike any he'd ever seen, in a cave underneath the Mouth of CharMaw. He couldn't activate the machine himself, but he kept it with the treasury in hopes he could discover its secret someday. He died before ever doing so."

"And how did you come to learn this alternate history of the god machine?"

"Soup," Greez snickered.

Krag looked sideways at the goblin. "Soup?"

"No, not the soup itself. He means the lady who lives in the soup," Millie said.

"I have a tutor, Lady Dissandra," Galvanius explained. "She's a master of the midnight arts and knows more about the ancient texts than anyone. But she's in another realm, and the only way I can access her is to cast a scrying spell with…soup."

Krag nodded in understanding, but then the corner of his lips twisted. "Why soup?"

"She says she likes the smell."

"Ah."

The conversation had helped the time pass, as the tunnel widened into a large, dark space. Krag put his hand against the wall, and ripples of firelight etched into the stone surface. Along the walls, fire crystals blazed to life in a warm, topaz glow. In a few seconds, the space was illuminated, revealing an expansive rounded cave hollowed out to shape a 100-foot high dome. It would have been a chamber worthy of a dragon's trove of centuries-amassed treasure.

However, it was empty.

Although, not quite—a few copper coins were scattered here and there, a few gemstones glistened on the floor, and there was a set of cast-iron pans and a tea kettle stacked on what appeared to be a rectangular brick oven.

"What…am I missing here?" Galvanius asked. "Where are we?"

"The Treasure of Dirge," Krag said as if it were obvious.

Greez's eye twitched as if he was having the onset of a mental breakdown.

"Uh, Sir Krag," Millie spoke up, "a treasure should have

treasure in it, right?"

Krag glanced around the room as if finally seeing the barrenness. "Oh. Yes, well…it has been a long time, and there are creatures around here good at slipping through cracks and tunneling through rock." He gestured upwards, and the group could now see several holes in the ceiling and along the cave wall. "Rock wyrms, stone scourges, small scavengers who grab a handful of coins at a time, but over the centuries, they must've subtracted more than I thought…"

A high-pitched scream escaped Greez as if it were his death cry. He collapsed, banging his fists on the floor. "I'm done, I'm done! We almost died a hundred times over, for nothing! I'm reporting this to the union!"

Swarmdog fetched a gold coin lying on the cave floor and dropped it next to Greez. The goblin sighed, plopping his head on the ground. "Good boy," he muttered.

Galvanius scanned the room again, his heart dropping. "I don't understand. Are there no more chambers? I was so sure it would be here…"

Millie shrugged. She looked at the brick oven. "Odd thing to have in a treasury. Maybe there were people guarding the treasure, and they built this oven so they could eat warm food. Which doesn't sound like a half-bad idea." She removed the pack she was carrying and rummaged around in it. "I still have flour and water. If we can light the oven, I can make us biscuits."

"If you need to light it, I would be more than happy to accommodate," Krag said. He lifted a finger and the tip ignited with a small tangerine blaze.

Galvanius groaned. "I don't want biscuits! If you would all get your brains out of your stomachs, we need to keep looking—"

Millie interrupted him as she yanked open the metal door over the oven's mouth. A flurry of ash sprang up, and she coughed as she swatted the debris away from her face. "Oh. There's something in here."

She struggled to pull out something covered in soot. When she finally did, it was an object four feet in length, shaped like a triangular cylinder, with each side of the triangle a foot wide. As she dusted the soot away, she revealed it was made of a lustrous green-gold metal, with strange markings all along its sides. On one end was an engraving of two hands, palms facing outward, each palm possessing an eye. The other end of the cylinder depicted a curled ram horn, and it encircled a full moon.

"The horn of Thealxethor!" Mille said, noting the horn-moon icon. "Keeper of Dreams! That's one of Rachdale's oldest stories. I always loved that one."

Galvanius took the cylinder from Millie, although it was heavier than he expected, and the weight nearly threw him off balance. "And the other end, that's the symbol of Libraya Nor, the Eyes of Truth and Deceit. One of the oldest gods in recorded history. This…this must be a clue! There must be something inside to direct us to the god machine…" He inspected the cylinder from top to bottom for a latch, or lock, or any means of opening it, but there was none. He grunted in frustration. "The clue must be in the engravings. If I can decipher it—"

Krag cleared his throat. "I should probably tell you—"

"If the icon of Thealxethor is on here, then it must have been engraved by dwarven metalworkers, although none of the glyphs on the sides look particularly—"

"Uh, Jimmy?" Mille nudged his elbow roughly.

Galvanius did not look at her as he said curtly, "Can you not bother me while I'm working?"

"I think something's wrong with Greez."

Galvanius tore his eyes away from the cylinder long enough to see that Greez was crumpled on the ground, his hands over his ears. His face was scrunched in pain.

"Would someone do something about that horrid whistle??" he cried.

Galvanius paused, straining to listen for any such noise in the cave. "What's he talking about? What whistle?"

Krag sighed, exasperated. "As I was trying to tell you, it would seem that the cylinder was walled up inside that stove because it is emitting a sound at a frequency that is only heard by sensitive goblin ears. In fact, I recall now what happened when Dirge first summoned me…he commanded me to flood the access tunnel with lava as he was escaping a rather nasty horde."

"A horde of what?"

"Goblins. And orcs. And goristros. It must be some alarm spell placed on the cylinder that attracts them."

A ripple of terror crawled up Galvanius's spine. "Just how far away can monsters hear this sound?"

Krag scratched his cheek. "We're pretty deep in the mountain, but the acoustics are good and can carry the sound…Oh, if you're asking if any nearby creatures would have heard it by now, oh yes, definitely."

Galvanius strained to keep his wits amidst his panic. "And I assume there has to be a way out of this cave other than the one tunnel you brought us through, right?"

The golem crinkled the corner of his lips. "You know what they say when you assume…"

Galvanius dropped the cylinder, doing the only thing he could think to do. He pulled out his canteen of soup—although he realized he left his bowl and spoon back in the other cavern. He snagged the tea kettle off the oven, poured soup into it, and then desperately banged his knuckle on the kettle while reciting the scrying spell as quickly as possible.

Dissandra's face appeared within the belly of the teapot, although it was fuzzier than usual as the spell had been done hastily. "Stop that banging, Galvanius! You'll rupture my eardrums! Now what's the problem?"

"I'm about to be attacked by goblins, I'm trapped in a cave with only one way out, and I don't want to die!"

Dissandra raised an eyebrow at him. "You're really bad at this, aren't you?" She squinted her eyes as if she had a headache. "Let me guess. You found the god machine?"

"I found this triangle prism with glyphs on it, with the symbols of Libraya Nor and Thealxethor on each end, but right now I need—"

"And you triggered an alarm ward that makes it emit a sound that infuriates goblins?"

"Uh…yes?"

"And now your only exit has a throng of beasts coming through it because you were dumb enough to not check for any wards before you grabbed that thing?"

Galvanius stared blankly at her. "Millie grabbed it first."

"Well, there's good news and bad news. The good news is, congratulations! You found what you were looking for. The bad news is, you're all about to be pulverized. Good luck." Her face flickered out of sight, leaving a wash of blood-red in the bottom of the kettle.

While her declaration initially seemed useless, it did have one helpful effect. Galvanius looked at the green-gold cylinder lying beside him, and a new resolve steeled itself in his veins. *This, THIS thing is the god machine…I found the god machine! I am not about to die now, not when I've found what I've been looking for all these years!*

A soft echo of a hundred tiny claws scratching against stone whispered from the tunnel, along with what sounded like a chorus of infuriated goats.

Millie's eyes grew wide. "Jimmy, I think we're about to have a whole lot of pissed-off guests who want to eat our faces."

Swarmdog whined, his form blurring as his insects began to fly into a frenzy.

Galvanius hefted the cylinder in his arms and turned to Krag. "Can't you fill that tunnel with lava to incinerate them, like you said you did before?"

Krag shook his head. "I need to be within close proximity of the lava pool to control it. I'm too far away from it here. And I can't detect any lava directly beneath this room."

"And our only way out is blocked?"

Millie glanced around the cave. "No, I don't think so." She pointed straight up to the ceiling. There was one tunnel above them that looked wide enough for them all to fit through, a shaft that possessed a pinpoint of light at the other end.

Galvanius's dread lightened. "There's light up there. That tunnel might take us up to the surface…but none of us have any rope long enough to go all the way up. How would we reach it?"

"The better question is, HOW ARE YOU GOING TO TURN OFF THAT THING???" Greez shouted, still clutching his ears and writhing on the floor.

Krag looked up the ceiling shaft, and then down at himself. "I believe, if I have done my calculations correctly, I may have a solution. I would just need a few moments."

Galvanius turned to Millie. "Millie, can Swarmdog give us some time?"

Millie's sweet smile shifted to a wry grin. She turned to her hive-hound. "Swarmy…go for the eyes."

Just as a cluster of gray-skinned, red-eyed goblins broke through the entrance to the room, Swarmdog dissipated into a shapeless blur and swarmed the intruders' faces, tiny bugs biting at eyes and ears. The buzzing was so ferociously loud that it drowned out the yelps of dismay and pain from the creatures.

Krag picked up Galvanius under one arm, Millie under the other, and grabbed Greez by the waist and held him in his hand. He positioned himself directly under the shaft in the ceiling.

"I don't suppose you plan to jump?" Galvanius asked. He had no idea how well golems could jump.

"Not quite."

Suddenly, Krag became quite warm. When Galvanius looked down at Krag's legs, he could see them heating up rapidly, glowing red to orange to golden yellow. The fieriness spread up the legs towards Krag's abdomen, and Galvanius could feel the heat blazing through his armor despite his heat-resistance charm.

"Krag, what are you—" Before Galvanius could finish, he was suddenly shot up, as if ejected by catapult, towards the ceiling. He watched as Krag's legs burst into a column of lava, sending them all skyward with the force of an erupting volcano. Their ascent was so fast that it took mere seconds for them to go through the ceiling, up the shaft, and break into the misty daylight at the surface of the mountainside. There was a momentary suspension of them being hurtled through the air, before coming to a heavy landing. Everyone rolled for several feet, but the ground was level enough that they each came to a stop rather than continue barreling down the mountain.

"Swarmy? Swarmy!" Millie got to her feet, despite having fresh cuts and bruises from the landing, and ran back over to where they had all exited the shaft. She continued to call for her pet while Galvanius and Greez rolled onto their backs and sat up, wincing and groaning. Galvanius still had the god machine in his arms, and he let out a sigh of relief. "At least it's still in one piece," he said.

"Unlike the rockhead," Greez replied, looking over at Krag. Or what was left of him. Head, shoulders, arms, and chest were still there, but anything below was gone. Traces of hot lava dripped from the end of what appeared to be his ribcage, but it quickly cooled and solidified into stone.

Galvanius got up and dashed over to the golem. "Krag! Good gods, are you all right?"

Krag wheezed but gave Galvanius a strained smile. "Eh, it's all just rock. More where that came from. Besides, you can fix it when you get that machine working."

Greez flattened his ears against his head and pressed his hands over them. "It's still making that noise! Shut it off!"

Oh great, more monsters will be here any second! And now we're exposed on the mountainside! Galvanius thought. He ran over to Millie, grabbing her arm. "Millie, we have to go!"

"No! Swarmy is still down there!" she cried, pulling against his grip.

"He's an elemental, he'll be fine!"

"But what about Krag? He has no legs!"

"He's a bloody rock! Who cares?? Let's go!"

Millie wrenched her arm from his grasp and squared her shoulders. She crossed her arms and gave Galvanius a glare severe enough to turn shadows white with fear. "James Domhnall, you are a Dark lord. Which means you are responsible for your crew. Which means you do NOT run away like a coward, leaving any of us behind. That includes Krag. He got us away from the ash goblins, that makes him one of us now. So STOP thinking about only yourself and start being a leader!"

Galvanius could not figure out, for the life of him, how this small, curly-haired dwarven girl could rattle him to his core. But worse than that, she was right. Before he could reply, a sharp banging distracted him. He looked over to see Greez beating a goblin-sized smithing hammer on the god machine with wild abandon.

"Will—this—bloody—thing—shut—off??" He screamed in time to each blow with the hammer.

"Greez!!" Galvanius ran over and grabbed the goblin to yank him away. "If you break that machine, so help me gods—" He paused, blanching as he looked over to the ridge near where they stood, and saw dozens of gray, grimy clawed hands reaching from beyond the edge, scrambling to climb up.

Greez made one more wild swing with the hammer, and it hit squarely on the left eye of the symbol of Libraya Nor. The eye sunk into the machine, and a rusty, gritty whirring began to come from the cylinder.

The top edge of the cylinder cracked open slowly. From within, six copper rods, like the spines from a great lionfish, extended from the gap. When they reached about five feet in length, an iridescent sheen radiated from between the spines, the light creating a dancing rainbow effect across it like soap film. There was something cosmic, hypnotic about the swirling colors, and deep from within the cylinder came a sound, like a tinkling of bells or glass. As the ash goblins poured up over the ridge and advanced on the group, they came to a halt at the sight of the brilliant display of colors. They stared, entranced, at the mechanical fan of light and sound, and Greez ceased his frantic ravings to stare dumbfounded at it. Even Galvanius found himself oddly captivated by it, unable to move.

What happened next seemed to defy all mechanical physics.

The crack of the cylinder opened wider, and a copper carapace emerged from under the shimmering spinal fin. The carapace curled like a hook, and as it rose into the air, it revealed a thin body adorned with six thoracic legs, reminiscent of a dragonfly, but at the end of each leg was a robotic humanoid hand. The head was an electrum-plated pyramid, the apex pointed outward like a beak, with more runic engravings decorating its bright yellow sides. Four transparent, elliptical wings unfolded from its back, shining with the same polychromatic glassiness as the spinal fin. Finally, at the end of the long, skinny abdomen, four black-green tentacles with soft, downy cilia unfurled. The bizarre insectoid machine hovered in the air, free of its impossible small cocoon—a twenty-foot leviathan of reddish copper, electrum and adamantine.

"Oooh, how pretty!" Millie cooed, while everyone else was too thunderstruck to speak.

The collective awe was broken as a tall, growling orc leaped up from the ridge and landed among the throng of goblins. His tusks curled up from his lips in a permanent snarl, his hair matted in locks of ash and dirt, his skin covered in hardened gray and brown clay-like armor. He paused upon seeing the god machine, but rather than marvel, he flew into an unbridled rage. In his hand, he carried a stone club, and he raised it over his head as he came charging at the divine device.

Galvanius drew his sword from its sheath and plowed forward at the oncoming orc. He brought his sword up to block the orc's swing, and while he stopped the club's trajectory, the orc's strength forced Galvanius down on one knee, his entire body rattling inside his armor. The orc smiled wickedly, bringing his club up once again to bring down on Galvanius's head.

Before he could, a thick swarm of stingers and pinchers smacked into the orc like a battering ram. The orc reeled back, cursing, flailing to free himself from the blinding mass of insects that were sneaking between the cracks of his clay casing to eat at his skin.

"Swarmy!" Millie cried joyfully.

That's our cue to leave, Galvanius thought. He sheathed his sword and turned to the god machine, racking his brain about what he was supposed to do with it now—put it back in its cocoon so he could carry it? Command it to follow him? Would it even take his commands? The machine hovered there, as if waiting for something, or maybe it was oblivious to everything around it.

"Uh, Jim…" Greez was slowly breaking free of the trance. "I think…we should go…"

Just as Greez was coming to, so were the other goblins. And they didn't look happy.

Galvanius felt something wrap tightly around his waist. He looked down and saw that one of the god machine's tentacles embraced him. He was slowly being lifted into the air as the machine began to ascend. The machine also grabbed hold of Millie, Krag and Greez, the last of which squealed and struggled wildly against his captor.

"Calm yourself," said Krag, who dangled by his arm in the machine's clutch.

"Calm myself??? I'm being hijacked by a giant metal bug!!" Greez cried.

Millie patted the metallic tentacle holding her. "I think it's helping us escape."

The ash goblins rushed them, but the god machine suddenly took off with an abrupt speed straight into the air, escaping the onslaught of claws, teeth and clubs. Swarmdog ceased his assault on the orc and flew off after the god machine. The monsters below screamed and cursed after them as the troupe flew off, away from the Ash Mountains and towards the vast plains that led to the Blackridge Sea.

*

Millie tilted her head to the side, her hands on her hips. "I take it you haven't figured out how to talk to it yet?"

It was nearly dusk, hours since the troupe had fled their adversaries, and they had taken refuge in a dilapidated cottage where the god machine had, for whatever reason, chosen to deposit them. There was not much to the property, save an ancient oak tree, a stone well, and a patch of dirt that might have once been a vegetable garden. Cobwebs filled every corner of the dusty cottage, and given the disorder of the place—broken plates on the floor, a single stray boot, old oil lamps on crudely built tables— whoever lived here before must have left in a hurry. The troupe was able to make themselves comfortable, with Krag lying near a bookshelf where he read one of its ragged books, Greez falling asleep on the quilt-covered bed, Millie taking a bucket to the well so she could wash up, and Swarmdog romping through the grass like a happy pup. Galvanius, meanwhile, had pulled the god machine inside by one of its tentacles—a bit like pulling along a large alien balloon—and puzzled over it for hours.

The dwarf, scrubbed clean, shook out her wet hair. "Why don't you take a break, Jimmy? I think we've all been through enough today. Doesn't look like the god machine's going anywhere."

Galvanius shook his head. "I am so close, Millie! I have it, right here! But it doesn't seem to respond to any verbal commands. I don't see any buttons, or levers, or cranks. I can't decipher these markings on its head. It's insulting to have the god machine and not know how to make it work!"

Millie frowned. "Say you figure it out. This thing grants you godhood. Then what?"

"What do you mean, 'then what'? Then I'm a god! Why do I need to think beyond that?"

The dwarf sighed, pulling a chair over, and sat down. "Do you remember how we met?"

Galvanius furrowed his brow at the random question. "I…believe so? Halesford, right?"

"The little well near the square. The one people would throw coins into, for good luck." She smiles, resting her chin in her hand. "You and I just talked and talked at that well for hours, while my father sold his brew to the local taverns."

"I know. What of it?"

Mille's smile waned, and she sighed. "It seemed like you used to be happy with your life back then. I can't figure out when you decided anything less than godhood wasn't good enough. Why did you become a Dark lord bent on being more powerful than anyone? What was so awful about being sweet little Jimmy?"

The god machine shuddered with a grinding moan. Its tentacles coiled into themselves and the machine hit the floor, causing the whole cottage to shake on impact. The spinal fin and dragonfly wings retracted into the carapace, and the whole machine started to tremble fiercely. The pyramid head was now two feet above Galvanius, and it was rotating in circles like a drill.

"What happened?" The Dark lord stood in front of the machine, frantically looking it over. "Why did it do that? Is it breaking?"

"It's going to explode!" shouted Greez, who scrambled under the bed for cover.

The six hands of the machine suddenly latched onto Galvanius, pinning his arms to his sides. He gasped as the machine hoisted him off his feet, bringing his face directly eye level with the pyramid head. The pyramid split apart at the edges, opening like a blossom, and inside was…a mirror? That's what Galvanius thought at first, for he was looking into a reflective surface that showed him the skeletal facade of his helmet. As he looked harder, however, he could see there were features of that chrome surface— depressions for eyes, a nose, a mouth, and with his visor reflected on it, it was as if the skull of Death was looking back at him.

"Wait, wait!!" Millie cried, tugging at one of the lower arms of the machine. "Don't hurt him! He's a good man! He may be a Dark lord now, but he wasn't always! Please, see the good in him! See the good I always saw! Put him down and don't hurt him!"

The machine paused as if considering the dwarf's pleas. Galvanius felt a surge of either terror or exuberance, perhaps both. He felt detached from himself, as if part of him was melded with this mechanical deity, as if he had become more than himself. The feeling was less than a second, however, as the machine released him, and the Dark lord clattered to the floor. Just as suddenly, the pyramid head snapped shut and fell from the body of the machine, landing at Galvanius's feet. The rest of the body jerked back to life, the wings extending and fluttering in a blur, the tentacles uncoiling, and the spinal fin unfurling. There was only a moment to take one last look at the mech marvel before it shot straight through the roof and disappeared from sight.

A long time of silence followed, as everyone stared open-mouthed at the hole in the roof.

Greez poked his head out from under the bed. "What…was…that...about?" he squeaked.

Millie walked over to the door and looked outside, scanning the sky. "It's gone."

"How peculiar," Krag said, walking over to the door on his hands. "I wonder where it plans to go now?"

The Dark lord stood up, fury burning throughout his being. "Are you kidding me?? It's just gone?? After all that work, after all that searching and fighting and nearly dying, it vanishes?" He let out a long, tormented scream before collapsing back on the floor. "The gods are wicked! They stole my glory away from me! This is their doing!!"

"Oh, stop being such a drama lord." Millie returned and picked up the pyramid, looking it over. "I wonder why it left its head. Did it say anything to you, Jim?"

"No! It just…I don't know! I thought it was going to work! I thought we were becoming one, but…" He rose again and snatched the pyramid from Millie. It was just large enough to fit a human head inside, but it was a great deal heavier. In his anger, he lobbed the pyramid across the room, and it collided with the bookshelf, knocking it over.

Millie retrieved the pyramid and held it with all the tenderness as one holds a baby. "Now don't be so violent. Obviously, it left its head behind for…some reason." She ran her fingers over the runic engravings. "Maybe it was trying to tell us something."

"I'm done, Millie. I'm done with that horrid thing. I'm done with the lot of it." Defeated, Galvanius sat down in the chair and held his head in his hands.

Krag came over and patted Galvanius on the knee. "Well, at least you have your health. And all your body." He looked down at himself, silently lamenting the sacrifice of his middle and legs. "Perhaps you can consult your soothsayer in the soup…your soup-sayer…heh, that's a rather good one."

Galvanius didn't reply. He arose, his body slumped in despair, dragged his feet over to the bed, and collapsed on it. Greez squeezed himself out from under the bed, snorting in anger that his sleeping spot had been usurped, but he didn't argue.

"Does he even sleep with his armor on?" Krag asked Millie.

Millie sighed. "He has his reasons. The armor makes him feel…strong, I guess. Well, how does everyone feel about dinner? 'Fraid it'll just be biscuits…"

*

The morning sunlight streamed through the windows and the hole in the roof, but a cheery dawn meant little to Galvanius, especially since every part of him ached from the previous day's adventure and he wanted to stay prostrated in bed. What eventually made him lift his head, however, was a strange melody coming from the kitchen of the cottage.

He knew what Millie's happy humming sounded like; this was not it. The soft song he heard was like a gentle rain falling on a meadow, or dandelion seeds on the breeze. The scents of cooking meat and warm bread wafted from the kitchen in the adjoining room. Galvanius rolled out of bed and crept to the kitchen door, because although he doubted an enemy would be cooking breakfast rather than slaughtering him, he knew fairy folk could roam these lands and he was in no mood for mischief.

In the kitchen, Millie, Krag, and Greez were all eating fried eggs, bread and fruit, while Swarmdog was buzzing around a pile of fruit rinds in the corner. At the stove stood a small girl who could not have been more than seven years old. Her skin was the color of earth, her long hair the color of sea foam that cascaded to her ankles. She wore an off-white tunic that covered her to her knees but little else, not even shoes. Tiny buds of white, pink and yellow crocuses were woven into her hair, and when she turned to look at Galvanius with her large, storm-gray eyes, she smiled. She brought him a plate of eggs, not saying a word, and then went back to cooking.

Galvanius lowered his voice, sharp with distrust. "Millie, who is this girl?"

Millie swallowed her mouthful of bread. "Isn't she sweet? She was making breakfast when I woke up. You were still out cold, so I didn't want to disturb you."

"Where did she, and all this food, come from?"

The dwarf shrugged. "I fell asleep in here last night after dinner, and I had the pyramid with me, and when I woke up this morning, there's the pyramid—" She pointed over to the area by the stove where the pyramid laid, now broken apart in four triangle pieces and a square on the floor, "—and there's the girl."

Galvanius went over to the pieces, noting how their engravings were now gone. Whatever mirror-essence had been inside was gone as well. He looked at the girl again, who gave him another smile. There was something oddly familiar about her…

"Did you…come out of here?" Galvanius asked the girl, pointing to the pieces. The girl cocked her head at him, and then went back to her wordless singing.

The Dark lord picked up the pieces, searching for clues. "Krag, you guarded this thing. What did it do? Why is this girl here?"

Krag, who rested against the wall, rested his chin in his hand.

"She does seem a tad unusual. Hasn't spoken a word to any of us. Just made us breakfast and hasn't eaten a bite herself. Perhaps she's of the Feywilds?"

"That doesn't make any sense. The god machine was supposed to make me a god, not hatch some fairy child!"

"I was a guardian. No one ever told me specifics about the position." Krag took a bite of egg, but a few seconds after swallowing it, it slid through his ribcage and splatted on the floor beneath him. He sighed. "Oh, right. I don't have a stomach anymore. Not that I ever ate anything other than lava and rock, but actual food was a nice change."

The girl stared at Krag, her eyes sorrowful. She came over to him, her fingers feeling along where his chest ended. She gently placed her hands on him and closed her eyes. From her fingers, green roots began to grow, entwining Krag's torso, and the roots gradually grew thicker, stronger, changing into wood and bark as it grew down. It took the shape of sturdy legs, with vines and flowers blossoming along the bark, and in a minute's time, Krag had a fully formed body, his arboreal lower half perfectly blended into his igneous top half.

The golem was speechless, and carefully pushed himself up onto his new feet. He wobbled at first, but found he was in control of the woody appendages. "My word! I have legs again! And the wisteria's a nice touch."

The girl beamed at his compliments of her work.

Galvanius blinked in disbelief. "What…how did she do that? Even fairy folk need to use an incantation or a channeling instrument to do a spell like that. It would at least exhaust them for a while. She did that with almost no effort!"

Millie suddenly sat up straight, a look of realization blooming on her face. "Jimmy! I think the god machine did exactly what you said. It didn't make *you* a god. It *made* you a *god*." She glanced at the child. "Or a goddess, in this case."

Galvanius stared at the child, who gazed back at him with a smile as if waiting for his reaction. He let out a long, exasperated breath. "That's—just—great."

"Come on, it ain't that bad," Greez said, as he shoveled more food into his mouth. "I mean, having a goddess on our side has got to give us a good payday, right? Can't she summon up a ton of gold or anything like that?"

Millie shook her head. "I think she's a nature goddess. She can do elemental magic, natural healing, help things grow. You know, harness nature and the like."

"Gold is nature!" Greez argued. "It's rock. Just ask her to call up gold and gems from the ground, that'll do me fine!"

"DON'T YOU IDIOTS GET IT??" Galvanius roared. "I was supposed to have the power! I don't want to have to defer to some kid! It was meant to be me! ME!"

Everyone stared at Galvanius in silence. The girl looked concerned, and she went to Galvanius and reached for his hand. He snatched his hand away and stepped back. "It's all wrong! Everything I fought for, everything I believed, everything is wrong!" He pivoted and stormed out of the kitchen, out of the cottage, out into the field beyond.

Millie patted the girl on the shoulder. "Don't you take it personally, dear. He's always had a short fuse. Give him time to calm down a bit."

*

The sun beat down on Galvanius, heating the inside of his armor to a roasting point, but he did not care. He sat out in the distant field, racking his brain over what he was supposed to do. Perhaps Greez was right; this new goddess seemed loyal to their troupe and eager to please. Could he not just order her to do his bidding—he could be a high priest of sorts—and get all the things he wanted? But what would happen should she become aware of her own godhood, if she wasn't already? Would she grow into some horrible, vengeful goddess who would do them all in? What if he couldn't keep control of her? It was too much to think about.

He needed advice. He still had his pack with him, and the canteen of what little tomato bisque was left. But he had no vessel, and he did not want to go back to the cottage—Millie would berate him for his behavior, and Greez would be irritable, and that little goddess, who knew what she might try to pull on him. With his hands, he dug a bowl-sized hole in the ground in front of him, and then poured what soup he had left in it. He drew his sword, tapped the hilt on the edge of the hole, and spoke the incantation.

A muddy vision of Dissandra appeared in the soup, and she hacked loudly. "Did you summon me in a dirty bowl? No, in actual dirt! What sort of third-rate sorceress do you take me for?"

"Sorry, it was my only option." Galvanius went on, describing all that had taken place—his escape from Ash Mountain with the god machine, its abrupt departure, the new goddess now living in the cottage with his team. Dissandra's expression remained stoic through his story.

"I see," she said when Galvanius finished. "Well, those ancient texts were rather vague about the machine's powers, weren't they? Although I suppose this situation can still be rectified…"

"Rectified? Do you mean, I could still gain my godhood?"

Dissandra smiled as a fox might smile at a rabbit. "Oh, yes, my dear Galvanius. There is a way. First, find me a decent vessel, not kettles or holes in the earth. Once you do that, you will brew a special soup, which I will instruct you how to make. Then you will summon me—you won't see me, but trust me, I'll be there. Finally, give the soup to the young goddess to drink. Once she does that, I can use my abilities to transfer her godhood into you."

Galvanius felt an odd, cold tingle in his forehead. "You can do that?"

"Of course. The goddess is still new, and not at her full powers yet. She is still vulnerable. So you will have to work quickly. By the time the moon rises tonight. After that, she may become too strong for even I to drain her essence."

The Dark lord thought on this. "But…what'll happen to her once you do that?"

Dissandra let out a light laugh. "Are you concerned for the little goddess? What have I always told you? A Dark lord with a heart is scarcely a Dark lord at all. Why does her fate concern you?"

Galvanius felt something like worms twisting in his gut, but he nodded. "Very well. Tell me how to make the soup."

*

Millie looked up from the garden where she and the young goddess were tending a score of fresh vegetables—the goddess had caused them to grow within a few minutes—and was surprised to see Galvanius walking across the field towards them. Swarmdog bounded happily over to Galvanius to greet him.

"Jimmy! I thought you wouldn't come back until dusk." Millie stood up, dusting the dirt off her skirt. "Krag and Greez went to go get some firewood. And Flora and I will make a lovely stew tonight with all these new vegetables."

The Dark lord paused. "Flora?"

"Oh, yes, Flora. She still hasn't said what her name is, so I thought to give her one."

The goddess, Flora, smiled at Galvanius, although there was a small hint of sadness in her eyes.

"Ah, Flora." Galvanius scratched the nape of his neck. "Say, Flora, you wouldn't happen to know where I could get some rue, sage, and some, uh…coriander, would you?"

Flora walked over to him. She tapped her foot in three places in front of him, and from each spot sprang small patches of the herbs he requested. She looked up expectantly at him.

Galvanius knelt and plucked the three herbs. He stood and said, "That'll do. Thanks. I was thinking, since Millie cooks so much, I would make some soup for us."

Millie looked stunned at his statement. "Oh my. I didn't know you…well, that'll be just fine, Jimmy. You can make a starting course and we'll make the stew the main course. Oh, we'll eat like kings and queens today!"

Galvanius went into the cottage, feeling Flora's eyes on him as he went inside. It dawned on him—gods were omniscient. Did she already know what he had planned? Would she not drink the soup if he offered it to her? Or was she aware of something he wasn't— maybe Dissandra gave him an inadequate spell and Flora knew it wouldn't work. Or perhaps…gods tried not to interfere with the will of men…

He rummaged through the kitchen for a good serving bowl, and eventually found a dusty, large wooden mixing bowl. It was arguably the nicest item in the cottage, with a nice finish and painted with small birds along the sides. It would have to do. Millie had already placed a cooking pot on the stove with some water in it, so he went about tearing off the parts of the herbs he needed.

Suddenly, Flora was at his side. Galvanius jumped at her abrupt appearance. *Oh gods, she knows!* he thought. But she did not look at him accusingly; she looked worried. Scared.

"What? What do you want?" Galvanius asked, a little too brusquely.

Flora took his hand and led him a few feet to the right. She stopped.

Galvanius raised an eyebrow in confusion. "Why did you—"

A massive hoof crashed through the ceiling of the kitchen, slamming right down on the spot Galvanius had been standing a few seconds ago. The cloven foot crumpled the stove like aluminum, splintered the kitchen table asunder, and consumed almost the entire room. The earth quaked as if it would turn inside out, knocking Galvanius and Flora off their feet. When Galvanius looked up through the demolished roof, he nearly passed out at the sight of a giant black ram, with the torso of a man upon four citadel legs and curling silver horns atop its shaggy head, glaring down at him with fiery eyes.

"**Where is the new god?**" the ram monster demanded.

"Jimmy! Jimmy!" Millie stood in the doorway of the cottage, shaking in panic. "Oh, thank goodness, you didn't get smushed! He just fell straight out of the sky! You know, he kind of looks like those old statues of Thealxethor—"

Galvanius snatched Flora under one arm, barreled out the door while grabbing Millie in his free hand. Swarmdog, knowing this was no monster he wanted to fight, followed his summoner, buzzing in panic. The Dark lord realized there was no cover out here. Where on earth were Greez and Krag? If they were collecting firewood, the only tree with any decent wood around here was that old oak tree—on the other side of the cottage. And now a ram beast was standing between him and it.

"The well, Jim!" Millie cried, pointing to the moss-encrusted stonework nearby.

Part of Galvanius cringed; he honestly hated the thought of going underground, again. But she was right; that was the only means of escape. Millie was a good tunnel-digger by nature, being a dwarf, so she and Swarmdog could hopefully tunnel a passage deep and far enough away from this monster.

Galvanius dashed for the well, looking down into it. There seemed to be no bottom—he couldn't even tell if there would be water to land in. This seemed of no concern to Millie. She took Flora from Galvanius, and with a quick, "Trust me!" she jumped into the well with the goddess in her arms.

The Dark lord, holding his breath, leaped in behind her, just as the ram god's hand reached for him. Galvanius felt the beast's fingertips brush his cloak, and then he was consumed by darkness as he plummeted down…down…

*

"Look! Look! Jimmy has returned!"

Galvanius opened his eyes, and at first, was greeted with darkness. Then several small, yellow lights flickered into view. He realized they were tiny lanterns, and they softly illuminated many small, round faces. The eyes of the faces were huge, and white whiskers and beards sprouted from their chins. These people were deathly pale and wrinkled, and their limbs and fingers were gangly. Each person stood about two feet tall, and they wore tattered, muddy miners' clothes.

One face loomed forward, wearing a pointed leather cap, and he smiled widely. "Jimmy boy, is that you? Well, gods of the underground be praised! I thought we'd never see you again."

Galvanius blinked, his eyes adjusting to the low light. "Skimble? Is that you?"

"Come now, you're not too high and mighty to give your old man a hug, are you?" The small man, Skimble Domhnall, helped Galvanius to sit up and clasped the boy in his arms.

It was then Galvanius realized his armor was gone, and all he wore was his quilted tunic and wool trousers. "My armor! What did you do with my—"

"Relax, boy. Even though your swarm elemental slowed your fall, you still landed pretty rough. We had to make sure you didn't have any broken bones or the like. Your armor's right over there." Skimble pointed, and Galvanius could make out his armor and sword piled up in a corner of the dugout room they were in. "I see it's held up well. One of the finest things I ever made, that armor. Not bad for an old toolsmith, eh?"

Galvanius felt naked without it, despite his tunic and trousers.

"Is Jimmy awake? Hey, Jimmy!" Millie came into the room, followed by Swarmdog. She held up a larger lantern which better lit the space. "Look who we found! I had no idea there was a knocker village under the well!"

The knockers had such a vast system of underground chambers, tunnels, and systems that they practically spanned all of Mirstone. Most of the other races had no clue how much territory the knockers lived in, right under their feet. Wherever there was a well, a knocker village would be nearby, due to there being a good source of water. Galvanius began to suspect that the god machine had brought them to that cottage because it wanted them to find the knockers.

"Your dwarf friend told me you are in a bit of a pickle," Skimble said, helping Galvanius to his feet. "Attacked by a ram god, were you? See, this is why you should've stayed with your family, Jim. Safe and sound underground, I always say. But you had to go a-questing, had to make your way in the world as an overlord. How's that going, by the by?"

Galvanius jerked in realization. "Wait…I left two of my comrades up there! Krag and Greez…they'll be pulverized by that monster!"

Millie laughed lightly. "No worries, Jim. There was a tunnel by the oak tree where they were collecting wood. The knockers pulled them under when they came to inspect the quake that Thealxethor caused. They're safe a few rooms down the tunnel, with Flora. Come."

As they walked down the tunnel—Galvanius needed to hunch over, almost doubling at the waist—Millie whispered, "Your family is so nice, Jimmy. I wish you had introduced me to them sooner."

Galvanius sighed. "You're not going to ask how a human has a knocker family?"

"I assume you're adopted."

"More like a pity case."

"Pity ain't got nothing to do with it!" Skimble retorted. "Jimmy was always a good boy. Can't be helped whoever was cruel enough to toss him down a well as a babe didn't know what a great kid they had. Their loss is our gain, that's what I say."

Millie gasped, placing her hand on her chest. "Someone threw you down a well? As a baby? That's horrible!"

Galvanius shrugged. "Hey, I don't need to be where I'm not wanted."

They all entered another room, lit by bioluminescent moss and mushrooms glowing bright green, creating a ghostly ambiance throughout the cavern. This space was large enough for Galvanius to stand up straight, and he did so with a slight crick in his back. Flora, Greez and Krag sat on some rocks beside a lantern, and the golem lifted the lantern to see who was approaching. Flora stood up and ran straight to Galvanius, hugging him at the waist. The Dark lord was taken aback by this affection and remained still until she released him.

"Hey Mill, glad to see you're not flattened—hey, who's the scarecrow?" Greez snickered.

Galvanius ran his hand through his sandy blonde hair. He figured the goblin's assessment of him without his impressive armor was about right; he was a twiggy man or twenty-some years, who had grown tall despite having spent his formative years in dark, small tunnels. He was just as pale as his knocker foster family, although having worn that Armor of the Violet Flame for the past couple of years had built up some traces of muscle.

Millie blurted out a laugh. "Greez, that's Jimmy! He just doesn't have his armor on."

The goblin looked gobsmacked. "*That's* Galvanius? Now I see why you never took that armor off. I've seen toothpicks with more brawn."

Krag lightly thwacked Greez on the shoulder. "Now now, Sir Galvanius is… hmm… *ethereal*," the golem said.

"Don't help," Galvanius muttered.

"Galvanius, that's right. Guess 'Jim' wasn't a good enough name for a Dark lord. Better than Skimble, I suppose." Skimble chuckled, patting Galvanius on the knee. "We'd love to have all you folks for dinner. We'll celebrate! My son has come home! You can tell me all about your adventures."

Flora looked up at Galvanius and opened her hands to him. Small green and yellow plants grew in her palms, and Galvanius recognized them as the three herbs she had grown for him earlier— rue, sage and coriander.

"It looks like Flora still wants that soup you were planning to make," Millie said with a smile.

Galvanius gently took the herbs from her, but he couldn't help but notice there was still a hint of sadness in Flora's eyes. If she knew what he had planned, why give him the herbs he needed? Was she testing him? Or…did she think giving him her powers would make him happy? Why would she care for his happiness?

"Yes, the soup," he said. "May I borrow some water and a pot?"

Two knockers fetched him a water-filled pot and ladle, and Skimble led him down a tunnel to a small makeshift kitchen, which was little more than a firepit with some hot coals in it. Once alone, Galvanius went about his cooking, adding the herbs to the pot of water, reciting the short incantation Dissandra had told him. He summoned up the nerve to bite the tip of his finger to draw a drop of blood, and he added it to the pot. Finally, he needed something from Flora—he hadn't even thought that far ahead, but as he looked down at himself he found one of her long hairs stuck to his tunic from when she hugged him. He figured that would do, and he put it in the soup. He recited, "She who drinks of this brew gives her powers to the one who claims it; what is yours will be mine."

The soup abruptly changed color, changing from a tepid green tea hue to a deep crimson, as if the pot were filling with blood. After a few seconds, it returned to its original state, although Galvanius swore he heard a whisper, a beckoning. Now he just had to make sure Flora drank it before anything else happened. He dipped the ladle in the soup—it was not much of a vessel, but it would do.

"Flora," he called down the tunnel. "Would you come here, please?"

Flora was suddenly before him as if she had anticipated his call. She looked up at him with those wide, innocent eyes.

"Would you…mind testing the soup? See if it tastes all right?" he asked.

Flora looked at the ladle, again, with an air of sadness. Then she looked Galvanius right in the eyes and smiled. That smile said it all—*If it's what you want.* She took the ladle from him and brought it to her lips.

Something inside Galvanius shattered like glass. It shrieked in his mind and burned in his temples. *What am I doing? Goddess or not, she's just a child! Without her essence, she could die!*

Galvanius knocked the ladle from Flora's grasp. The soup

splashed against the wall of the room and the ladle rolled across the floor. Flora stared at him confused at first, but then she wrapped her arms around him and buried her face in his tunic.

"You knew, didn't you?" Galvanius asked.

"OF COURSE SHE KNOWS!" screeched a voice from the pot.

Galvanius spun around to see a wine-red vapor leaking from the pot, filling the room with a foul bloody smoke. Dissandra's face formed in the vapor, except it was clearer than it had ever been—it was as if a viper were turning human but stopped halfway through transformation. Her eyes were yellow and beady, her face ashen and bony, her mouth a blackened slit that reached back to her ears. The Dark lord's breath caught in his throat.

"You couldn't do this one, simple thing for me," she hissed. "All this mindless teaching, and you've wasted all I taught you because you have a conscience in that thick skull. Make her drink the soup, so I can finally be free of this miserable place!"

Galvanius gaped at her. "I…I'm sorry? Free you?"

Dissandra narrowed her eyes on him. "Did you think I trained you as my Dark lord for fun? Because I'm nice? I need someone to free me from this horrible limbo I was banished to! But if I told you what the god machine really does, how it would produce a new god who then I could use as a vessel to transfer my essence, then you wouldn't have found it for me, would you have?"

"Wait, what? I don't understand!"

"Of course you don't. You're an idiot, *Jimmy*. Now, tell your goddess to drink the soup so I can become one with her and I can finally be free. Otherwise things will become very unpleasant for you both."

A fire built up in Galvanius' stomach, searing through his veins and into his spirit. "You used me this whole time. But I'm a Dark lord, and I'm in charge. You're at my mercy, and I will never summon you again!"

Dissandra let out a high, blood-curdling laugh, flashing her sharp teeth. "That's cute. But please, call me by my true name—

Libraya Nor. Or, at least, what's left of her. I am her Oculus Dolo, the Eye of Deceit. I'm afraid her Eye of Truth is long lost to the world. But what do you care for truth, Jim Domhnall? You gave yourself a false name, a false title, false friends—even your heart is false. You think you care about this weak goddess, but you only care about yourself."

"That's not true!" Galvanius went to kick over the pot, to sever Dissandra's connection for the last time. But he found his body locked. He couldn't move.

"You surrendered your soul to me for my secrets. Let me show you what's truly in your heart!"

Galvanius felt as if currents of lightning were ripping through his body. His blood…he had put his blood in the soup, the soup that Dissandra used as a link to his world…she had control of him. He gasped and spasmed, as his insides boiled and twisted in knots. He dropped to his knees and hands, his skin blistering over as if his flesh were dissolving. He looked helplessly at Flora, and the girl's eyes were wide in terror. She tried to place her hands on Galvanius as if to heal him, but she snatched them back with a soft whimper. Her hands steamed at his touch. Libraya Nor was an ancient goddess, and Flora was no match for her, even with Libraya Nor trapped on another plane.

Flora's terrified look switched to calm resolution. She picked up the ladle from the floor.

"Flora…sto…" Galvanius couldn't form the words. He couldn't move to stop her.

Flora went over to the pot. She dipped the ladle into the soup. She lifted the ladle to her mouth.

Stop! Please, stop! Gods, why did I let it get this far? Why did I want power so badly that I put the people I care about in danger? Where's Millie, and Greez, and Krag? I need help! Flora needs…

There was a soul-shattering cry that turned Galvanius' blood cold. Dissandra's face was gone from the vapor. The smoke slowly dissipated, fading into the walls and floor. There was a long silence as if time had stopped. Slowly, Flora turned and faced Galvanius.

She approached him, expressionless, soundless.

Galvanius braced himself for whatever punishment he was in for. *Just get it over with quickly*, he silently begged. Flora bent over, touching one finger to his forehead.

In an instant, his blistered skin was fully healed. The agonizing pain in his gut subsided. He breathed deeply and found he could speak again. "Flora?"

The goddess showed him the ladle. A fly floated in the soup, buzzing in spurts and struggling to free itself from the liquid.

Millie's voice echoed in the tunnel. "Swarmy! Where did you go, boy?"

Galvanius and Flora looked at the entrance to the kitchen. There floated the swarm elemental in dog form, somehow silent instead of the droning cacophony he normally was.

"Swarmdog?" Galvanius looked at the fly in the ladle. "Is this fly…yours?"

The swarm elemental whined.

Flora pointed at the fly, and then at the pot.

"Wait, you didn't drink the soup. The fly…" Relief flowed through Galvanius, and he smiled at the elemental. "Swarmy, you genius!"

Swarmdog buzz-barked happily. Millie appeared in the tunnel behind him. "What's all this now? I thought I heard a commotion. Are you two all right?"

Galvanius put an arm around Flora. "We're fine. I'm afraid I spoiled the soup, though."

"Is that all? For gods' sakes, all that screaming over spoiled soup? Remind me to never ask you to cook again, if you're going to be so high-strung about it." She came over and looked in the ladle. "Oh, I see! Swarmy got mixed up in it. Can't keep every fly under control, I suspect. Sorry 'bout that."

She picked the fly out of the ladle and crushed it between her fingers. Galvanius winced.

Millie wiped her hand on her skirt. "Now come on, the others are waiting."

Galvanius started to follow Millie and Swarmdog, but Flora took his hand to halt him. He knelt to her level. "Flora, I'm so sorry—"

She placed her hand on his chest and smiled at him.

Galvanius could hear words in his mind. *A Dark lord with a heart is no Dark lord at all.*

"I guess I'm not cut out for this gig, huh? I suppose I'll have to retire my name," Jimmy said.

*

"Um, Jimbo? Would you do something about the giant sheep-man who just ripped off the ceiling to our dining hall?" Skimble sounded remarkably calm, given what he said.

It seemed that Thealxethor had grown impatient waiting for his quarry to reemerge from underground, so he had decided to reach down and tear up the cottage grounds. A few handfuls had been enough to expose the knockers' main dining hall as well as several mine shafts, and the knockers scrambled, more so because of the sharp sunlight rather than the looming ram centaur.

The renounced Dark lord and his troupe walked into the dining hall to show themselves—except for Greez, who chose to hide behind Krag's legs.

"**Where is the new god**?" Thealxethor reiterated, his voice crackling like thunder.

"Oh my," Krag said, shielding his eyes to look up. "And I thought CharMaw was gargantuan in stature."

Jimmy gulped, looking down at Flora. She was calm, and she held his hand reassuringly. He turned to Millie. "This is a dwarven deity, right? Does he mean to harm Flora?"

The dwarf fidgeted with her fingers and bit her lip. "I suspect if he meant to harm Flora, he'd just smash us right now. And Thealxethor is a god of dreams, a herald to adventure. I've never heard of him being the wrathful, crush-your-bones type."

"Just give him the kid!" Greez squeaked, "before he *does* become a crush-your-bones type!"

Flora released Jimmy's hand and willingly stepped forward. Thealxethor lowered one of his huge hands, large enough to hold a skiff, and placed it palm up so Flora could step onto it. She did so, and he raised her all the way up to his ear-level. They seemed to converse, the ram god's voice so low now it sounded like distant rumbling to everyone on the ground. After a few minutes, Thealxethor lowered Flora back down, where she hopped off his hand and returned to Jimmy and Millie.

"So? What'd he say?" Millie asked.

Flora pointed straight up to the sky and shook her head.

"What does that mean?" Jimmy asked.

Thealxethor noted the confusion of the mortals, and he rapidly shrank in size, his black fur shifting to a steel-blue tone. When he shrank to ten feet tall, he leaped down into the dining hall and stood before the others.

"Sorry to give you all a scare," the ram god said, scratching the back of his head. "When I detected a new god was present in Mirstone, I had to be sure it wasn't a threat. I've feared the return of Libraya Nor's Evil Eye for centuries. But I see now I had no reason to worry." He tenderly patted Flora on the head.

"Was it really necessary to be that giant? You could've just talked to us like this from the start," Jimmy said.

Millie elbowed Jimmy in the side. "Show some respect! You're talking to a god, you know."

"No, he's right. We gods tend to come off a little aggressive at times." Thealxethor made an awkward smirk. "I told your…Flora, is it?…that she is welcomed into my pantheon, the realm of the gods, but she has declined my offer."

Jimmy looked in disbelief at Flora. "Are you sure you want to pass on that? You're a goddess. You should be with the gods."

Flora shook her head.

"Why on earth not?"

The ram god chuckled. "She says she wants to learn more about mortals and about Mirstone. That she wants to live among your people, to understand your ways, to understand your truths. Only then can she grow into a proper guide for your people."

Jimmy grinned—apparently, the god machine knew what it was doing when it made Flora. "Thealxethor, could you tell me…why did the god machine give Flora to us? What determined what kind of god it would make?"

"You determined that," the ram god replied. "The god machine viewed you with the Eye of Truth. What you truly are, deep in your soul, is what Flora became."

"But Dissandra said the Eye of Truth was lost a long time ago."

Thealxethor leaned in close to Jimmy. "The Eye of Truth lies within all of us. Libraya Nor, when she was whole, sacrificed her Eye of Truth to dwell in all living things. This goddess was born and shaped from your true nature, the truth of you. There is good in you, Jim Domhnall, a good that could change all of Mirstone, if you let it."

Flora squeezed Jimmy's hand.

Millie smiled from ear to ear. "See? I told you, nothing's wrong with being sweet little Jimmy."

The ram god pawed at the earth with a hoof and shook his shaggy mane of hair. "Take good care of the young goddess, mortals. I had no doubt we'll cross paths again. Adventure's always calling you!" And with that, he bounded away up out of the ground, into the air as if he weighed nothing, and soon vanished into the meadow of clouds in the sky.

"That was weird," Greez said as he crawled out from behind Krag.

"The gods tend to be such," Krag commented. He approached Flora and knelt before her. "Goddess Flora, if it be within your power, may I ask…one divine request?"

"That's right, your wish!" Millie said. "And for all of the help you've given us, I hope it's something we can grant you."

Flora nodded to the golem.

Krag suddenly got flustered, his molten face blushing a bright orange. "There's only one thing I ever truly wanted, and because I'm a golem, I thought it couldn't ever come true, but if you could, could you make me…an accountant?"

Jimmy snorted to hold back a laugh. "An accountant? That's it? That's your big lifelong wish?"

"Yes, an accountant," Krag repeated firmly. "I love numbers and equations. But no one ever creates a golem for that. I don't know what kind of magic it would take, but I—"

"You know," Skimble said, coming over from the far end of the room where he had been listening. "I might have an opening for you. We knockers could really use someone to keep track of what all's in our coin rooms for us."

Greez snapped his head toward Skimble, his ears perking forwards. "Did you say, 'coin rooms'? As in, rooms full of coins?"

The knocker grinned. "Well, more like caverns full of coins. So many folks over the centuries have been tossing coins down wells for wishes, and they wind up in our tunnels, and we haven't really had a use for them. We just keep gathering them up and throwing them in our coin rooms. Don't think anyone's ever really accounted for everything in there. Might be good to have a fella keep track of all that."

Krag's face lit up, literally, at the knocker's offer. "Oh, that would be wonderful! Centuries of accounting to catch up on, how delightful! I'll need some tablets, and a chisel, and an abacus if you have it—"

"That'll be a lot of numbers to crunch, Krag ol' buddy," Greez said coyly. "Maybe you could use an assistant. Goblins are very good at organizing, particularly us U.U. goblins."

The golem leaned over and placed a hand on Greez's shoulder. "Are you offering your services?"

"For a nominal fee, of course," the goblin said. "Five gold coins a day should do just fine."

*

Jimmy stretched out his legs and leaned back on his hands as he sat in the field, watching the morning sun change the sky from purple to blue to gold. Millie, Swarmdog and Flora sat to his right, and the little goddess watched with wide-eyed amazement at the oncoming sun.

Millie turned to Jimmy. "So, what's the plan now, m'lord? It looks like Krag and Greez are happy to stay with the knockers for now. What will the four of us do?"

Jimmy knotted his brow in thought. "Flora wants to know more about Mirstone. I think we should show it to her."

"Ooooh, a trip!" Millie cooed. "I've wanted one of those for a while…without the fighting horrible beasts and going to ungodly places. We can stock up in the next town. I still have some food and tools in my pack—oh! You'll need to fetch your armor from your dad."

Jimmy smiled at Millie. "I don't think I need it anymore."

THE END

Your Wish, My Cage
Richard Fierce

1

I sat at the back of the small fishing boat, puffing on a smoke-stick as we drew closer to the Cursed Cay. The small plot of land rested a few miles offshore and was overgrown with thick vegetation.

"What was your name again?" the fisherman paddling the boat asked.

"Natavia," I replied, blowing a stream of smoke over the side of the vessel.

"That's an odd name. Does it mean anything?"

"Not that I know of."

The man harumphed and continued rowing. He hadn't asked for much in payment, but he was only willing to take me to the edge of the island's arm. He'd muttered something about bad luck and dark curses. I wasn't sure what he meant.

"What do you want to see the ruins for, anyway?"

"You ask a lot of questions," I said.

"Not many people come out here is all. And nobody asks to be taken to the ruins."

"I have my reasons."

I leaned back and stared at the island we were approaching. It was larger than I expected, but my only frame of reference had been a drawing on an old map. Something jutted out into the water, gently bobbing up and down. A light breeze stirred the water's surface, and if I wasn't heading into the unknown, I might have enjoyed the trip. As the boat drew closer to the island, I realized the thing protruding from it was an old dilapidated dock. It didn't look like it had been used in years. I swallowed hard, questioning whether or not this was still a good idea.

"We're here," the fisherman said. "Do you want me to wait for you?"

"Does that cost extra?" I asked.

"Depends on how long I have to wait."

I snorted and stood, fishing a few coins from the purse that hung at my waist. The man held his hand out eagerly and I dropped the coins onto his palm. He was giddy at the sight of the money like a cloverweed addict I'd seen in an alley once. I almost pitied him. I'd have paid much more to be brought here.

"Wait for me," I said. With any luck, my task would be simple.

"Yes ma'am."

Attached to the side of the dock was a rope ladder. It rested in the water, mostly hidden from view in the murkiness. I stepped onto the edge of the boat and leaped through the air. My feet landed on the last plank, and I had to windmill my arms to keep from falling backward against the boat, or worse, into the water. I caught my balance and stepped lightly across the dock. It creaked under my weight but held firm.

"You've got some guts!"

I didn't bother responding, mainly because it was all I could do to keep from turning around and running back to the boat. There was a darkness here that was almost palpable. It felt heavy, and I questioned again why I'd decided to come here. Small waves hit the dock, and the blasted thing shifted each time. It was a marvel that anyone made this place their home, especially a race of creatures supposedly gifted with magical powers.

I cursed as I reached the end of the dock. It didn't quite touch the shore, and a thin rope ladder stretched from the dock to a stone pillar that rested in the sand. The ends of the rope were tied securely around metal rings that had been driven into the stone. It seemed safe. After a long moment of struggle, and more cursing, I managed to find the right place to put my feet and quickly ran across the flimsy makeshift bridge.

Once I was standing on the shore, I felt a little better. I glanced over my shoulder to make sure the fisherman hadn't left. He was still there, though he looked at the island as if it were about to come alive and devour him and his boat. I rested for a brief moment and continued.

A path was evident, despite the overgrowth, and I followed it toward the center of the island. If the map I'd seen was correct, the remains of a stone building should be here. I pushed deeper into the island and came upon the ruins.

The building, or what was left of it, had crumbled. Judging by the amount of moss growing on the stones, it had happened long ago. Set against a small hill was an arched doorway. The door itself was circular in shape and made of bronze. I stared at the swirled design engraved on it. A book I'd read said that this was the home of the *Tabaxi*.

Sweat trickled down my forehead, the humidity in the air adding to my discomfort. But I was here. I walked to the door and spotted an aperture on the upper part of it. It was now or never. I knocked three times. There was a screeching noise, followed by a muffled voice.

"I don't understand," I said, looking around for the source of the voice.

"Up here."

I looked up at the aperture and saw that it was open. A single eye peered at me.

"Do you have an appointment?"

"No," I replied. "How would I?"

"You'd come to the door and ask for one."

My left eye twitched, but I caught my tongue before I said something obscene.

"Well, I've just arrived and haven't had time to request one."

"Ah. Well then, I suppose we can take your request now."

"Fine. Can you fit me in for today?"

"I'm afraid not. We're booked solid."

"When's the next available time?" I asked.

"Six months from now."

I paused. Six *months?* That wasn't going to work for me.

"I need to see someone today. Tomorrow at the latest."

The eye blinked, and the aperture closed most of the way. There was a hushed conversation on the other side of the door, but I couldn't make out the words. Finally, the grate slid back open and the eye peered out again.

"What's your business here?"

"I'm looking to commission something," I answered.

More whispered conversation.

"I have plenty of coins to spend," I added.

"Money is of no importance," the voice replied.

"Speak for yourself!" Another voice chimed.

"Well, if money isn't important, then I suppose I can take my request elsewhere. Maybe to the gnomes in the Floating Isles, I suppose?"

I turned and started to walk away.

"Wait! Come back. No need to be so hasty. Come back, come back."

I turned around. The grate closed and there were several loud sounds, then the door swung open. The hinges squealed in protest. The door stopped just short of hitting the rock wall and a long feline figure stepped into the daylight. He was roughly six feet tall and looked just like a large hunting cat, except he walked on two legs.

The Tabaxi waved toward the entrance, seeming flustered. Another Tabaxi waited across the threshold.

"Come in," she bade. "We don't turn away money here." She glared at the male.

I smiled. No matter the race, everyone had a weakness for money. Well, almost everyone. My weakness was for revenge.

2

I followed the female Tabaxi deeper into the hill. We traveled along smoothly carved tunnels until we reached a steel contraption with a sliding door. The Tabaxi pulled a lever and the door opened. She stepped inside, motioning for me to do the same. I eyed it warily, unsure of whether to trust it based on the rope ladder outside, but I entered anyway.

The Tabaxi pulled another lever. The door screeched as it closed, then the entire apparatus began to descend slowly. There was no railing to hold onto, so I balled my hands into fists and hoped I didn't vomit as my stomach churned.

"I'm Trigani," the Tabaxi said.

"Natavia," I replied through gritted teeth.

"What are you looking to have commissioned?" Trigani turned her white eyes on me.

"A lamp," I replied.

She furrowed her brow. "You could have gone anywhere to get one of those."

"Yes, but I need it to do something specific."

"Such as?"

This was the part I wasn't sure the Tabaxi would be able to accommodate. Crafting a lamp itself was easy, even for non-inventive races. But I needed something more … magical.

"I need it to grant a wish."

"You want to capture a djinn?" Trigani's face had transformed into what I assumed was a scowl, but it was difficult to read her expression.

"No. I need the lamp itself to grant me a wish."

"We are not sorcerers."

"I'm aware of that, but you do have some magic, don't you?"

Trigani stared at me mutely for a moment. I wondered if I'd crossed some sort of cultural line and offended her, but she finally nodded slowly.

"Yes, we have magic, but nothing like that. You may be better off going to see the people of El-Tal."

I had considered that already, but I'd decided to check with the Tabaxi first. The Cursed Peninsula was closer, and from what I'd heard whispered about El-Tal, I wasn't sure it was somewhere I wanted to go.

"Is there not a Tabaxi capable of such a thing?" I asked.

"As I said, we're not sorcerers."

The metal box we were in stopped and Trigani pulled the lever to open the door. I followed her out and found myself in a completely different world. A small city was built within an enormous cave, and a plethora of sounds filled the air. Smoke rose from various buildings, funneled into large tubes overhead that disappeared into the rocky ceiling.

"Welcome to Guun," Trigani said proudly. "The best city in all of Mirstone."

"Better than the gnome cities in the Floating Isles?"

"Of course. Those isles can sink, you know. This island *can't* sink."

I didn't know the isles could sink. I'd glimpsed them once from afar, but I hadn't been close enough to see any of their details.

"How would the isles sink?" I asked.

Trigani shrugged. "There are many reasons, but gnome business is not Tabaxi business. Follow me."

Trigani walked along a wide path that led between a string of buildings on both sides. She stopped in front of a small, square structure that was old and dirty. The paint was chipped and the wood seemed to be deteriorating. I could feel my hopes being dashed already.

"This is Dorlin's workshop," Trigani said. "He's the best suited for your project, assuming anyone can do it."

I eyed the building as I slowly walked to the doorway. Three ramshackle steps brought me to the door, and I knocked twice. I could hear sounds inside, but no one came to the door. I knocked again, louder this time. There was a clang, followed by cursing. I was on the verge of leaving when the door swung open and a short Tabaxi covered in black soot greeted me. He looked just like the one that had greeted me at the door.

"Oh."

He seemed taken aback by my presence and stared up at me for a moment, then peered around me and spotted Trigani in the street. She waved cheerily.

"I take it you need something, then?"

"Yes," I replied. His tone wasn't rude, but more curiosity. "May I come inside?"

"If you don't mind getting dirty. I've been rather busy and my shop is covered in this stuff." Dorlin waved at the soot that covered his clothes.

"I don't mind."

"Well then, come in."

He left the door, and I stepped inside. A glance showed he wasn't exaggerating. There was soot *everywhere*. It stained the walls, the ceiling, and the floor. Dorlin cleared a space on a table and looked at me expectantly. I retrieved a folded parchment from my coin purse and uncreased it, then laid it out on the table. Dorlin looked at it in silence, then eyed me with an air of annoyance.

"Is this a joke? Who put you up to this? Was it Feldon? By the whiskers of Idris, I'll—"

"It's not a joke," I said. "I need a lamp."

"My talents are highly prized here, my dear. I'm afraid making a lamp is … well, it's not something I'm interested in."

"It's not a normal lamp. I need it to grant a wish."

Dorlin's face wrinkled. He looked at the design again, then shook his head. "I'm not sure what you were told, but I'm no summoner of magic. What do you want something like that for, anyway?"

"That's my business alone," I said. "I have plenty of coins."

"It's not about the coin," Dorlin grumped. "It's about the magic. I don't know the first thing about spellcasting. We Tabaxi can do small magic, and only once a year. I wouldn't use my magic on something this trivial. I'm sorry."

I sighed. "Is there nothing I can do to persuade you? I'll pay double your rate."

Dorlin pushed the parchment across the table to me.

"It can't be done."

3

"I take it you didn't find what you were looking for?"

The fisherman pulled his paddles out and dropped the ends into the water. Was the disappointment that evident on my face? I shook my head, not in the mood to talk.

"Ah, well. That's life sometimes. Back to the mainland?"

I nodded, and the fisherman began rowing. He turned the boat around and we headed back to the coast. Once we docked, I left the boat and wandered aimlessly for a while, trying to figure out my options. Trigani had mentioned seeing a sorcerer in El-Tal. Perhaps it was worth checking out. I nodded to myself, making up my mind.

"El-Tal it is," I muttered.

At the local inn, I found a merchant who was heading that direction and paid him a small fee to ride along. Five days later, I found myself standing outside the gates of El-Tal. It was the most exotic place I'd ever seen, though to be fair, I hadn't traveled very far from home in my short life.

Guards stood at attention near the open gates, but I walked into the city without harassment. I'd heard many tales about the place, and none of them were good. Hope had a way of making me do foolish things, though.

"Excuse me," I said, stopping a young woman who was carrying a basket full of fresh bread. The scent made my mouth water despite having already eaten.

"Where can I find a sorcerer?"

"The guild is that tall building there," she replied, nodding toward it with her head.

I turned to look and spotted a tower that rose high into the air. It was cylindrical, with oddly shaped stained-glass windows that dotted the exterior like glimmering rose petals.

"Thank y—" my words faded as I turned to see that the girl was gone. I glanced around, but she was lost to the crowd that congregated among the market. I shrugged and made my way toward the tower. On the way, I stopped at a stall and bought a smoke-stick. The vendor lit it for me, and I puffed on it as I continued along the cobbled street. The aroma smelled of chocolate, which I found intriguing.

I reached the tower's entrance and noticed guards in similar attire as the ones outside the main gates were on duty. There was something about them that I couldn't quite figure out, but I shrugged the thought aside and stepped into the building.

The antechamber was a large space, filled with empty chairs in orderly rows. A desk was near a staircase that led up to the next level, and a black-haired woman in plain robes sat behind it. She looked up as I approached and I offered my best smile.

"I'm here to see a sorcerer," I said.

"I would assume so," the woman replied. "This is the sorcerer's guild, after all."

"Right. Is there someone available that can help me?"

"That depends. What do you need?"

"I'm looking to have an item created."

The woman pulled a blank parchment from a pile and grabbed a quill, dipping it into an inkwell. "What sort of item?"

"A lamp."

The woman scribbled something onto the parchment. "Do you have a specific design in mind?"

I pulled my own parchment out and handed it to her. She unfolded it and set it to the side, scribbling again.

"And what types of spells should the lamp be imbued with?"

"It needs to be able to grant a wish."

I waited for her to say it wasn't possible, just as the Marid had.

Instead, she continued to write on her parchment.

"The cost will be steep," she said.

"How much?"

"It depends on who crafts the item, but I'd say around 5,000 gold coins."

My heart skipped a beat. That was much more than I expected. While I was carrying a small fortune for most people, it wasn't nearly enough. I hadn't even brought half that.

"Will that be a problem?" the woman asked.

I don't know why, but I shook my head. "No, not at all."

"Very good. And what is the intended purpose for this lamp?"

"Revenge."

"Interesting. Revenge upon …?"

"My father's killer. He was murdered."

The woman pursed her lips. "Was the killer a man?"

"Yes."

"That's going to put a damper on things."

"Why?" I asked.

"Well, we don't like men. Or rather, we prefer to keep them only as slaves and lovers, but nothing more. You want revenge upon a man, which is a worthy cause, but it's revenge *for* a man. That simply won't do."

"He was my father," I protested.

"Even so, the laws of El-Tal must be followed. We are, after all, a matriarchy."

Her words not only crushed my last bit of hope, but they didn't make any sense. They refused to help me because the person I wanted to avenge was a man?

"There must be something you can do," I said. "I traveled five days to get here."

"I'm sorry, but you've come all this way for nothing."

Tears of frustration welled in my eyes, but I refused to let them fall. I gritted my teeth and nodded, then turned to leave. What would I do now? There was no other place I knew of that I could go. Perhaps my desire for revenge was wrong. That would explain why every place I went had an obstacle that kept me from reaching my goal. I was almost to the door when the woman called out.

"Wait."

I paused and tried to compose myself before turning around. The woman had left her desk, and she had something in her hand.

"Take this," she said.

I realized I'd forgotten my parchment with the drawing of the lamp on it. I took it and offered a sad smile.

"Thank you."

"Though we cannot help you with your revenge directly, perhaps this will guide you."

With that, she went back to her desk.

4

I stood outside the tower, fighting against the overwhelming feeling of defeat. If only I'd have known that the women here didn't like men, I could have lied about the purpose of the lamp. Then again, I didn't have the exorbitant amount of money they asked for, either. I blew out a long sigh and unfolded the parchment.

At the bottom, a crude map had been drawn. I looked back at the tower, realization dawning on me. The woman had chosen to help me after all. Even better, the map's location appeared to be just outside the city.

Welling with excitement, I hurried along the street to the city gates and left, turning right and following the worn dirt road that went south. I walked for an hour before I spotted the rolling green hills. On the map, there was a large X that marked the location. It was the centermost hill. I picked up the pace, jogging the rest of the distance.

When I reached the hill, I didn't see anything out of the ordinary. The hills were covered in tall grass that swayed gently, but there were no buildings or people. A sinking feeling filled my stomach and I assumed the woman had tricked me. Had she done this simply to get me to leave the city?

That thought took the forefront of my mind, but I refused to believe it. I stalked ahead, marching up the hill that the X indicated. Roughly halfway up, there was a small cluster of trees. I paused under them to get out of the sun and rest my legs. I folded the parchment up and stuck it into my coin purse, then sat down on the ground.

That's when I noticed the hole. Or rather, the tunnel. It was outlined with stones that were clearly carved by mortal hands. I crawled toward it and stuck my head inside and listened. It was quiet, but that didn't mean there were no animals inside. Since this was the correct hill on the map, this had to be the spot the X indicated.

I threw caution to the wind and crawled inside. After a few feet of darkness, the tunnel opened into a large cave. The ceiling was covered in moss that glowed with a bright green luminescence, bathing the chamber in a blanket of emerald light. I'd never seen anything like it before.

A stream flowed on the far-left side, the babbling sound of the water adding to the peaceful ambiance of the place. Carved stones, like those at the tunnel entrance, covered the floor. It was apparent that this place had been created by someone, though for what, I didn't know.

I followed the stream with my eyes and saw that it came out of the wall. Assuming it was safe to drink, I walked over and knelt beside it, splashing water on my face and drinking a few handfuls. When I stood back up and turned around, I saw something that hadn't been there before.

It was a stone column, roughly four feet high. Atop it, something was covered with a red cloth. There was no one in the chamber with me, yet I knew for certain the column wasn't there a moment ago. Had it appeared by magic? My curiosity overrode my uncertainty and I slowly approached the pillar.

"Is someone there?"

The voice echoed off the walls and made my heart leap in my chest. I whirled around, looking for the source, but no one was there. Was I losing my mind?

"H-hello?" I called out.

"Aha! I knew these old ears of mine still worked."

I surveyed the cave, turning in a slow circle. Still, I didn't see anyone.

"Where are you?" I asked.

"I'm technically stuck in a metal case of emotions," the voice replied, chuckling.

"I don't understand."

"Forgive me. It was a joke."

"Right. Are you a ghost?"

"Hardly."

"Then why can't I see you?" I asked.

"Because you have to summon me. Do you see a lamp?"

"No."

"It should be on a pillar of stone. It keeps me from, uh, falling loose. Yeah."

I eyed the cloth covering the top of the pillar warily. I grabbed the edge of the cloth and slowly pulled it off. A gasp involuntarily escaped my lips. It was a lamp, similar to the one I had drawn.

"Are you inside the lamp?"

"That's correct!"

"Are you a djinn?"

"Something like that. I'm a Marid."

I did it. I found a way to get my revenge. Reaching out, I touched the handle of the lamp, careful not to rub it just yet. I'd heard that djinn were tricky beings and loved to grant wishes in unexpected ways.

"Well, what are you waiting for? Let me out of this thing."

"Not so fast," I replied.

"And why not? Do you know how long I've been in here?"

"No, and I don't care. Before I let you out, I want to set some rules."

"I'm listening."

"Good. No tricks. Give me your word."

"Tricks? What are you talking about? Marid don't perform tricks. We grant wishes."

"You know what I mean," I said. "You may grant wishes, but you pervert the original intent."

"I have never done that," the Marid replied, sounding insulted.

"Be that as it may, I want your word there will be no trickery."

"Very well. No tricks."

"I also demand that you be honest with me."

"Simple enough."

That was easier than I expected. Satisfied, I rubbed the side of the lamp. It began to tremble, and I almost dropped it. A tendril of multicolored smoke snaked out of the lamp, forming into the shape of a man-like figure.

Fully formed, the Marid hovered in the air in front of me. He had an amphibious head and green skin, and he wore flowing, colorful clothing that made him look like a merchant. Where his legs should have been was nothing more than a churning blue dervish.

The Marid clapped his hands and rubbed them together.

"Let's get started, then, shall we? You get one wish, and only one. What's your wish?"

I smiled. "I want vengeance."

5

"That's a desire, not a wish," the Marid said.

I considered how I wanted my father's killer to die. Or did I want him to suffer instead? To let him feel the grief I had felt? Now *that* was an idea. Then again, I would feel a lot of satisfaction if I could take the killer's life myself. There were so many possibilities I hadn't considered before.

"I haven't got all millennia," the Marid complained.

"Sorry, I'm trying to decide."

"Maybe I can help? After all, I've been around for quite a long time. What kind of revenge do you want? Something painful? I know plenty of torture methods."

"I've spent all this time thinking about making him pay for what he did, but I haven't thought about the exact method," I said. "Perhaps you could bring him here and I could do it myself."

"Is that a wish I hear?"

I paused. What if I couldn't do it? Did I really have what it required to kill another person, regardless of my hatred for them? After a moment, I decided I didn't.

"No, that's not my wish," I replied. "I couldn't kill someone."

"No? I've killed before. It's easy once you get used to the screams."

I stared at the Marid. There was a look in his eyes that told me he wasn't lying. His looks alone were imposing, but he was also a magical being. Perhaps I should let him do it. I could even watch, to ensure he didn't trick me into thinking my father's murderer was dead.

"I like that idea," I said.

"You may not have it in you to kill, but I do. I could give you my ability to do it, if you'd like? Then you get your revenge, and it would be at your hands. You would become me, and I would become you so to speak."

Now *that* was an intriguing idea. If the Marid could give me his murderous desire and experience, my revenge would be perfect.

"I'm in."

I considered how to word the wish. I didn't want to be tricked, so I needed to be clear and concise.

"I wish for you and I to exchange …" Exchange what exactly? Powers? No, that's wasn't it. Desires? No, that's wasn't right, either. Abilities? Absolutely not. "Places?"

Before I realized I'd said the word aloud, the Marid grinned like a fiend.

"As you wish it, so it becomes," he said.

He pressed his long fingers together, forming a dome, and I knew something was amiss. A light glowed within his hands, and then it exploded in a brilliant display that blinded me. I stood still, waiting for my sight to return. Once it did, I saw the Marid was gone. I didn't feel any different, though. Would I experience murderous rage once I saw my father's killer? I supposed that's how it would work.

I headed for the tunnel that led out of the chamber. As I tried to crawl through it, an invisible force stopped me. I tried to force myself ahead, but whatever was in my way wasn't budging. The green amphibious face of the Marid appeared at the end of the tunnel.

"That was easier than I expected," he said. "Humans are always easy to fool, but you? You fell into that trap all by yourself." The Marid laughed.

"What's happening?" I asked. "Why can't I enter the tunnel?"

"Did you forget your wish so quickly? You asked for us to exchange places. Now you are stuck here, and I am free to roam the world again. Foolish human!"

Gods, no. He was lying, he had to be. And yet, I knew the truth. He'd tricked me.

"Please don't do this," I begged.

"I didn't do anything. It was you who made the wish."

"Then I take it back."

"Sorry, it doesn't work that way. I hate to leave you like this, but I've got a whole world to see."

With that, the Marid left. I stared at the end of the tunnel where he'd been, wishing that this was all a nightmare and that I would wake up, but no, it was reality. I was going to die in here, and no one would ever know. What had I done? There had to be a way to escape. I had no magical inclination, but that wasn't going to stop me.

I was going to find a way out of here, and when I did, that Marid was going to regret it.

THE END

Once Upon A Crossroads
A "The Knight, the Witch, and the Warhorse" Tale
Jeremy Hicks

No matter the planet in the multiverse, one caveat proved true all too often: Well-behaved women seldom made history. Bruttia proved to be no exception. One of those dark days before she became a household name, the raven-haired woman stared down an Inquisitor of the Lumen, a fancy title for yet another man who dared judge her for living her truth. She ignored the rough hemp rope cutting into her wrists, the Luminaries stacking wood around her, and even the crowd gathered at the crossroads. She focused on the Inquisitor as he prepared to read the charges.

Witchcraft, a capital crime in the nation of Balsinor, topped the lengthy list of heinous acts attributed to her. Murder of the unborn came next, an erroneous accusation made by an esteemed citizen, along with a half dozen lesser charges associated with her arrest and the destruction that ensued when the Luminaries came to take her into custody.

The mask of serenity on her faelike countenance hid Bruttia's roiling inner turmoil about the coming firestorm. She knew the look well. She had practiced it in front of the vanity mirror often during her childhood on the family farm. Despite their differences, she regretted not being able to see her parents and siblings one last time. She writhed under the rope binding her to the pole at the center of the crossroads.

Thinking back on a young life full of regrets, Bruttia recalled the worst of them, sacrificing her unborn child to save the world. Layers of fabric and the coil of sturdy rope concealed the scar, but she could see it clear as midday in her mind's eye. Visceral images of her desperate act flooded her conscious mind. The bloody malformed babe had not died quietly. It fought with the same murderous, cannibalistic intent as its father, her infernal attacker and former master.

She shuddered as she recalled the only sound her child had

made in this world before departing it, an inhuman keen. Her child's cry haunted her till this very day, each tone communicating hunger, rage, fear and confusion. The pain and isolation she felt at the time bloomed inside her again. Her mask of passivity slipped. Sudden tears stung her eyes.

"Behold! Even a stone egg can be cracked," said the Inquisitor, an oafish man draped in the gilded robes of the Lumen, the Lighthouse of Helioptera, once a benevolent goddess of enlightenment and learning. Her modern incarnation had been cast as cruel and judgmental as her clergy. "The witch knows what fate awaits her in the Underworld."

Someone from the mob shouted, "She *should* cry!"

"Fry, baby-killer, fry!" another screamed.

Baby-killer. If only they knew the whole story.

As the beak-nosed official condemned her to die in his nasal, officious tone, she realized she'd sentenced herself to this fate by joining the coven. Despite her crimes, she would not go quietly, much less easily into the waiting arms of death.

The local Conservator of the Peace and his deputies tossed torches onto the pyre, forcing Baeb to call upon the powers of the Aethyr that yet availed her. Inhaling deeply, she imagined her lungs were like the giant air bladders used in gnomish airships. Exhaling, Bruttia envisioned herself as bellows pumped by a muscular smith. She focused her will on putting out the fire around her rather than fueling it.

A collective gasp rose from the bewildered mob when the fire flared in intensity before dying. The citizens of Balsinor knew magic and mysticism when they witnessed it. Most of them tolerated non-sanctioned magic-users about as well as they tolerated strong, willful women. That is to say, not at all.

Before she could turn her efforts on her rope bindings, someone in the mob hurled a stone at her. Sharp pain exploded in her brain when it impacted her skull. She struggled to regain her senses, but a hail of stones pelted her breasts, ribs, and thighs. Each impact hurt less, instead of more, as she ebbed toward unconsciousness or death.

"Stay your hands, citizens!" The Inquisitor urged, raising his empty palms for emphasis. "I would not have the taint of this witch's murder on your souls. Let this purifying fire—a gift from Mother Sun—do it for us."

The bearded priest chanted in the Old Tongue, petitioning Helioptera with his prayer. The timber and tinder piled around Bruttia burst into flames. The crowd roared anew as they praised the efforts of the so-called holy man.

Rivulets of sweat washed the blood from the gash on Bruttia's forehead into her eyes, obscuring her vision. She fought to blink away the caustic combination of blood, sweat, and tears. Failing at that, she shook her throbbing head like a dog fresh from a bath. A howl of rage rose in her throat.

Acrid smoke curled around her, stinging her nostrils. She forced herself to calm down despite the pain. She had to breathe smoothly, sparingly. Otherwise, she'd asphyxiate and miss her chance to be burned alive while surrounded by a howling mob.

Fear ate at her resolve as the swirling winds fed the fire, driving the flames closer to her dress. Raising her eyes to the sky, she cast her gaze away from the scene of her fiery demise. She imagined herself becoming smoke, rising forth into the heavens.

Hope had all but fled when she cast her bloodshot eyes on the pale image of Luna. Ever the defiant daughter, the Moon Goddess lingered in the sky despite the burning presence of Mother Sun. Bruttia marveled at the rare daytime appearance of the celestial Silver Lady.

Her thoughts fled once again to the past. She recalled her grandmother sitting with her under the stars, teaching her how to read the phases of the moon, predict the changing seasons, and use astrology to chart people's fortunes.

Her grandmother's voice echoed in her mind.

Luna is the protector of all, even the unworthy. She chose to disobey her parents, leave her mother's house, and serve as a source of light in the darkness. No matter what happens, look to the Silver Lady at your direst hour.

Bruttia failed to find the words. It had been too long since she'd prayed to any of the gods and goddesses of Mirstone.

Even as her words remained below, her thoughts rose through the Aethyr to the heavens above. She lamented her past actions, truly regretting her orgiastic activities with the coven and her compliance, however brief, with their dark agenda. When confronted with a series of hellish, revelatory visions, she had chosen to believe them and act. They had prognosticated the unholy events that would surely unfold if she allowed the demon spawn brewing in her belly to enter the world.

Had her sacrificial act saved her from damnation or merely condemned her to an eternity in the Nine Hells? Until Bruttia laid eyes upon the moon inhabiting the sky alongside the sun, she would have bet on the latter. Ever the defiant daughter, the Moon Goddess lingered to spite her mother.

Though she could glimpse her runaway child, Helioptera could never quite catch her. Why did the Sun pursue the Moon? Did Mother Sun want to punish her daughter or forgive her for her disobedience?

As the smoke and flames arose around Bruttia, so did the clatter of metal-shod hooves on flagstone. The crowd parted to avoid being ridden down by an armored horseman approaching the crossroads at a gallop. A tall cavalier sat astride a stout warhorse covered in expensive barding. A masked chainmail coif hung from his helmet, obscuring the knight's identity.

When the mysterious rider slowed to a halt at the base of the growing conflagration, Bruttia's gaze settled on the pearlescent moonstone inset into the pommel of the sword worn on the knight's side. Fighting the panic rising in her chest, she believed the Lunar Knight's arrival no mere coincidence.

The townspeople seemed to take it as a sign as well. Though a few looked baffled by the masked cavalier's sudden appearance, most hung their heads, obviously ashamed to be seen at the scene of her execution. A stubborn, hateful few, led by boisterous old

Scipio, the aggrieved party responsible for Bruttia's current predicament, seemed angered by the knight's intrusion.

Common folk viewed the Moon Goddess as their protector, so they saw the orders of knights dedicated to the Silver Lady as living embodiments of her divine mandates. Her holy warriors did not take kindly to injustices, especially those visited upon women and children. The circumstances of her situation demanded that the knight intercede on her behalf.

The Conservator shouted, "This is none of your business, sir knight. Kindly allow us to dispense of this troublesome witch. She's sentenced to die, but we've no quarrel with you."

The Inquisitor added, "She must die by fire. It is the only way to cleanse the taint upon her soul."

Steered by silver spurs, the laconic knight's steed edged closer to the fire. The well-disciplined warhorse did not shy away from the nearness of the flames. Despite their bold words, none of the citizens moved to stop its progression. Holy men, city officials, and their armed thugs retreated a few steps.

Finally, a deputy conservator reached for the horse's bridle. The charger reared on its hind legs, dragging the swordsman forward and allowing the knight to slip from its flanks. The horse lashed out with its forehooves, while the knight drew both sword and axe. Their aggressive posturing drove back both the mob and the deputies.

The stockier of the two deputies present at the execution rushed forward, swinging his curved blade downward in a chopping motion. The Lunar Knight caught the scimitar with crossed sword and axe. A vicious kick to the knee destabilized the deputy and allowed the knight to disarm him. As the scimitar skipped across the flagstone, the cavalier backhanded the muscular deputy to the ground, and blood flew from his mouth.

Meanwhile, the warhorse flummoxed the Head Conservator and the other deputy by lashing out with its steel-shod hooves again, causing them to retreat. To Bruttia, the fierce creature deserved the label of hero as much as its master. Despite the flames crawling along her garments, she shouted words of encouragement in the mind speech common to all beasts.

The horse neighed, drawing the masked knight's attention back to the pyre. The burning witch's eyes widened when her aspiring savior hurled the axe in her direction. It sailed past her, whipped around the pole, and then sunk into the rope securing her hands behind her back. The knight snapped with his free hand, and the axe reappeared in less time than it took Bruttia to blink. Once she did, she took note of the enchanted axe's crescent shape and silver gleam.

Thanks to the magic axe, tension on the coil slackened. She wiggled, strained, and almost fell face-first into the flames when her hemp bonds snapped. Using her momentum, she tumbled from the pyre and landed on the unforgiving flagstones below. Fresh pain shot through her tiny form, but the sensation served as a powerful reminder. Though bruised and burned, she still drew breath, for now.

The towering knight reached down, grabbed her hand, and snatched her to her feet. The warrior pulled her close and then spun her, like a child's top, in the direction of his warhorse. Dizzy from blood loss and smoke inhalation, she fought to keep from fainting as she twirled away from the knight.

Nearing the steed, she spied something that alarmed her. The Head Conservator maneuvered around the pyre to threaten the knight's vulnerable flank. Bruttia screamed through the gag.

Her muffled warning almost came too late for her savior, but it allowed the knight enough time to get into position to intercept the incoming attack. The cavalier blocked the enemy's swing, before elbowing the official in the nose.

The Head Conservator lost his balance and staggered backward. When he dropped his guard, the cavalier's horizontal swing all but severed the bearded official's head from his neck. His head flopped at a sickening, impossible angle. His eyes blinked in surprise. Bruttia wondered if it was because he was seeing his own arse for the first time without using a mirror.

The knight stopped, taken aback by the sudden, surprising end to the duel. The masked warrior stepped back from his ghastly handiwork. Hesitation left the knight vulnerable once again. As the other deputy struck from behind, Bruttia ripped the gag from her mouth and called to the flames. The fire blazed outward and engulfed the advancing foe. He screamed in anguish and staggered about before pitching over onto the flagstones. His screams died along with him.

The few citizens still in the vicinity fled before the onslaught unleashed by the knight, the witch, and the warhorse. In the wake of their flight, Bruttia stood at the crossroads with the masked savior and barded charger. She had never been more grateful to have allies by her side, even if a duo of strangers.

Humbled by their acts of bravery and compassion, she did not know what to say. A simple "thank you" did not begin to cover what they had risked to save her worthless hide. She locked eyes with her knight-in-shining armor across the carnage around them. She could not help but be taken aback by the pain and anguish she found in the stranger's gaze. It felt like home.

Was it a heavy burden or some secret sin carried by the Knight of Luna or merely a reflection of her sorry state? At the moment, she did not know nor did she have time to care. She wanted to flee this land and never return.

"We have to go," Bruttia pleaded. "The others will send for reinforcements."

The hazel-eyed knight glanced toward the town and then down at the decapitated conservator. Taking the warhorse by the reigns, he offered his other hand to her.

Using the gauntleted hand to steady herself, she boosted herself up onto the back of the warhorse. In a single fluid motion, the Lunar Knight stepped into a stirrup and then swung his leg over the flank of the broad-backed mount.

The muscular thighs of the knight tightened around her narrow hips as they galloped away from the conflagration at the crossroads. Her pulse quickened with their pace. Wholly inappropriate thoughts ran rampant in her frazzled, damaged brain. Before shock gave way to slumber, she managed to eschew her notions as an irrational, immature byproduct of being rescued in such a storybook fashion, a true rarity in this savage age.

*

Bruttia awoke from her uneasy dreams to find herself staring up at the starry night. Pale moonlight filtered through the trees to illuminate the glade where she lay upon a makeshift pallet of woolen horse blankets. Her head ached enough to make it difficult to focus. She could not discern much beyond the glade's edge, but the sound of flowing water betrayed the presence of a nearby stream.

A soft rustling led her attention to the shining silhouette of the cavalier's armor-clad charger. The horse eyed her while it nibbled at a patch of clover. The warhorse paused for a moment, as Bruttia gained her feet, and then returned to eating.

Disappointment filled her when she did not find the knight bedded down in the glade. *Too bad*, she thought, *far worse things than a stranger's warm embrace on a chilly night*. She decided to settle for a less satisfying alternative and wrapped herself in the thick cloak that had served as her blanket.

Easing closer to the grazing animal, Bruttia spied a helmet and armor displayed upon a spare horse blanket. The silvered steel gleamed in the moonlight. No visible traces of blood remained on the helmet or the hauberk's chainmail links.

Gently touching her fingertips to her brow, Bruttia found that the blood had been cleaned from her wound as well. Judging by the feel of the material, the knight had bound it with a silk scarf. *Considerate, courageous, and wealthy.* Exactly the type she had always desired, but never believed herself worthy to pursue, especially after her unholy ordeal with the coven. *Perhaps this was different.* Maybe the fates had provided her mysterious savior as a divine reward for her ultimate sacrifice.

Was it cosmic confirmation that her desperate, sanguine act had been in the best interests of all humankind? Or was it a case of the Knight of the Moon being in the right place at the right time, fortune rather than fate?

Bruttia did not pretend to know. At the moment, she merely wanted to find her savior and display her gratitude. But where had the masked cavalier gone? Not far surely. Not without mount or armor.

Bruttia padded toward the sound of running water, watching her every step. Responding to her conscious desires, the vines and branches snaked away from her which made her path much less treacherous. The peat moss beneath her feet responded to her will as well, muffling the sound of her footfalls. She came to an abrupt stop when she spotted a surprising sight illumed by the full moon.

A lone figure stood waist-deep in the shallow pool formed below the fall line of the waterway. Alabaster skin stood in stark contrast to the straight dark hair cascading down the imposing individual's bare back. Muscular arms rippled as they labored to wash intimate areas concealed from her point of view.

Aching for a closer look at this person, her savior judging by height and breadth, she slipped closer to the exposed shoreline. Unable to take her eyes off the form bathing in the moonlight, she became entangled in the one thing in her path that did not respond to her desires: the knight's weapon belt.

Bruttia stumbled and plunged headfirst into the creek.

I always did know how to make a helluva entrance.

Her senses caught fire as the bone-chilling cold enveloped her as completely as the waters of the stream. She shielded her face as best she could with her flailing arms, hoping to avoid another blow to the head. Bruttia collided with the gravelly streambed, and pain exploded anew in her elbows and wrists.

Alarm, anger, and embarrassment propelled her to the surface. Breaking the plane of the water, Bruttia screamed a stream of nonsensical obscenities at the offending stream. Her mouth had detached itself from her brain and decided to work against her best interests. She spewed slurs and curses that would make the most foul-mouthed field hands blush.

First, her balance had betrayed her lack of courtly grace by pitching her off the bank in a most undignified fashion. And now her foul mouth betrayed her low-class upbringing. She fought to collect herself, but the scene unfolding before her became too much for her frazzled, stone-addled mind to bear.

Bruttia's vision focused on the nude figure she had seen bathing in the moonlight. The reality of the situation did not meet her fantastical expectations. The truth sent her reeling.

"Holy shit!" She exclaimed, unable to control her cursing anymore than her wide-eyed reaction. "You're a—"

"Woman," the curvaceous individual said. Her crossed arms covered her pendulous breasts but served to amplify the effect of her generous cleavage. The female knight's wide hips remained beneath the dark waters of the stream, preserving some semblance of modesty. Instead of appearing embarrassed, her furrowed brow and clenched jaw projected annoyance, possibly anger.

"Would you accept 'warrior goddess carved from the finest marble'?" Bruttia asked, unable to avert her gaze.

"Says you." The knight blushed from brow to waterline. However, her eyes remained fixed on Bruttia. Once again, she observed a familiar sadness there. A smile touched the edge of her savior's lips, before slipping away.

Bruttia realized that they were sisters of a sort. Neither one of them saw the beauty in themselves that others observed. The statuesque giantess would be a prized corn queen back in Bruttia's rural shire, fit to pull a plow and birth many a babe to a fat, happy husband. The mystery woman preferred swords to plowshares, though. Like the witch, the knight rebelled against the roles that society expected them to play.

"I'm Bruttia. Thanks for saving me. Not that I needed—"

"Spare me the bravado. Or the gratitude for that matter," her savior responded. "We are not men, so neither of those is required to satisfy our egos. I am Baebiana Agryffa, and though I may have spared your life for a time, I am not convinced that it is by any means saved. Walk a fine line with me."

"I hear ya, Baeb," the witch gibed, hoping to defuse the sudden tension between them. "I'll toddle along after my iron maiden like a good little babe."

Baebiana's standoffish expression evaporated. She erupted into raucous laughter. Her bittersweet smile returned, peeking out like the moon on a cloudy night.

"Perhaps the Luminaries should revise their dogma," Baebiana replied. "Suffer a witch to live, but only if she has a good sense of humor."

"Why spare me if you might have to kill me later?"

"I have need of your particular services."

"You've done so much for me already," Bruttia said. "Ask it and it is yours."

"I need you to talk to a horse about a man."

The witch stopped in her tracks, confusion furrowing her injured brow. Finally, she asked, "Isn't that normally the other way around?"

"This is no joke."

"Seriously?"

"Seriously," Baebiana said. "Ulixes, the steed that I ride, served as my father's faithful mount more than a *decadus*. If the official report of his death is correct, this horse was the last soul to see him alive."

"I'm not sure I understand what you want."

"You don't need to understand. You merely need to perform the required feat of sorcery. Then we are square."

"How do I know you won't kill me after the deed is done?"

"You don't," Baebiana said, stepping within arm's reach of Bruttia. Taking the smaller woman's hand, the knight held it to her heart and said, "All I can do is to swear upon the only thing of value left to me in this world: the honor bestowed upon me as the noble daughter of a late Knight of Luna.

"As the Silver Lady's light protects us during Mirstone's long nights, my oath shall protect you from harm…so long as you hold true to purpose. But beware. Betray me or my quest, and your life is forfeit."

Bruttia found the woman standing before her to be a true conundrum. One moment, Baebiana acted gruff, haughty, and aloof. And the next, she seemed grave, sincere, and intimate.

Could the grieving woman be trusted? Probably. Was the wannabe knight in over her pretty head? Most definitely.

Bruttia smiled again. Diverting her eyes from the other woman's intense gaze, she realized her hand rested on Baebiana's impressive bosom. This time Bruttia blushed.

A coarse, masculine voice called from the shoreline, "Ya gonna kiss her or not?"

"Yeah, we ain't got all night," said another.

Baeb wheeled around at the sound of the strange voices. A trio of armored men emerged from the undergrowth along the banks of the stream. Two of them carried sturdy iron maces; the third man shouldered a cocked-and-loaded crossbow.

The crossbowman said, "That'll be enough of that. We're here to enforce morality, not encourage corruptions of it."

Bruttia recognized him as one of the Deputy Conservators at the crossroads. The press of the crowd fleeing the scene had prevented him from aiding his fellow deputies.

Tugging at his beard, one of the mace-wielding deputies replied, "Noble Justinus, always the honorable one."

Keeping his crossbow trained on Bruttia, Justinus said, "Stow it, Iulus! Be productive and go inform the Inquisitor that we've caught his witch. And her confederate."

"Sure you and Virgil can handle these two dangerous ladies on your own? After all, you've let them escape once already."

"Confident as I am that the next smartass thing you say will be your last, Iulus. I'm in no mood."

Justinus's stony gaze shifted, enough for the sharp-tongued heckler to see the same gleam that had given Bruttia pause.

Iulus fell silent.

Justinus repeated his order, louder this time. The mouthy deputy nodded and then disappeared into the bushes without further commentary.

Though they stood on opposite sides of this conflict, Bruttia admired the crossbowman for having enough self-respect to silence his critics. Throughout her short, tumultuous life, she had been forced to ignore more critics than she'd ever managed to silence.

Just another entry on her growing list of regrets, Bruttia lamented. But having secured a new lease on life, she decided to do something about silencing her critics.

Starting now!

The witch called upon one of the first powers taught to her by her grandmother, a simple but effective charm that proved indispensable when dealing with the weak-minded.

She injected her voice with a tone as sweet as honey when she said, "If your duties include policing morality to uphold decency, I entreat you to return my companion's tunic. It's there on the bank."

"A reasonable request and one I shall see obeyed," Virgil replied. He retrieved the garment and edged toward her.

Her bewitching suggestion failed to sway Justinus. His will was strong, but he was distracted nonetheless. Turning to his comrade, he said, "Don't get near them. It could be a trick."

Stopping at the edge of the stream, Virgil tossed the silk tunic. As it danced through the space separating the opposing parties, the pearlescent material caught the moonlight perfectly. The shimmering sight distracted almost everyone.

A sudden, sharp snap arrested Bruttia's wandering eyes. A whirl of motion crossed her vision. Her focus settled on the familiar gleam of the knight's axe as it struck Virgil in the chest. Baebiana caught the tunic with her outstretched hand.

Undeterred by the death of his fellow deputy, Justinus fired the crossbow leveled at Bruttia's chest. Acting as her savior again, the knight jerked the witch out of the bolt's path, nearly wrenching the smaller woman's arm out its socket in the process.

Despite the pain, Bruttia concentrated on disabling Justinus before he could reload his weapon. She called out to the dense undergrowth around him. The flora responded, snaking around his legs to his torso and arms. The bewildered deputy struggled against the vines and saplings, but her magic held.

Baebiana strode boldly toward the entangled man. As the bare-assed woman cleared the water, she snapped her fingers and recalled the axe. Justinus flinched as she lifted the weapon aloft. She struck him once in the temple, with the backside of the axe, and his eyes rolled back in his head. The enchanted vegetation held the unconscious man upright, his feet mere inches from the ground. To Bruttia, he looked like a discarded marionette left dangling from its strings.

Convinced the threat was neutralized for now, the witch watched as the knight slipped the simple yet elegant tunic over her head, shoulders, and breasts. The long shirt fell to the middle of her thick thighs, clinging wetly to every curve on the voluptuous woman's body. For a moment, Bruttia wondered if she would be the one who ended up being bewitched.

Baebiana appeared oblivious to Bruttia's lingering gaze. After retrieving her weapon belt, the knight said, "Come on! We don't have long before that fool returns with an entire posse of armed men howling for your blood and mine."

Without waiting for a reply, the knight plunged into the undergrowth and disappeared into the darkness beyond the banks of the stream. Bruttia followed, unwilling to be left behind.

Back in the glade, Baebiana finished dressing in a hurry. Bruttia squired for her, albeit ineptly, knowing neither arms nor armor beyond cudgel or dagger.

As she struggled to fasten the knight's undercoat that went below the chainmail hauberk, the witch commented, "How in the

Nine Hells did you get this over your girls without help?"

Scowling, Baebiana said, "Normally, I bind them before armoring up and gallivanting around on horseback."

"Where's the binding? I don't see it anywhere."

"It's on your head. I used it to stop the bleeding."

Bruttia brushed her fingers to the silk scarf bound about her forehead and blushed again. She smiled sheepishly.

As Bruttia reached up to untie it, Baebiana said, "Keep it. I have a spare in my saddlebags, but there's no time."

Baebiana snapped the last fastener on her undercoat and then wiggled into the roomy chainmail shirt that stretched from her shoulders to the top of her knees. Bruttia held the knight's weapon belt ready. She fitted it around the taller woman, securing it above her hips.

"At least the armor is roomier than the padding."

"It belonged to my father," Baebiana said. "He was a titan of a man, even compared to an ogre of a woman like me."

"You loved him a lot then?"

"As much as any daughter could love her father."

"Probably more than I loved mine. He wasted his life in the fields, only to see most of what he grew go to support greedy lords, corrupt officials, and this withered, dying country."

"My father slaved away every day for the state, eventually sacrificing himself for it, if that is to be believed. That's how I knew he loved me. He sacrificed so much for me."

Bruttia's cheeks flushed with warmth. Fresh tears welled in her eyes at a sudden, painful epiphany. Her father had probably labored his life away for the same selfless reason. The young witch desired nothing more than the loving embrace of her father, but she might as well be dead to him because of the way she'd lived her life.

Bruttia's father had made that clear after the death of her

grandmother. He had never approved of his daughter being taught hedge magic and herbalism, but limited his criticisms to groaning and grumbling when the old woman was still alive.

In the wake of her grandmother's death, his paranoid delusions about Bruttia embracing an immoral life and consorting with demons and spirits had prompted him to cast her from his household. Storming away with naught but the clothes on her back, she had set the barn ablaze and then vowed never to return. In her mind, she could never return home, especially not after his worst fears and delusions had become her reality.

Baebiana broke the uncomfortable silence between them. Drying her own tears, she asked, "Can we bemoan our tortured pasts away from here?"

"Yes, please." Bruttia sniffled. "Where to now?"

"That's up to you and Ulixes. Where *are* we going?"

The warhorse snorted and nodded at the mention of his name. When the witch extended an open palm and edged toward him, he pawed at the ground. In Bruttia's experience, animals perceived Aethyr energies better than most humans, though not as well as elves, magic-users, or other fae. The knight's steed proved to be no exception. The horse whinnied and backed away.

Bruttia said, "You remember me, don't you, big fella? We touched minds at the crossroads. You were so brave to rescue me. If you can be brave for me now, we can help Baebiana find out what happened to her father, your former master."

Ulixes took a few tentative steps forward. Snorting, he dipped his armored head, allowing Bruttia to touch his muzzle, to touch his mind. Though she did not require physical contact to converse with mind-speech, it facilitated her ability to read the thoughts and feelings of both people and beasts.

"Where's the last place you saw your master alive?"

A barrage of images flooded the witch's mind after asking the question. From the point-of-view of the warhorse, she watched as Ulixes crested the rise overlooking the bustling twin cities of Themis and Theophania. Identical spires on the banks of the

Celestial River marked the boundary for each city. The broad river running betwixt the Twin Cities served as the sole water route through the mountains to the Fool's March, arid grasslands named for the countless ill-prepared travelers to meet their fates there.

Until Ulixes broke contact, Bruttia imagined she could hear the voices of the dead wandering the Fool's March. Once the shared scenery faded, ghastly moans became the howls of hounds. The posse had returned in force by the sound of it.

Fortunately, the witch had gleaned enough for now. Though she had their destination, she provided Baebiana with nothing but a cardinal direction…for now anyway. The wannabe knight seemed honorable enough, but Bruttia wanted to be far from their pursuers before she told the other woman too much.

"We head north, along the coast," Bruttia said.

Baebiana mounted Ulixes with ease despite the layers of padding and armor. She smirked as she settled into the saddle.

"North it is then," she said, nudging Ulixes forward.

The horse sidled away from Bruttia as the dogs drew closer. The witch looked skyward, locking eyes with Luna in all her glory. Big and bright, the moon shone down upon them. The Lunar Knight and barded charger gleamed brighter than any previous sign the powers of Mirstone had ever provided.

"All right! It's the Twin Cities."

Baebiana reigned in the warhorse. The avenging daughter responded by extending one gauntleted hand. Gathering the hem of her dress, Bruttia ran toward the pair of armor-clad warriors. Taking the proffered hand one more time, she climbed onto the saddle and joined them for a midnight ride through the heartlands. They rode for their lives, guided by Luna's silvery light and Ulixes' nimble hooves. If they made it to coast alive, Baeb vowed to kiss the feet of the Moon Goddess's statue at the famed Temple of the Silver Lady in Theophania.

*

The next day, fiery Helioptera glared down upon them. Her

withering gaze forced Ulixes from a gallop to a trot to a halt. Bruttia empathized with the poor animal. The foam-covered warhorse had to be exhausted. Ulixes had run for countless leagues, until starry night had given way to break of day.

If its legs were half as sore as her ass, she could not understand how the charger could remain on its feet. Ulixes had borne their combined weight, along with gear and armor, through the night and morning. Hoping to provide them all with some sort of relief, Bruttia slid from the saddle to the ground.

Bruttia followed, moving stiffly, throwing one leg over the saddle with visible effort. She wobbled as she put foot to flagstone. Though the cavalier towered over her, the shorter woman's lower center of gravity helped her to steady her savior.

"Looks like we could all use a rest," Bruttia observed.

"Agreed. We'll have to be back on the road by midday. Those riders may not be far behind. Whatever you did to rile them up must've been pretty bad."

"I provided specialized services to my fellow citizens, as I'm doing now."

"Whore around and anger the wrong wife, did you?"

The witch said, "I'm no whore! That particular service is free of charge to the right parties, thank you very much."

Bruttia stormed off in the direction of a thick copse of trees on a hilltop some distance from the road. That small grove would have to suffice for cover. It would also serve as an ideal vantage point to spy upon the road. She concentrated on her leaden footsteps rather than her simmering anger at the pompous, presumptuous bitch.

Baebiana caught her before she reached the woody summit. She laid a heavy hand on Bruttia's slender shoulder. The witch wheeled around, ready to curse, fight, or possibly even fuck the woman who'd confused her with endearing and noble acts, only to follow them with hurtful accusations about her character.

Instead, Bruttia looked into Baebiana's sad, haunted eyes and connected once more. Her resolve faltered. Words failed her. The witch considered herself to be a damned soul unworthy of the time and energy it had taken the knight to save her from the flames' embrace.

Have I damned Baebiana, too?

So far, her savior had murdered two Conservators of the Peace. If nothing else, the knight deserved to know why both of them might be wanted women. If nothing else, the Luminaries would seek vengeance for Baebiana's interference.

"I sold a preparation to a woman with child who did not wish to carry it to term. Is that what you wanted to know? I didn't realize that she'd been knocked up by the richest, most influential old man in the whole town! Much less that he had no living heirs."

Baebiana said, "You must mean Noble Scipio? His name is known to me. The House of Agryffa did brisk trade with that town, until its noble daughter beheaded its Head Conservator. Now, who knows?

"He is called Noble Scipio, but he is little more than a merchant whose ego bloats faster than his purse. Various plagues took wives and children but left him. Evidence the good fall from the vine while ripe, leaving the old to wither and rot."

"I swear I'd never heard his name until they snatched me from my bed at the inn," Bruttia said. "My first night's sleep in a warm bed in a fortnight, and it's interrupted by a trial without jury and a public execution. I sold a number of potions, poultices, and preparations that day, but Scipio was the only citizen to complain. He proclaimed me to be a witch who'd murdered his unborn child. I did not force her to do anything."

"Ridiculous! Similar remedies to those same troubles exist in every city, town, and dale. If they had burned you as a witch for it, the Luminaries of Helioptera might as well burn every apothecary, midwife, and wizard in the whole damn empire. But then we'd be no better than barbarians."

"Exactly!" Bruttia exclaimed. "I simply provide a service, a vital and necessary one. Countless women die trying to alleviate the symptoms of an unwanted, unnatural, or unhealthy pregnancy. Countless more die because they cannot or will not do anything about it. Even when the choice is made, it is anything but easy, anything but desirable. It is what it is."

"Choice, instinct, or mistake, it's a woman's decision to make. The bearer of Scipio's unborn heir made hers. If I have to die—or kill—to preserve that freedom for her, for you, I will. Being the kept concubine of a nobleman is no sort of life for any woman. My own mother was a full participant in her marriage. She misses her partner even now, and I quest with her blessing."

"Do you think her correct for following her instincts?" Bruttia asked. "Scipio's concubine, not your mother. Was she right to free herself of one unwanted bastard forced upon her by another?"

"That's between her and the gods in my opinion," Baebiana said. "Every case is different. But if there is no love, no affection, what kind of life is that for a child? For in the absence of love and light, hatred and darkness take root in the heart of the young, twisting them towards mischief and evil."

Embracing her, Bruttia repeated, "So you see. So you see."

I knew she was my knight in shining armor.

The witch had found a genuine friend in the impostor Knight of the Moon, someone who would accept her despite her lengthy list of past sins and transgressions. Baebiana could look past an act that Bruttia herself found repugnant but wholly natural—even necessary at times. *Perhaps I'll find a way to forgive myself...someday.* Until then, Bruttia decided to focus on helping Baebiana discover what happened to her father. As the witch drifted off to sleep in the knight's arms, another lesson her grandmother taught her echoed from the past: Having good friends is easier when you are a good friend. *I'll try, Baeb. I'll try.*

THE END

Hinter Wizard
David Jones

Promathan Kurent tied his horse next to three others at a hitching post along the wet, cobblestone street. He had considered paying to stable the hateful creature, he disliked the idea of leaving his saddlebags unattended, but he couldn't spare the coin. Besides, the town of Halesford looked reasonably safe, and anyone who stole the spiteful mare deserved what they got. She tried nipping his ear, but he dodged the attempt, mindful of her evil ways.

A constable dressed in leather, a blackjack tied at his waist, stood nearby. He eyed Promathan. "You an exterminator?"

"Yeah." Promathan withdrew his staff from the special saddle holster he had commissioned of an elf artisan in Vaelkesh.

The constable placed a hand on his weapon, his dark eyes gone wide. "That's a hell of a spear. I can't let you go inside wielding that thing. The mayor and sheriff are in there."

"It's not a spear. It's a staff." Promathan snapped his fingers to produce a spark in the air that sizzled like a snuffed ember. "I'm a wizard."

"I don't care if your Billy Howe, King of the Dwarves, you're not entering the conclave carrying that thing." The constable, who stood a head and a half taller than Promathan, pointed to a gated alcove built into a nearby wall. An assortment of swords, maces, knives, and sundry other weapons lay inside behind a wrought iron fence secured with chains. "All exterminators must relinquish their weapons to enter the conclave."

Promathan considered arguing the point. Larger or not, he figured he could take the constable in a straight fight, with or without magic. He had come up on far harder streets than these. But bloodying the man's nose for doing his job didn't seem genteel, and Promathan was late.

He handed the man his staff. "Understand, this staff means more to me than your life."

The constable's nose flared, and he tried to stare Promathan down. That lasted perhaps three seconds before he straightened and took a step back, eyes wide. He gestured nervously over one shoulder at a solid wooden door behind him. "The meeting's in there, wizard."

Promathan favored him with a nod and stepped inside. Though it bore no particular signs on the outside, he recognized the type of building he had entered the instant he cleared the threshold. Most large cities possessed this sort of place, an unmarked—and likely unremarked—prison to house criminals the town proctors wanted to forget...or torture. The scent of burning tobacco and unwashed bodies permeated the air.

Sixteen people sat on two rows of benches facing a sallow-faced man dressed in a fine, if faded, red suit illuminated by a handful of oil lamps dispersed about the room. Behind him stood six prison cells, all empty, separated by a heavy wooden door.

"Exterminator?" Demanded the man in red.

Promathan nodded.

"You're late. I'm Dannald Willison, the mayor hereabouts. Sit there." He pointed to an open spot on the rear bench next to a mountain of a man wearing black leather armor festooned with rusty spikes.

The giant glared at Promathan who let the look slide off him. It meant nothing. In ten years hunting and killing exotic—often magical—creatures, Promathan had learned one thing for certain: there existed no true *camaraderie* between exterminators. Every rival in this occupation represented the chance at a lost payday. Any you could mean mug into leaving off the pursuit, you wouldn't have to fight later.

"As I was saying." The mayor ran a hand through what remained of his gray hair. "Whatever foul beast has been terrorizing the city, it's proven untraceable for our hunters. The sheriff and I have organized no fewer than twelve searches for it in the last forty days without success, and still, the thing continues to kill. The situation didn't seem dire when it was taking livestock and damaging farmland, but of late it seems to have gained a taste for human flesh. Two weeks ago, it killed a young lass of twelve right here in the city without any witnesses. Then, just last night, it savaged a young shepherd on a farm three miles east of here."

"Bear?" Suggested a lean rugged man on the front bench. He wore a circle within a circle tattoo on his left cheek, the guild sign of an assassin out of Talwaes or one of the other human cities west of Fool's March.

"We wouldn't call on outside help for a *bear*." A tall, broad-shouldered man stood up from the front row. He wore a black tunic and leather britches with a golden brooch in the shape of a blackjack on his chest and a real one tied loosely at his hip.

"Roguern Sten, our sheriff." The mayor gestured at the speaker.

"Could be a griffon," said an elf on Promathan's row. "We've seen them come out of the dwarf mountains into Lawaes before."

The mayor shrugged one shoulder."Frankly, we don't care what it is so long as it's dead within the fortnight. We have a spring festival to host in a month's time, and Count Rasven Gelsulloch plans to attend, or had done anyway. The count has voiced his concerns about bringing his family to Halesford with a ravening beast on our doorstep."

"If there truly is a beast," rumbled the sheriff. He walked his gaze back and forth across the gathering, his lips pressed into a thin line. "Ten years ago, a band of unscrupulous crooks duped the city council into believing we were under siege from a pack of dire wolves. They staged sheep attacks and planted evidence, all in an effort to steal the reward money we offered."

Promathan grimaced. Scammers like that gave honest exterminators a bad reputation. Not only did their tricks fray customer confidence, it made them reluctant to hire legitimate help when a real threat arose. They made Promathan's life harder, a sin he would happily punish given the chance.

"As you can imagine, we're eager to avoid making that mistake a second time," the mayor said. "Therefore, we are assigning an overseer for each exterminator."

A general groan of disapproval filled the air.

"You don't like it? Leave." Sheriff Sten waved a meaty hand at the exit. "We're paying two hundred gold for this job. We expect results, and we won't be duped. Your overseer will accompany you at all times during your hunt. If you should give your overseer the slip, or do anything they find unscrupulous, you will immediately lose your chance to collect the bounty."

"And you'll be escorted from the city. Now, let's have a count." The mayor waggled his fingers as if doing sums, his gaze roving back and forth across the benches. He scrunched his nose, brows furrowed, and pointed a stubby finger at Promathan. "You're an extra. We only brought eight overseers for the teams who had already arrived."

"Good," Promathan said. "I'll work alone."

"Not a chance." Sheriff Sten turned to the mayor. "We could bar him. We already have eight."

Promathan bristled, but the mayor came to his aid.

"Why lessen our chances? Surely, we can come up with one more observer." He rubbed the stubble under his chin. "How about that orphan boy who works for you?"

"Modi?"

"That's the one. Where is he?" The mayor looked around as if he had misplaced something of little consequence.

Promathan resisted the impulse to rise—the sheriff would probably take that amiss—but he leaned forward on the bench. "See here, ours is a dangerous line of work. I won't be saddled with watching after some child."

"He's mucking out cells below." Ignoring Promathan, Sheriff Sten threw open the door at the back and leaned his head into a darkened staircase. "Ay! Boy! Modi, get your ass up here."

Quick footsteps sounded from below, preceding a lanky youth of perhaps seventeen years. His careworn clothes fit well enough, but appeared secondhand—maybe third—with many patches and permanent stains. Dark-haired and slim to the point of starvation, the kid looked like a street urchin crafty enough to have survived puberty.

"Yes, Sheriff?" Modi whipped off the cap he wore.

"You're to go with this man." Sheriff Sten pointed at Promathan. "Note everything he does, make certain he isn't cheating the city, and report it all back to me."

"Yes, sir."

Either Modi understood what the sheriff meant by 'cheating the city' or else he was too afraid to question the directive. Probably the latter. Relieved the kid was no child at least, Promathan favored Modi with a nod. He wanted no minder at all, but if the mayor and sheriff insisted on saddling him with one, better an obsequious teenage servant than some self-righteous constable who would likely question Promathan's every decision.

"Very well," Promathan grumbled. "I'll have him along. But you better not slow my work, boy."

"I won't, sir!" Modi nodded enthusiastically, thought better of the action, and switched to shaking his head with the same vigor. The kid looked delighted at the prospect of breathing fresh air.

"Then it's settled." The mayor gestured at the exit. "Everyone outside. We'll mount up, and the sheriff will lead you all to the scene of the first attack."

The group filed outside into the street, the assorted exterminators and observers formed into a semi-circle around Sheriff Sten and Mayor Willison. None of them looked any better by the afternoon light than they had in semi-darkness. Modi, blinking hard, kept stuck close to Promathan's side, though he thankfully said nothing. Good kid.

"Constable," Sheriff Sten said. "Give the exterminators their weapons back."

"Aye, sir." The constable who had given Promathan grief over his staff unlocked the iron gate securing the bricked-in alcove and begin handing out instruments of death.

"Hinter wizard."

The words made Promathan turn around slowly like a cat, jaw tight. Behind him stood a slight man dressed in a robe the color of ripe wheat. He wore a conical hat, the tip bent at a right angle, a silver medallion strung about his neck, and a scraggly beard which he had at some point dyed gray though the roots showed a quarter-inch blond.

A guild wizard.

From the glyph etched on the man's medallion—a bull thrashing impressively long horns against an oak tree—he belonged to the Taurus Maginarium, a pompous lot more enamored with the mystery of magic than its actual use. A stuffy troupe of assholes every one. Though, in their defense, Promathan found all guild wizards that way. They couldn't help it.

"Didn't think I'd recognize the stink of fakery about you, eh? Thought you could sneak under my nose?"

"Why not? You snuck under mine." Promathan grasped the thick lapels of his own tunic and regarded the wizard for a moment before hawking a wad of spit an inch from the man's soft boots.

The wizard jumped back, his face gone red with fury. "Challenge! You will die for that, street mage! I demand a duel."

"Gentlemen!" Mayor Willison moved between them, scrawny arms outstretched. "This isn't the time for wizardly politics. We want no duels here."

"Your city has signed the Taurus guild accords. We have the right to exact justice on those who practice the Art without sanction."

"He's right, Dannald," Sheriff Sten said before locking a stern look on the guild mage. "Though the guild will be responsible for any damages."

"Of course, Sheriff." The guild wizard smiled like a fat man eyeing a particularly decadent dessert.

"What is your name?" Sheriff Sten produced a small pad bound in leather and a bit of sharpened charcoal from a pocket. "I'll have to make an official report about this."

"I am Elain Yohonsen, member in good standing of the Taurus Maginarium, wizard of the seventh degree, holder of the chalice of—"

"That will do." The sheriff turned to Promathan. "You?"

"Promathan."

"No other titles?"

Promathan shook his head.

"Fine and dandy." Sheriff Sten waved to the crowd of exterminators which had grown appreciably with the addition of townsfolk come to investigate the hubbub. "Move back, people! We're to have a wizards duel here. The city will not be responsible for any harm that befalls spectators. You get turned into a salamander that's your own business! Wizards, on my word you will begin."

"Is there something I should do for you as your minder?" Modi asked.

Promathan shook his head, touched by the kid's earnest question. "Nah. Just move back. This should be over quick."

The crowd circled around Promathan and Elain though they gave them ample room given the sheriff's warnings. Modi joined them off to Promathan's right so he could watch the action.

Elain, who had already retrieved his staff, a gnarled bit of hickory with an irregularly shaped knob on one end, took the weapon in both hands. "Make ready, pretender. I promise not to do you any lingering harm, I'd like to leave you the option of joining the guild after I've taught you some real magic."

Promathan tossed his head side to side eliciting several pops in both directions. "I make no such promises, shit for brains. You challenged me."

Elain scowled. "Enough talk! Let's see what sort of underwhelming tricks you've learned on the streets!"

"Begin!" Shouted the sheriff.

Elain started mumbling some nonsense as all guild wizards

were wont to do when casting. A dark cloud formed around the knobby end of his staff, condensation dripping off the wood onto the cobblestones. Flashes of silver-blue static-like jagged fingers sizzled inside the mist.

Promathan mumbled no words. In fact, he gathered no magic. Why bother? With his opponent focused on his burgeoning spell, Promathan took four long strides to close the distance, set his feet, and punched Elain on the jaw with all the strength he could muster. The blow produced a satisfying POP that echoed along the narrow street. The crowd erupted with a mix of sympathetic groans, surprised exclamations of delight, and pleased whistles.

Elain, unconscious, hit the cobblestones, his mouth bloody. His staff rolled out of hands, though given its odd shape, it didn't go far, leaving a damp trail in its wake.

Sheriff Sten looked from the crumpled guild mage to Promathan. "Can't say I'd call that fair. You didn't use magic."

"Sure I did. This here's a sleeping potion." Promathan held up his fist.

The sheriff threw back his head and laughed. The crowd joined him, though the mayor remained sober.

"Someone drag the wizard out of the street, would you?" The mayor gestured at a couple of young bystanders who hurried to obey. "The rest of you exterminators, form up around my carriage there and follow me to the first attack sight."

While the others busied themselves gathering weapons and saddling mounts, Promathan pulled his overly spirited horse and young Modi off to one side. "Think you could lead me to the most recent attack instead?"

Modi, whose brown eyes kept darting to the prostrate Elain—only now beginning to rouse—nodded absently. "The Vernon farm. Yes, I know the way."

"Quick now, before anyone notices we're gone."

"Shouldn't we tell the mayor?" Modi looked pained. He struck Promathan as the type of young man fearful of breaking a rule—

any rule.

"No, boy. That's rather the point. Hurry now."

They made good their escape by turning down a narrow alleyway that brought them to a wide dirt road on the west side of the city where traders in makeshift stalls hawked their wares.

"No one saw us leave," Modi said, sounding astonished. "Did you work some sort of magic on them, sir?"

Promathan considered saying yes, but fooling a kid this innocent felt dirty. "In my experience, a pound of distraction is worth a ton of glamour. Why waste time on magic to disappear when the people you're evading aren't looking your way?"

Modi nodded, a faraway look in his eyes. "The same reason you didn't bother with a spell against that guild wizard?"

"Exactly. Old guard mages rely too much on spells and conjuring and all that muck. Granted, some of that stuff has its place, but when it comes to dealing with a problem, magic usually isn't the answer."

They walked in silence for several minutes, Promathan leading his mount to keep pace with the young errand boy. Surprisingly, the mare behaved. Most times, when Promathan attempted to pull it by a leader line, the hateful thing would spend every moment bobbing its head or tugging back to test its master's grip. Today, it walked peaceably. Maybe he had finally broken the creature, or maybe it was lulling him in order to make a break when it got the chance. He really needed a new horse.

The road narrowed as they traveled, the city's cramped buildings giving way to thick forest on either side of the path. Crows cawed in the high branches and somewhere not far off a woodpecker beat a steady tattoo in search of breakfast.

"How did you come to work for the sheriff?" Promathan asked to bridge the silence. He felt sure the boy wanted to speak but feared asking questions. "You're not his son are you?"

Modi shook his head. "I was a foundling—grew up at the orphanage. The sheriff took me on as an apprentice when I was eight. Gave me work."

"Apprentice or slave?" Promathan eyed Modi for a moment and the boy dropped his gaze.

"I'm free," he said without a speck of conviction.

"Free to starve should you try making it on your own? What skills have you learned during this apprenticeship?"

Modi shrugged one shoulder, embarrassed to answer.

"Sweeping, mopping, scrubbing? All the things that make for a good lawman I take it?"

"I know how to shoe a horse. Old Taberal, he's the watch smithy, he's promised to teach me some metalwork...sometime."

Promathan nodded sagely. He had seen this sort of thing before—a poor boy raised up to a poor position and expected to thank his betters for it. The sheriff had no intention of deputizing Modi. Why jeopardize his free servant? It was a damned shame.

"That the farm?" Promathan gestured at a flat spread of pastureland where several oxen and a herd of sheep and goats grazed.

Modi nodded and the two of them made their way to a ramshackle farmhouse fenced off from the pastures. A barrel-chested man, his brown skin glistening with sweat, answered the door when they knocked.

"Farmer Vernon," Modi said with a deep nod that bordered on a bow. "I'm Modi, the sheriff's ward, and this is Promathan. He's one of the exterminators that's been hired by the mayor. We're here to see Troaden if that's alright with you."

Vernon eyed the boy for a long moment, causing Modi to look down before he turned an intense gaze on Promathan. "You come to kill whatever murdered my farmhand?"

"If I catch it, I'll kill it." Promathan met the taller man's gaze. Most of being a wizard and a hunter of exotic creatures balanced on knowing how to deal with people. Vernon liked directness, and that suited Promathan fine.

Satisfied by whatever he saw, Vernon stepped onto the porch, shutting the door behind him. Setting a brisk pace, he marched into the yard and around the back, obliging Promathan and Modi to keep up. They crossed a horse paddock to a barn easily three times larger than Vernon's house.

"We put the body in here," he said as he lifted the door latch. "Would've buried it already, 'cept the sheriff said there might be people interested in seeing the wounds."

The scent of horses, hounds, and death met Promathan's nose the instant he stepped inside the barn. Though the afternoon heat wasn't unpleasant—the days were cooling with Autumn on the approach—the barn's interior was stifling. No doubt, that added to the stench.

"Is it in the loft?" Promathan asked.

Vernon shook his head and set about untying a hempen rope cinched in one corner. Promathan followed the line with his eyes to a rapidly descending bundle of cloth, brown where it wasn't red with blood.

"I had to suspend poor Troaden," Vernon said as he gently lowered the wrapped corpse to the barn floor. "Didn't want whatever killed him coming back to finish the meal."

"Did you see the creature?" Promathan asked.

Vernon set about loosening the dead man's shrouds the way he might unwrap a summer sausage, his expression grim. The smell intensified.

Modi's face paled and he swallowed rapidly, though to his credit he remained where he stood.

"Didn't get a good look." Vernon stood from his grisly task and folded his arms. "I caught the beast on the attack though. Heard whatever it was screaming, just the same as poor Troaden, like it was mimicking him. Found 'em in the back pasture, right by the woods at dusk."

"The creature screamed?" Promathan bent to examine the farmhand's body. Troaden still wore a woolen shirt which had been split into three ribbons from the divot at his throat to a finger's width below his belly button. Whatever had cut him had sliced through his flesh and the organs below.

"Yeah. Sounded like a bird if you ask me, except larger." Vernon watched Promathan. "Sheriff laughed when I said that. I notice you ain't laughing."

Promathan shook his head. "No. Can you show us the place this happened?"

Vernon led them across an open pasture to the forest's edge where something, likely the doomed Troaden or else his attacker, had churned up the dirt and uprooted several hand-sized patches of grass.

"Your bird attacked the farmhand and then made to drag him off." Promathan squatted to examine the grass more closely.

"How do you know that?" Modi likewise bent to examine the ground.

Promathan pointed at a long gouge. "See here. Even though he was gutted, Troaden attempted to anchor himself against something large enough to slide his body weight."

"That's why I didn't get a good look at it," Vernon said, shaking his head. "It was half in the woods by the time I got here, and I was seeing it by torchlight. Damned thing fled before I could make it out, and left Troaden to die after six hours of pure hell laying in his bed screaming for relief."

"I think we've seen enough, sir." Promathan patted the big farmer's shoulder. "We'll see ourselves off your land."

Vernon nodded and swiped a callused hand across wet eyes. "Me and the misses are going to bury Troaden before sunset. I don't care what the sheriff says. Poor boy deserves a respectful send-off."

"That he does," Promathan said.

"I hope you find whatever did this and take its head, hunter." With that, Farmer Vernon turned on his heels, shoulders thrust back, and headed for the barn at a hard pace. Promathan got the feeling he didn't enjoy letting others see him cry.

"Do you know what did this?" Modi tilted his head to one side.

"I have an idea." With Vernon gone, Promathan ran his hands through the grass near the longest of the furrows poor Troaden had gouged with his naked fingers and came up with a small, green object. He had spotted it earlier but hadn't wanted the farmer questioning him about it. Thankfully, Vernon hadn't noticed it, likely because its color nearly matched the long grass that verged the forest.

Modi looked expectantly at the thing sitting in Promathan's palm but held his tongue. A trait beat into him by the sheriff? Or was the young man patient enough to curb his questions on his own? Promathan couldn't decide which, but he respected the young man's forbearance.

"Ever seen one of these?" Promathan asked.

Modi shook his head. "No, sir. Should I have?"

"Not unless you frequent a dragon eyrie. It's one of their scales."

Modi's look of astonishment made Promathan grin. Had his own master experienced this sort of enjoyment from shocking his young pupil?

The boy's look magnified when he dropped his gaze back to the ground and immediately freed a similar scale from a tangle of grass, this one sky blue and shining. "Look, another!"

Now it was Promathan's turn to stare in shocked disbelief. "Shit. There's two of them."

*

They followed a trail of broken tree limbs, scattered footprints hidden in the ubiquitous pine needles, and disturbed undergrowth deep into the forest. Continuing its unprecedented docility, Promathan's horse left slack in the leader line as it followed gamely behind him. Any minute, he expected the beast to nip his shoulder or go wheeling off for no reason, but it never did. Insane creatures, horses. Harder to gauge than a snake.

"Promathan?" Modi said, after they had walked for some time under the dappled forest shade. "Shouldn't we—shouldn't you—get some help if you plan to face two dragons?"

Promathan drew his horse around a particularly wide oak tree to avoid a patch of briers. "Without question. If these were grown dragons, I'd just as soon find something else to hunt. But those scales we found came from hatchlings—probably not much older than fifty or sixty years."

Modi, who had found a walking stick tall enough to reach his shoulder, tapped it lightly on the ground near a set of double claw prints in the dirt. "Do dragons usually hunt in pairs when they're young?"

The boy asked cogent questions, and he seemed to take the dragons' long lives in stride. Shame he was a near slave to the town sheriff. He should have been apprenticing as a clerk somewhere, learning to read and write and think.

"As a rule, no," Promathan said, keeping his thoughts to himself. "Dragons are solitary creatures on the whole, but sometimes a couple of brood mates will live together for a few decades—gives them a competitive advantage. Sooner or later, once they've grown smart enough to start speaking, they split up."

"Dragons talk?" Modi asked.

"Takes a long time, more than a century in most cases, but yes. Clever beast, your dragon. Smart, but more than that, wily in ways only the most sinister of humans can ever match. I don't tangle with grown ones. Too risky. Hatchlings though, they've got the brains of a particularly smart hound. Dangerous, but not cunning."

"Have you ever faced a full-grown one?" The eagerness in Modi's gaze pled for Promathan to say yes.

"Yes. Once."

"Wow."

"But don't go thinking me some hero of the ages. I was new to the job. Thought I could take on a real beast to prove myself. It didn't go well."

"Something must have gone right. You're still alive."

"I'm alive because I had the good sense to run when I got the chance. One wizard against a mature dragon? That's the recipe for broiled wizard. I thought I could kill the thing while it slept."

"Seems the most reasonable time to me," Modi agreed. "I assume it woke?"

"The blasted thing was never asleep." Promathan ground his teeth at the frightful memory. "It lulled me into thinking I had caught it unawares in a cave. It was toying with me. I escaped with my life, but only because I was small enough to slither through human-sized passageways. I'll never tangle with an adult dragon again."

Modi nodded, seemingly deep in thought.

Promathan pushed through a curtain of ivy that had spread across two trees and beheld a clearing filled with knee-high grass. At the far end, sunning themselves on a large, flat rock, the green and blue adolescent dragons glistened like irregularly shaped pieces of metal. Heatwaves perturbed the air around them.

"Huh," Modi said, his eyes wide with fright, his voice stammering. "Sleeping dragons. Any chance these are pretending?"

"Young ones aren't that smart," Promathan whispered. "Here." He pressed the horse's lead into Modi's limp hand and set about slowly, quietly, extricating his staff from the saddle holster. It came away with a soft hiss, the metal head gleaming as if in anticipation of a kill.

"Can they smell the horse?" Modi asked. "Or...us?"

"Wind's blowing the wrong way," Promathan said. "And despite what you might have heard about dragons, their sense of smell isn't all that keen. Probably has something to do with spitting fire I'd imagine."

Modi started to giggle but covered his mouth to stop the noise. The kid was nervous. Promathan couldn't blame him. His own palms were a little sweaty. He had taken on a juvenile dragon before, but only singles, never a pair. This kill would require finesse.

Dragons, even small ones like these eight-footers, enjoyed a high resistance to magic. Promathan attributed that to their scales which mages the world over considered valuable for their arcane properties. Regardless of the reason though, the hatchlings' resistance gave him pause. He doubted he could keep one of the beasts asleep while he dealt with the other. That meant his first strike must kill, else he would end up facing both monsters at once, an outcome he would just as soon avoid.

"You should head back to town," Promathan whispered. He considered asking Modi for the blue dragon scale but dismissed the idea. Let the young man keep a piece of his first adventure. Perhaps such a memento would inspire him to greater things.

"I'm staying with you." Modi screwed up his courage enough to clear most of the fear from his eyes though his cheeks remained pallid.

"If I fail, and these dragons catch sight of you, they'll happily abandon my corpse for a fresh kill."

Spying the long dagger Promathan kept sheathed on his saddle, Modi drew it and stood resolute. "I'm not leaving."

"Alright then, kid. Stay, but keep to the trees and don't follow me. If all goes to plan, I'll kill both dragons and you'll have nothing to fear. If not...well, maybe you can sneak away while they're busy rending me limb from stem, eh?"

Modi favored Promathan with a strained grin and a nod. "Good luck."

Promathan stepped into the clearing careful to keep his footfalls as silent as possible. Striding forty feet had never taken so long nor passed so quickly. Every step Promathan took sent a spasm of fear coursing from his laboring heart into his throat. He worried the whisper of tall grass against his trouser legs might rouse the beasts, but they remained motionless aside from the gentle rise and fall of their chests. Before he knew it, he stood next to the blue-scaled fiend, his staff raised above its unsuspecting head. One quick thrust and, if his luck held, he could end the green before it snapped him in half.

The sound of splintering wood and cracking timbers brought Promathan up short before he could strike. He twisted about to find a towering, winged figure tear through the screen of trees, not twenty feet from where he stood. A head the size of a wheelbarrow, its scaled visage ringed in heatwaves preceded a body red as a cardinal's feathers. The adult dragon growled, and Promathan felt the rumble in his boots.

"Oh, shit."

Roused by the tumult, the juvenile dragons sprang to their feet, their wings spread, their fanged mouths opened to emit hisses of alarm. Luckily, they appeared more concerned with their giant counterpart than the puny human standing within striking distance. Both scrambled off the rock and made for the forest, casting worried looks behind as they fled.

"It was a trap, eh?" Promathan called, surprised at the lack of squeak in his voice.

"Just so," the dragon rumbled. Head lowered, twin streams of white smoke issuing from his nostrils, the beast drew a step closer to Promathan as his lips spread in a gruesome smile filled with too many dagger-sized teeth to count.

Promathan held his ground though it took every speck of fortitude he could muster. But then, what was the alternative? Run and die instantly? Better to stand while the dragon gave him leeway to breathe.

"You didn't think I would forget, did you vermin?" The dragon squeezed its armored eyes down to slits.

"No, Jouroth. I never thought that."

"You tried to kill me while I slept, wizard."

Promathan nodded, acutely aware of the iron grip he held on his staff, unable to relax it. "It was my duty. You murdered a hundred elves—for sport."

"I only eat the young ones. Past fifty, they go sour."

"So it's revenge you want?" Promathan asked for no better reason than to keep Jouroth talking. He saw no way to escape death at this point. Magic was all well and good, but it meant nothing compared to a dragon's strength, claws, teeth, and unholy fire. Knowing that didn't stop his mind from flailing for a means to best the creature, even if from a forlorn hope of survival.

"You are too small and pathetic to warrant my revenge, wizard. I should just as soon take revenge upon a housefly for all that you mean to me."

"And yet you laid a trap for me." Out of the corner of his eye, Promathan spotted movement. Modi, perhaps suffering a fit of insanity brought on by seeing a dragon for the first time, had mounted Promathan's devil mare. "Perhaps I'm a small-minded human, but that alone puts the lie to your claim."

Unaware of Modi, who was now urging the reluctant horse to break from the forest, Jouroth lifted his head to peer down at Promathan, growling. Accusing him of caring about a human, even enough to kill said human, appeared to be getting under his scales.

"You are meaningless to me, scum!" The dragon boomed, shaking the very ground with his unearthly voice.

The sound masked the horse's thundering hooves as it galloped across the clearing, young Modi clinging to the saddle with just his legs, Promathan's knife in one hand, and his own walking stick in the other. What the boy planned to do, Promathan couldn't fathom, but he had to keep the dragon distracted as long as possible else Modi would surely die.

Against his better instincts, which yammered at him to abandon Modi to his fate and beat a path for the forest, Promathan summoned magic to strengthen his arm, and hurled his staff at Jouroth's breast in a cone of light brighter than the noonday sun.

The dragon spotted the weapon in time to jerk sideways, no small feat for so large a creature, but he could not wholly escape harm. Rather than pierce Jouroth's heart, the staff's silver blade struck sparks as it bit into the thin scales surrounding the dragon's right forelimb at the shoulder.

Jouroth roared as hot blood spurted from the wound. He wrenched the staff free with his teeth and flung it to one side, incensed by the pain and the pure effrontery of this upstart human who had dared injury him. The dragon drew breath to flame.

Promathan smiled despite his impending doom. Even if he died in the next second, he had at least inflicted a little damage on the undisputed king of monsters. He figured he could divert Jouroth's flames for perhaps five seconds with a spell he knew, but after that, he'd be charred. He called for his magic, hands pressed together as if in prayer to the gods. Futile or not, he would give it a try.

Jouroth reared back in preparation to spew flame and something slim pinged off one of the massive horns protruding from his skull.

Modi's walking stick.

The boy was mad.

"Hey, you great red, scaly rat!" Modi screamed, the devil horse rearing beneath him while he brandished his puny dagger. "Your mother was a lizard and your father was a stoat!"

Promathan had never known a dragon's expression could look so comical, nor so dumbfounded. Interrupted mid-flame, Jouroth belched yellow fire over the human's heads, hot but harmless, and narrowed his eyes to get a look at the flea haranguing him from horseback.

Seizing the opportunity for a second volley, Modi flung the dagger, which struck Jouroth's nose broadside. Though it did no damage, it seemed to give the monster a fright. He jerked back like a scolded dog, his long neck bent almost in two.

Promathan, as surprised at the servant boy's actions as the dragon, stood for a moment in transfixed awe. Had Modi really just hit a dragon with a stick and a knife? For that matter, had he really convinced that malevolent horse to charge a dragon in the first place? The mare pranced under Modi, obviously nervous, but nonetheless held its ground, nostrils flared, muscles bunched, breast heaving.

The moment stretched on in burning silence for what felt like a week, but shock could not long hold the dragon. Injured, bleeding, and insulted, Jouroth cried his rage to the heavens in a gout of smoke and fire.

The horse screamed in fear, as did Modi, though both somehow held steady. Bereft of a weapon, the boy took up the horse's reins and stared defiance at Jouroth like an innocent man facing the gallows with the stoutest of hearts. Not that bravery could long sustain him.

Jouroth drew breath again, his head ringed with torturous heat, and opened his mouth to erase Modi and the horse from existence.

Promathan's mind raced for some way to save Modi. Clever, brave, and cloistered, the boy deserved a chance at living his life. Surely he was meant for greater things than so ignominious a death as this! Promathan's staff lay too far away to reach, and its shaft looked cracked from the dragon's bite. Desperately, he padded his pockets, searching for something he might use to help Modi, though in his heart he knew the chances were next to zero.

From his tunic pocket, he withdrew the small green scale he had found on Vernon's property. Magic flowed from it, endemic to the dragon who had formed it. Eyes wide, heart full of hope, Promathan seized it, added to it, molding it from a nascent force into a harness of intention.

With all the might of his body, all the weight of his magic, and all the strength of his urgent desire, Promathan took aim at the rearing Jouroth, set his sights on the creature's open mouth, and flung the scale that direction. Aided by the dragon's in-flowing breath, the scale flew unerringly past Jouroth's teeth into his throat.

Jouroth's breath stopped with a titanic hitch that shook him crown to tail. His monstrous jaw opened wide, he jerked in place, heaving to dislodge the scale, but couldn't. His golden eyes widened with pain and not a little fear.

Like an acrobat trained by mummers, Modi bounded from the saddle and hit the ground at a run headed for Promathan's broken staff. Seemingly unaware of the danger posed by Jouroth's convulsing claws, he snatched up the gleaming blade and plunged it into the dragon's heart with both hands.

Jouroth shuddered in choking silence, heaved one last time, and dropped to the grass with a boom. His armored tail thrashed twice before he lay still, smoke rising from his open mouth and nostrils.

Promathan headed for Modi, but the horse beat him there. She nuzzled Modi's hair, whinnying her approval and nipping playfully at his shirt. He scratched behind the beast's ears and she settled, though she kept her muzzle draped over his shoulder to receive more pats and assurances from the servant boy.

"Are you okay?" Modi asked.

"Me?" Promathan shook his head. "I'm not the one who rode headlong at a dragon. I can't believe you did that."

"Seemed the only way for us to survive was a distraction. I couldn't think of a better one."

Promathan glanced at the blade protruding from the dragon's breast before turning back to the boy and the horse. "You know, kid, I have a title for you, and it's not servant."

Modi lifted one eyebrow. "What is it?"

"Hinter wizard."

THE END

Us Gnomes Stick Together
pdmac

Skeeter stood at the end of the bridge connecting Ynys Bari to Ynys Denligh, wondering if the tale was true. Old Alvyn Wrenchman said that there were islands that actually rose up out of the ocean, that gnomes once traveled on ships that used the wind and sails to make them plow through the water from one island to another. What old Alvyn said next had to be stretching the truth. He said the airships gnomes now used were little different from the ships back then.

Skeeter shook his head, trying to imagine a gnomish caravel hoisted by a large gas-filled envelope, thrust forward by two whirling propellers at the back of the sterncastle, bouncing along on top of the water. What sane captain would want to do that? The water would just slow him down as well as bounce the ship and cargo all over.

Besides, why would anyone want to sail on top of the water when they could sail high above the water like the birds in the sky? And why would anyone want to go below the floating islands anyway? Life was perfect right here. Well… almost perfect.

That's why he was here, studying the bridge.

He had admired the bridge from the moment he learned that his great-great-great-grandfather Jebido Bolthead had built the first bridge connecting the two islands. While his father claimed it was an engineering feat, others pointed out that there wasn't much engineering involved.

"That might be true," his father admitted, "but it took his genius to make it happen."

Grandpa Jebido had convinced the skeptics that the two islands could be brought closer together. After all, they were less than a quarter-mile apart.

"They're floating islands," Jebido had pointed out. "Sure, they tend to stay in one spot, but that doesn't mean they can't move. All we gotta do is move one."

When asked why they needed to move the island in the first place, Jebido answered, "Us gnomes gotta stick together. There's gnomes there; there's gnomes here. Don't see the sense of living apart."

His solution was simple – ropes and winches.

When Skeeter asked why didn't they just use airships with ropes attached to the island, his father explained that airships hadn't been invented yet.

"So how did they get the rope across?"

"Cannon," his father proudly said. "After they spent almost a year making two ropes as thick as yer wrist and just about as long as this island, Grandpa Jebido rigged up two cannons that could fire spear-like projectiles. Attached the ropes to 'em and fired 'em off. Took a couple o' tries to get the powder load right. First three shots fell short. But, on the fourth try, hoo boy! Once folks on the other side dodged out the way, they wrapped the ropes around fifty of the stoutest trees they could find. When they finished, they sent a pigeon across tellin' us they were ready. Well, Grandpa got them winches turnin' by riggin' up a pulley system, each pulley with big teeth in 'em like in a gear clock."

"How many gnomes did it take to pull the rope?"

His father slapped his knee and laughed. "Just about everyone who lived on this island. They'd pull and pull and inch by inch the two islands started movin'."

Skeeter loved the tale so much that it was his favorite bedtime story, especially the part where it took nigh two weeks to pull them closer until they were so close that you could just about reach across and shake hands.

That was when the tremors started.

"Ya brought it too dang close," the island council exclaimed, wringing their hands.

"So, what did they do?" Skeeter asked, repeating the same line with the same fervor.

"Well," his father said with a knowing smile, "Grandpa told 'em to hush up 'cause he got it all figured."

"It's the gas below mixin' and interfering with each other," Jebido explained. "What we gotta do is build a spanner bridge."

"A spanner bridge?" Skeeter asked on cue.

"Yup," his father answered. "First, he built a wooden bridge to connect the two islands, but in the center, he had sections like giant corkscrews. That's when the fun began."

"How did they twist the screw?"

His father burst a laugh at the telling. "Tied ropes around themselves and attached the other end to one of the levers."

"And jumped right off," Skeeter announced, filling in that part of the story.

"Hoo boy, that had to be a sight," his father guffawed. "All them gnomes jumpin' off the bridge."

"Weren't they scared?"

"Course they were. That's why the ones that did are remembered for bein' so brave."

"Did any die?"

His father grew solemn and nodded. "We lost two brave gnomes then, but Grandpa pushed the island away just far enough that the tremors stopped."

"Then what happened?"

"Why they built a permanent bridge and it's been there ever since. Folks called Grandpa a genius and a hero. And when they saw that it worked so well, they did the same thing for the other four islands close by. That's why we only use airships for the islands too far away to be pulled closer. But what do we learn from all this?" His father narrowed his gaze and smiled at his son.

"Us gnomes stick together."

That's why Skeeter was here today to study the bridge.

For hundreds of years, the connected islands had enjoyed a

tranquil peace and prosperity unequaled in their history. But that peace was threatened, for one of the islands was sinking.

They discovered it a month ago when someone noticed cracks in the masonry. Thinking it a result of age, they repaired the cracks and thought little more about it… until two weeks ago when the cracks reappeared, worse this time. Surveyors took measurements and experts were called. The result?

The island, the biggest island, was sinking.

According to the experts, based on the severity of the cracks, it would probably be only a few months before the island sank all the way down to the ocean to float away to who knew where?

"It's running out of magairite," one expert opined.

"No, it's not," another expert countered. "It's because of the additional population that's adding weight to the island and pushing it down. All we have to do is move folks to the other islands and the problem is solved. Remember, the simplest solution is more often the right one."

"We've offended the gods," a cleric intoned, "and this is the result."

Ignoring him, the experts continued their debate, finally settling on reducing the weight by having everyone on the island cross a bridge to another island, When nothing happened after five days, the experts regrouped.

"Definitely a problem with the reduced amount of magairite," they expostulated.

"What's magairite?" a young gnome asked.

"It's the gem that acts as a catalyst with the caliche of the islands," an expert loftily replied.

"What's a catalyst and what's caliche?"

The expert narrowed a frown at the young gnome. "Don't you have someplace you need to be?"

"No, not really," he cheerily answered.

"Humpf, well, I don't have time to explain it all at the moment. If you're really interested, come by my work."

"That still doesn't solve the problem," a council member from the sinking island moaned. "What are we going to do?"

"We dig up magairite from the other islands and bury it here," another expert suggested, which caused a round of hysteria from the other island councils.

"That would cause all the other islands to sink," the councils cried out.

"Whatever happened to 'Us gnomes stick together?'" Skeeter asked.

"We do," an older gnome replied, "but in this instance, it makes no sense for the many to suffer for the few. Besides, they can always move to one of the other islands. That's gnomes sticking together. I say let it sink and be done with it."

Quite naturally that did not sit well with the residents of Ynys Denligh.

"What about getting magairite from somewhere else?" Skeeter interrupted.

"Other than these islands, the only other source of magairite is Ynys Malfor," an expert replied, which sent shivers through the crowd.

"That's where the Tynelings live," a voice wailed.

"They're vicious giants, headhunters and cannibals," another voice added

Skeeter's face hardened. "Suppose someone was able to bring back some magairite? What would do with it?"

"We dig a hole and bury it," one expert answered.

"How far down?" Skeeter narrowed his gaze at him.

"Uh… as far as possible."

There was an awkward pause before another gnome spoke. He was an older gnome with bushy white brows and a thick white beard that fell nearly to his belt buckle.

"That's not gonna work. The reactions that cause the gas to provide buoyancy and stability occur far below the surface… too far for us to dig We're gonna need someone to take the magairite and toss it into the cauldron of reactions to stabilize the island until we can come up with a better plan."

"But that… that's suicide," a gnome sputtered, "on two accounts. We need someone either brave enough or stupid enough to get the magairite from the headhunters then fly over the side of the island and down to where he can toss it into the churning inferno. Who's crazy enough to do that?"

"I will," Skeeter answered.

A stunned silence evaporated to cheers and whistles until the elder gnome pointed out, "He'll need a crew. Can't sail the airship by himself."

After a thick silence engulfed the crowd, a voice called out, "I'll go."

A tall gnome by gnome standards pushed through the crowd, followed by muted voices saying his name, "Torgil Iron-Sprocket."

Torgil was two handspans taller than Skeeter, with a full thick dark brown beard that went to the middle of his stout chest. Where Skeeter had the glow and exuberance of a gnome just entering his adult years, Torgil had the look of a gnome used to working with his hands, bending metal to his will… a strong, brave and fearless gnome who, despite an appearance of sober reticence, some said could also be bit reckless.

"Thank you, Torgil," Skeeter said with heartfelt appreciation.

"That only leaves seven more," the elder gnome said.

When no one else stepped forward, he sharply shook his head and growled, "I'll go."

"What?" many in the crowd mocked. "You're an old gnome, Cormun. How can you help?"

Several others called out that the only reason he volunteered was because he was old, that this was a suicide mission and he just wanted to be remembered for being brave. Yet a few others were conscience convicted and three more stepped forward, effectively silencing the crowd.

Folding his handing over the top of his ornately carved cane, Cormun slowly scanned the crowd. Ticking his head at Skeeter, he said, "This lad's right. Us gnomes stick together. At least we used to. We've grown soft from living the good life… no dangers, no outside interferences, just us going about our daily lives enjoying the blessings of peace and prosperity. But now there's a danger and a problem, it seems like it's every gnome for himself. I said we'd need seven more, but if we use one of the old scout ships, the five of us can do the job." He cocked an eyebrow and curled a lip. "Then the rest of you can go back to pretending none of this is your business."

If his words were meant to cause guilt, they failed miserably as the crowd cheered the rescue team. Rolling his eyes, Corman beckoned the others to follow him. Twenty minutes later, they stood in front of a large storehouse next to Cormun's cozy home with a high-pitched roof of polished bark.

"Wait here while I fetch the key."

Another twenty minutes later and Cormun ambled out the bright red door, a thick iron padlock key in his hand. "Forgot where I put it. Been a while since I was in there." He handed the key to Skeeter. "Here. You go ahead and open it."

Admiring the ornate scrollwork on the handle, Skeeter inserted the key into the lock, which easily popped open. Opening the door, he led the way into the dark storehouse.

"Unbar the main doors there," Cormun commanded, "and let some light in."

Torgil and Skeeter lifted the crossbar off and swung open the main doors. Sunlight flooded into the storehouse.

There in the middle of the storehouse, propped on eight boat stands of varying heights, rested a gnome-sized brigantine scout ship… a very old scout ship.

"You want to sail in that?" one volunteer exclaimed, suddenly having second thoughts on the whole affair.

"Yes, Warvyn," Cormun proudly replied. "She may not look like much at the moment, but she was the fastest scout ship in her time."

"What? A thousand years ago?" Warvyn stared at the relic then cocked an eyebrow at Cormun before relaxing and chuckling. "Good one."

"Good one what?" Cormun replied, puzzled.

Warvyn continued chuckling, shaking his head. "You had me going for a while. Where's the real ship?"

"This is it," Cormun answered with a frown.

"Very funny," Warvyn said, tilting his head back and looking down his large bulbous nose at him. "Where's the real ship?" Craning his neck to take a quick scan around the storehouse, he tsked. "It's not even in here. Where is it?"

"Where is what?"

"The ship."

"It's right there." Cormun poked his cane at the vessel.

"C'mon Cormun," Warvyn said, starting to get tired of the joke. "You've had your fun, but enough's enough."

Cormun twisted his head to frown at Skeeter. "What is he talking about?"

"I think he thinks you're not serious," Skeeter said, "that this is a prank."

Understanding swept through Cormun and he scrunched his face in anger. "At a time like this, do you actually think I would make jokes?"

"But... but," Warvyn lamely replied, "this ship ought to be in a museum. Can it still fly?"

"It's really not that bad Warvyn," another gnome interjected. He was a slender forest gnome from Ynys Muhr. Unlike his city cousins, he was clean-shaven with curly strawberry-blond hair that came to his shoulders. Tall for a forest gnome, he was still a handspan shorter than Skeeter.

Warvyn shot him a 'don't-be-daft' look. "Really, Jerbo? I'll give you 10 shillings if this can fly."

"I don't think we have a lot of options," Torgil stated. "No one's going to volunteer their precious ship with the possibility of never seeing it again."

"Sure, there is," Warvyn pooh-poohed. "I bet I can find another ship in less than half an hour."

"Go ahead," Torgil replied. "While you're wasting time looking for another ship, the rest of us will get to work on this one here."

Two hours later, a frustrated Warvyn shuffled back into the storehouse only to be surprised at the improvement in the formerly dilapidated airship.

"No luck, eh?" Torgil said, knowing the response.

"I can't believe it," Warvyn moped. "Not a single gnome had a ship we could use."

"Forget it," Skeeter said from above, leaning over the port railing. "We're almost finished here. While the decking might not look brand new, it's in good shape. But the engine and mechanicals are all smooth and in excellent shape."

Warvyn stepped back to study the airship. Brigantine in style and design, its length, not counting the bowsprit, was about twenty-five gnome paces, with a beam about ten paces. The engine was below deck, just forward of the quarter deck. Three large propellors gave it speed: one mounted behind the quarter deck and the other two mounted on extended metal arms on opposite sides of the hull, the drive chains looping around the drive sprockets then disappearing through holes in the hull. The hull, originally painted barn-door red, had faded to the color of rust. Shrouds connecting the hull to the air envelope unfurled over the rails and down to the floor, waiting to be connected to the envelope, which Jerbo and the other gnome carefully unrolled on the ground.

"You gonna stand there and gawk or you gonna help?" the other gnome asked. He was a young gnome like Skeeter, with dark wavy brown hair and like Skeeter, smooth-shaven.

"Leave him be, Nimble," Cormun spoke up. Leaning forward in his chair and resting his hands on the top of the cane, he stared directly at Warvyn. "He's not sure he's going with us."

His jaw jutting out, Warvyn objected, "Who said I wasn't going with you? I just said we needed a reliable ship."

"And you can always blame the ship if we fail," Cormun replied.

"We can't fail," Skeeter said. "They're depending on us."

"Forget the ship," Jerbo interrupted, his gaze focused on Warvyn. "What about the Tynelings? We'll be lucky to get out alive."

"What do you know about Tynelings?" Cormun asked.

"They're headhunters and cannibals and offer gnome sacrifices to their gods," Jerbo replied in a rush.

"How do you know that?"

"Everyone knows the stories," Warvyn answered for him. "Not only are they cannibals, they're huge, giants ten times the size of us."

"Bosh," Cormun scoffed. "Those are just stories."

"Do you know what they look like?" Skeeter asked.

"No one does," Cormun said. "The island is at least a five-day voyage to the northwest. No gnome has sailed any farther than our own islands in over a hundred years,"

"How do we know how to get there?" Jerbo asked.

Cormun answered with a knowing smile, curling his fingers for them to follow as he shuffled over to an oak cabinet against the far wall. Sliding out one of the wide slender draws, he pulled out a map from the bottom of the drawer and placed it on top. The others crowed around to gaze in wonder at the vellum, faded to a dull tan.

"These are our islands." Cormun pointed to a cluster of six islands on the right side of the map. "This one is Ynys Bari." He then traced his finger to the left across the blank space on the map to another island about the size of Ynys Denbigh. "This is Ynys Malfor." He poked a finger at each location. "From here to here is a five-day journey one way. Ten days round trip with however many days on the island. We need provisions for at least two weeks."

Silence settled for a bit as each pondered the trip to Ynys Malfor until Warvyn broke the quiet.

"What's the plan once we get there?"

"Go down and get some magairite," Skeeter answered.

"Just like that," Warvyn said, snapping his fingers. "Hi. Give us your magairite. Thanks so much. Bye."

"We'll figure it out when we get there," Cormun said. "For now, let's get this ship afloat and stock up.

Provisioning the ship was the easiest part for once word got out, everyone wanted to contribute for the privilege of saying they had provided for the intrepid voyagers. Gnomes dropped off foodstuffs, ale barrels, live pigs and chickens – enough food for Skeeter and company to be away for months, far more food than the little ship could carry. Cormun finally had to corral Ynys Bari's Burgomeister to place guards near the storehouse to shoosh good-intentioned gnomes away.

When departure day came, crowds surrounded the scout ship, newly painted its former barn door red. Thanks to the generosity of another gnome, the former patched and repaired gas envelope had been replaced with a gleaming silver one that extended beyond both bowsprit and stern.

The Burgomeister gave an inspiring speech wishing them a safe and successful voyage, commending them for volunteering, and thanking those who contributed to the endeavor. Impatient to be gone, Cormun smiled with only his lips and waited to give the command to release the docking lines. As the Burgomeister droned on thanking each particular family or individual, Cormun's patience evaporated and when the Burgomeister paused to catch his breath, Cormun called out,

"Release the docking lines."

Before the Burgomeister complained that he wasn't finished, the grounds-gnomes released the lines and the airship floated into the sky.

"There," Cormun grumphed. "That's done at least. Heed to boys. Set a course for Ynys Malfor." When they stood and stared vacantly at him, Cormun uttered a long-suffering sigh, realizing he was the only one who knew how to sail this ship. Oh, they had practiced at the various stations on deck, but that was in dry harbor. Now that they were aloft, it became painfully clear that none of them had ever been higher than a ladder.

As the ship drifted higher, Warvyn went below and started the engine, causing it to cough and sputter before catching. With the engine running, he engaged the drive chains to drive sprockets and soon the propellors whirled, pushing the little ship away from the islands.

Skeeter was the first to understand Corman's importance as both navigator and pilot and had paid close attention to Cormun's instructions. By the second day out, Cormun felt comfortable enough to let Skeeter navigate while he slept.

By day three, Jerbo commented, "I don't know about the rest of you, but with nothing but water as far as the eye can see, I'm glad I'm an earthbound gnome."

"Me too," Warvyn readily agreed.

"We still don't have a plan," Torgil reminded them, his mind on the future.

"We'll decide when we get there," Cormun said with a frustrated sigh, repeating the mantra of the past several days. "We know nothing about the place or the environment or the Tynelings. We'll know better when we've had a chance to scout it out."

"Still like to have some idea," Torgil grumbled.

Apprehension and nervousness grew as the fifth day's dawn

rose bright and clear. Jerbo, posted as forward lookout, scanned the horizon with a spyglass, sweeping a tight angle to the front. Several hours later, his efforts were rewarded when he called out,

"Land ho!"

Cormun immediately powered up the engines, tilting the wing flaps at the same time, pushing the ship higher in the sky. Too soon they were circling high above the island, a mountainous affair, heavily forested.

"We need to go lower," Skeeter commented, shivering in the cold altitude. "All I can see are trees and some lakes."

Cormun tilted the flaps and the ship began its descent and was soon edging the island perimeter as they searched for signs of inhabitants. Yet signs of life eluded them.

"Surely someone has to live close to the edge here," Jerbo said, "like they do at home."

By the time they circled the island, the sun had dipped below the horizon, the last bits of light fading to evening. Cormun powered the engines to gain altitude and soon the ship was high enough to crest the tallest mountain.

Picking a thickly treed crest, Cormun said, "We stay here for the night. Nimble, go ahead and tether us to something solid below."

"Aye, aye, captain." Nimble saluted and hustled forward to toss a thick tether line over the side. Waiting until it hit the ground, Nimble swung over the side and slithered down, the rest of the crew leaning over the railing to keep a look out.

As Nimble disappeared into the darkness below, Jerbo mumbled, "Suppose there's no one on this island, that the stories were all wrong?"

"We've just started," Skeeter replied. "Give it a chance."

They felt a tug on the tether line and leaned over to see Nimble climbing back up the rope.

"What's it like down there?" Torgil asked.

Nimble shrugged. "It's too dark to see much of anything."

*

It was during the second watch, Warvyn's watch, that the ship nearly capsized when someone or something gave the tether line a hard pull, causing Skeeter and the others and everything else not secured to tumble across the deck to whack against the portside railing.

"Cut the tether line," Cormun yelled.

Torgil scrambled forward, knife in hand when another yank caused him to tumble sideways. He would have fallen overboard had not Warvyn grabbed him by the trousers. At the same time, Skeeter crawled to the helm, grabbed hold of the wheel, and hoisted himself up to power up the engines and adjust the flaps to prevent whatever it was from dragging the ship down to the ground.

The yanking continued on the tether line as Torgil struggled forward, finally grabbing hold of the rope and furiously slicing until the last strands of line broke, immediately freeing the ship which jerked upwards.

Skeeter swore he heard a high-pitched cry of surprise.

Safely aloft, their hearts pounding, they readjusted and secured supplies as they searched the skies for possible intruders.

"Well, at least we know something's down there," Nimble remarked with understated nonchalance.

"Think of the size of the creature to pull our ship like that," Warvyn exclaimed. "Thank the gods that it didn't pull all the way down."

"What do we do now?" Jerbo fretted. "They know we're here."

"We regroup and explore more to see if we can find a spot to land," Cormun said.

"Are you nuts?" Warvyn blurted. "They're giants. They see us and we're dead."

"We're gnomes," Cormun shot back. "We use magic to get

what we need. You do know how to use magic."

"Of course," Warvyn replied, unconvinced.

"Good," Cormun grumbled. "Instead of whining about how big they are, think of spells we can use to trick them into giving us what we want."

"Illusion spells," Nimble brightly added. "I've been practicing a dragon one." He began laughing. "Tried it out on Orrlyn. Made him pee in his pants. Boy was he mad, but he's such an easy target. That gnome's afraid of his own shadow."

Cormun nodded and smiled. "See? That's what I'm talking about. Creative ideas. They have giants down there? We make them think we're giants... or something else to give them second thoughts."

"We still need to figure out how to get the magairite," Skeeter pointed out. "We'll need some sort of reveal spell, something that will make them show us where it is."

"Good idea," Cormun agreed, impressed with Skeeter's coolheaded approach. "For now, let's all get some sleep."

"I'm too wound up to sleep," Warvyn said. "I'll take the first watch."

*

Skeeter woke when Torgil poked his shoulder. "Your turn."

Rubbing his eyes and standing, Skeeter frowned as dawn rimmed the horizon. "Why'd you wake me so late? The sun's coming up."

"I wasn't tired and figured you all could use the sleep. I'll catch a nap while we're searching for a place to land."

Skeeter glanced down at the others, curled and tucked into bedrolls, sound asleep. Cormun lay on his back, snoring softly.

"You want to sleep now or are you up for acting as lookout while I pilot us lower to look for a spot."

"I'm good," Torgil answered, stepping around his sleeping

companions as he headed towards the bowsprit.

Striding to the helm, Skeeter flipped the engine switch, feeling the hum vibrate the ship. Deciding the best course of action was flying low, he adjusted the flaps and angled the ship on a gentle descent, leveling out fifty feet above the shoreline.

Nimble was the first to waken, yawning and stretching before scooting out of his bedroll to walk over and stand next to Torgil.

"You're supposed to be asleep," he commented.

"Too restless to sleep," Torgil shrugged.

"See anything yet?"

"Nothing much. Looking for a clearing to make it easier to get in and get out."

Silence settled for a bit as the two gnomes concentrated on the landscape before them, a thick forest of pines and hardwoods that came right up to the edge of the island.

"We'll probably have to go a little higher," Torgil pondered out loud. "Can't see much of anything at this level."

"If we can't find a spot, we'll have to tether like we did last night while some of us go aground, which means someone will have to stay with the ship."

"I recommend Cormun," Torgil said without hesitation. "He may be the smartest one of us, but he's not as fast as the rest of us. And I got a feeling speed is gonna be important."

"You got any magic up those sleeves of yours?" Nimble said with a smile.

"I'm counting on our talent to make ourselves *invisible*." He made quote marks with his fingers. "A good gnome always knows how to not be seen. We use that skill and add in a couple of diversionary monsters and hopefully we'll be able to get what we need and get out before our illusions are discovered."

"Hopefully." Nimble turned when he smelled the aroma of eggs cooking and saw Jerbo laboring over a metal box full of sand in which a small fire provided enough heat to cook the eggs in the cast iron skillet. "I'll take mine sunny-side-up," he grinned.

"You'll take yours scrambled like everyone else," Jerbo shot back.

"What kind of outfit is this?" Nimble moaned in feigned annoyance. "Next you'll be telling me we have to go to some island populated with giants to fetch some mineral to save the world."

"There," Torgil shouted and pointed. "Right there."

A wide meadow opened up in the midst of the forest. Wildflowers in golds and reds and blues rippled in the wind. Curiously, a low split-rail fence edged the side of the island as though reminding whoever that it was a long way down to the ocean below.

"That'll do," Cormun called out. "Hold 'er steady, Skeeter. Everyone better get something to eat now. It may be a long time until the next meal."

All too soon, Skeeter maneuvered the ship to hover above the meadow. A single tether line dropped to the ground.

Cormun called them together. "Climbing up and down ropes was easy when I was a younger lad, but I'm not as young as I used to be, and besides, I'd only be a hinder. Since one of us has to stay with the ship, we all know it has to be me. That said, we're not leaving until *all* of you are back on board."

"No gnome left behind," Skeeter resolutely added.

"Right," Cormun said with a brisk nod then inhaled a slow deep breath. "Us gnomes stick together. Alright then. Let's get this over with."

Torgil led the way down the rope. The four gnomes had no sooner touched the ground when the forest in front of them shook, followed by a cacophony of weird sounds.

"Get ready," Skeeter commanded.

The branches parted and a giant creature looming high above them pushed into the clearing.

"Now," Skeeter yelled.

Immediately, illusionary dragons and monsters swirled in the meadow.

A chorus of terrified screams erupted followed by the giant falling face-first onto the ground, the head tumbling off to the side.

"What the –" Torgil sputtered, looking down at the prone 'giant', a scarecrow of a creature stuffed with straw.

Nimble boldly strode over and pulled some of the straw from the neck where the head once perched. "I hope all our giant slaying is like this."

Frowning, Skeeter strode past the tall mannequin and headed to the edge of the clearing. "We're not here to harm anyone. We need your help. Please." When no one answered, he repeated his plea. "Please. We need your help."

Silence met his appeals. Turning around he made a slashing sigh at his neck. "Nix the monsters."

Waiting as the others broke the illusion spells, he turned back to the forest. "They're not real… the monsters… just like your giant. They're not real. Will you help us?"

"Who are you?" a voice called out.

"We're gnomes. I'm Skeeter. Who are you?"

There was a pause before a small creature stepped into the clearing. He stood a little shorter than Skeeter and wore dark green tights tucked into leather boots. His dark brown leather vest covered a short-sleeved shirt, revealing tanned and sinewy arms. His long auburn hair was held back by a leather headband, revealing pointed ears.

"We're halflings. I'm Pimstoke. Why are you here?"

"Halflings?" Torgil blurted.

Ignoring him, Pimstoke focused on Skeeter. "Why are you here?"

Skeeter studied him a moment before announcing their real

intent. "Magairite, We come from the gnome kingdom five days travel to the southeast. We live on islands like yours. One of our islands is sinking and we need magairite to stop it. Will you help us?"

Pimstoke studied him for a bit. "How many more of you are there?" He ticked his head at the ship.

"Just one more, an elder gnome who has much wisdom."

At that moment, Cormun leaned over the railing. "Halflings," he exclaimed. "How wonderful. You can trust them Skeeter. They've a wide reputation for honesty."

Flattered, Pimstoke dipped his head then turned to Skeeter. "We might be able to help you. But… there are conditions, essential conditions that must be agreed and adhered to. Otherwise, go back to where you came from."

"What conditions?"

"I'll explain in a moment."

"What about the giants?" Warvyn interrupted.

"Giants?" Pimstoke frowned then relaxed in a grin. "There are no giants. That," he said pointing the straw-stuffed scarecrow, "was just to scare you away."

"What about the giant that yanked on our ship last night," Warvyn countered.

"Oh that?" Pimstoke snorted a laugh. "That was us. Took about twenty of us to get any weight to it. Figured we'd have some fun. Figured we'd yank on it a while and give you a scare. Caught us by surprise when you cut the rope. Banged up a couple of us pretty good. Got three still with the apothecary."

"That was you?" Warvyn said, somewhat disappointed. "You nearly capsized our ship."

"Didn't mean to. Just wanted to have some fun and give you a scare at the same time."

"Conditions" Skeeter interrupted.

"Ah, yes," Pimstoke thoughtfully nodded. "Why don't you all come feast with us and we can talk about it. Bring the old one with you."

Immediately on guard, Skeeter replied, "Can't. He's too old to slide down the rope and get back up again. Also, we need someone to stay with the ship."

"You can set it on the ground here," Pimstoke said, waving a hand at the meadow. "There's plenty of room."

"Even if we could," Skeeter explained, "we'd still need someone to stay with the ship. Someone has to monitor the engine."

"Engine?"

"The machine that makes the propellors move."

"Propellors?"

"Those things." Skeeter pointed to the propellors slowly spinning at the sides of the ship.

The branches parted and another halfling stepped into the meadow, a very attractive lady halfling, dressed much like Pimstoke whose immediate deference told Skeeter that the lady was someone of importance. Her long blond hair was held back with a braided leather band. She smiled at Skeeter, her emerald green eyes scrutinizing him.

"This is Skeeter, Lady Kithzina."

"So I heard."

Skeeter was immediately smitten for her voice was like a gentle zephyr.

"What brings you to our fair land, noble gnome?" She took a step closer to him, her perfume, the bouquet of lilacs, lazily wafting and surrounding him.

When Skeeter didn't answer, Nimble frowned at him only to see his entranced face mesmerized by the lady halfling before him.

"Magairite," Nimble said, breaking the spell.

"Why do you need magairite?" she sweetly asked.

"Their island is sinking," Pimstoke explained, "and they flew her to steal some of ours."

"No we didn't," Skeeter snapped, surprised at Pimstoke's about-face. "We brought money to buy what we needed."

"What good is gnome money here?" Pimstoke scoffed.

"So," Nimble calmly said, "halflings don't use gold?"

Skeeter saw the flash of surprise, along with a flicker of greed, cross the halfling faces. He turned his attention to Pimstoke. "You said there were some conditions. You do realize that now that we know who lives here, we could simply return with a gnome army of thousands of airships and take what we wanted. It would be a war of annihilation. Is that what you want?"

Kithzina's face hardened. "Who are you to come here and make demands?"

"I merely point out the obvious. We came peacefully, looking to trade gold for magairite. But he," he thrust a finger at Pimstoke, "accused us of being thieves." Spinning around, he headed back to the tether rope, curling hand at the others. "C'mon. We've seen enough."

Marching back to the ship, Nimble grinned and whispered to Skeeter, "Nice one. A war of annihilation, eh? We'd be lucky to get another scout ship to come with us."

Jerbo had tether rope in hand when Kithzina called out, "Wait."

Skeeter turned, his arms folded across his chest. "Yes?"

"Careful," Nimble whispered out the side of his mouth. "She's using some sort of magic."

Skeeter replied with a quick nod.

"Will you meet us halfway?" She took a step forward.

"Stay here Jerbo," Skeeter ordered as he and the other two marched towards the halflings.

"Why not come to our village for a feast and we can talk this all out like civilized beings," Kithzina said with a warm smile.

Skeeter felt the same entranced feeling as before and purposely steeled himself against it. "Because we don't have time. One of our islands is sinking. We've been gone for six days now. Who knows how much farther down it's gone? If we don't return quickly, it may be too late."

Pimstoke cocked an eyebrow. "Your kingdom is falling apart and yet you threaten us with invasion?"

"It's not a threat," Skeeter coldly answered. "It's a fact. Yes. One island is sinking. There are still five more where we can resettle amongst other gnomes if necessary. We prefer to save the island."

"Why?" Pimstoke asked, realizing the halflings were in no position to argue. They would have to bluff their way to get what they wanted.

"Homes and livelihoods and memories are there."

"And so you flew all the way here to save your island," Kithzina said.

"Yes."

"There are still conditions," Pimstoke interjected.

"Name them."

Pimstoke turned to Kithzina who gave him a regal nod.

"First," he said, addressing Skeeter, "we are willing to give you the magairite in exchange for these following conditions. First, no one must know that halflings live here, that there are no giants like you believed. The tale must stay the same that giants rule the island."

Skeeter looked back at the others who nodded in unison. They were willing to stretch the truth to get what they needed. Warvyn was already thinking of a cover story.

"OK," Skeeter replied to Pimstoke. "We agree. Second?"

"Once we give you the magairite, you can never return."

"Suppose we need more?" Skeeter argued.

"We will give you enough to last you far beyond the lifetimes of your great-great-grandchildren."

Surprised, Skeeter nodded. "Agreed." Assuming that was it, he was about to thank him for the magairite when he realized Pimstoke wasn't finished.

"Anything else?"

"Yes." Pimstoke narrowed his gaze at him. "One of you must stay here as a guarantee."

"But… but," Warvyn burst. "That means never going home again."

Pimstoke folded his arms. "Those are our conditions."

Stunned, Skeeter blinked in weight of the demand. To never go home again… to never see family or friends ever again. He looked at the other gnomes whose looks told him they too weighed the consequences of accepting the terms. Part of him reasoned that Cormun was old. Maybe he would volunteer to stay. After all, it wasn't like he had many years left and the rest of them here were younger gnomes. Yet, he knew he couldn't ask Cormun to do that. He had as much right to live out his years with family as the rest of them. Then for some unexplained reason, an abrupt peace settled over him and he turned to Pimstoke.

"I'll stay."

"*You* will?" Warvyn blurted, relief washing over him.

"Are you sure?" Nimble stepped around to face him.

"Yes, I'm sure." He stared past Nimble's shoulder to look at Pimstoke. "Any other conditions?"

"No," Pimstoke replied, impressed.

"Then we need to hurry. Each minute we spend away from the island, the further it sinks."

"Why don't we ask Cormun if he'll stay," Jerbo interrupted.

"The decision has been made," Pimstoke firmly asserted. "Like he said, you're wasting time. You all will wait here while we get you what you desire."

The halflings disappeared into the forest, leaving the gnomes alone with their thoughts.

"Are you sure about this, Skeeter?" Nimble repeated.

"What choice do we have?" Skeeter answered with a resigned sigh. "We have to save our island."

"What do we tell them back home?" Torgil said, stating the obvious. "What kind of story do we tell them, especially with you missing? We can't say that you were killed."

"Tell them I'm missing," Skeeter replied, "that you don't know where I am. In all the excitement of getting the magairite, we lost contact with each other. In a sense, it would be true, and your tale would not need too much expanding."

Pimstoke stepped into the clearing, a small box of finely crafted silver in his hands. Kithzina and several other halflings followed behind him.

"Here is your magairite." He held the box out to Skeeter.

"That's it?" Warvyn harshly said. "That little box is supposed to last us for generations?

Skeeter opened the lid to gaze inside at the sparkling onyx-colored gems, each the size of a thumbnail.

"Your cities and towns will fade away long before you run out of magairite," Pimstoke shot back. "Be thankful for our generosity."

"How much gold do you wish in return?" Skeeter asked.

Staring intently at Skeeter, Pimstoke solemnly replied, "You have already given your word…and your life. Is that not enough?"

Exhaling a resigned sigh, Skeeter nodded. "Thank you." He handed the box to Nimble. "You better get going."

*

The last they saw of Skeeter was him being escorted into the forest by the halflings. The five-day journey back was a quiet affair, each gnome pondering Skeeter's great sacrifice. They would write poems and songs about him. They would make sure his legacy never faded.

Still, they needed to concoct a well-thought-out story and spent the five days attending to the details of the tale, each one adding tidbits as necessary, ensuring all repeated the same account.

Their sober and somber reflections were swept aside for a time when they saw their home islands and the raucous crowds that gathered to welcome them home. The joyous cheers and shouts gave them an overwhelming satisfaction that they had saved the island, that their quest had been a success.

That lasted until Nimble, the first to disembark, presented the precious magairite to the lead expert, a middle-aged gnome with a salt and pepper beard that ended at the belt in his trousers.

Surrounded by other experts and the growing crowd, the gnome cleared his throat with the air of self-importance. Opening the lid, he dipped his head, impressed.

"Yes, well… I see you were successful. Turns out we were wrong. Discovered that two days after you left. It wasn't magairite that we needed. It was merely a magnetic imbalance. Simply by expanding the bridge network connecting the islands, we've managed to correct the problem. Is everyone OK?"

Nimble's jaw had dropped and he dumbly blinked at the expert.

"Are you OK, lad? Answer my question. Did all make it back safely?"

Shaking his head, Nimble handed him the box. "Skeeter didn't make it."

A wail pierced the air as Skeeter's mom collapsed.

"Ah, that's a pity," the expert said. "He was a good lad. Well then, welcome back." He turned and handed the box to an assistant. "Label it and store it with the rest of the minerals."

*

Several weeks later, after the excitement faded and retelling the fable became a chore, the intrepid adventurers gathered at Cormun's home. Cormun busied himself pouring mugs of cold ale before returning to the dining room and distributing the brew. He then turned to Nimble.

"You sure about this?"

"As sure as the sun rises in the morning." Nimble lifted his mug and swallowed a satisfying gulp.

"But we gave our word," Cormun reminded him.

"I know," Nimble firmly answered. "But that was based on false premises. One's word isn't any good if it's based on a lie. What we were told about our islands wasn't true. Surely we can't be expected to stick to the conditions based upon what we know to be wrong."

"I say we steal the magairite and return it," Jerbo said. "An even trade. Skeeter for the magairite."

"One of the conditions was that we couldn't return," Cormun pointed out.

"We have to break that condition to rescue him," Warvyn said, stating the obvious.

Cormun studied the faces of the younger gnomes, all with a look of determination… even Warvyn.

"You are all sure about this?"

"Yes," they answered.

"Then I think Jerbo is right," Cormun said. "We take back the magairite. An even exchange. We'll need all the illusions and stealth we can muster because they won't be happy if they discover us again. That could put Skeeter's life in danger."

"We have no other choice," Nimble said. "We can't leave him there. Remember, us gnomes stick together."

THE END

The Armor of Dusan
A.G. Porter

Human.

Those words had been spat in Zanna's face since she was a child as if it were a curse. Her life amongst the fair folk was full of enchantment and wonder, but there was an underlying resentment from those around her. While her adoptive family loved her, she knew in her heart she would never truly be one of them. After all, she was only human.

Still, her father, Dorthran, was a High Lord and trained all of his children in the ways of Vaelkesh. It made no difference, he said, what was in her blood, it mattered what was in her heart. She clearly had the heart of a warrior.

"Move it, Little Fire," a sharp voice yelled as she hit the ground. "You're being outmatched."

Zanna knew that. Her father had pitted her, once again, against her oldest sister, Keres.

Just as the air returned to Zanna's lungs Keres' sword came down towards her head. She only had a moment to stop the blade from severing her head from her shoulders. Anger wheeled inside her chest and she pushed the sword away with all her strength and somehow made it back to her feet.

"Are you yielding so soon, Little Fire," Keres used the nickname like a taunt, still Zanna could see the stunned look on her sister's face.

"Never," Zanna smiled and lunged forward, swinging wide.

She knew that it left her wide open, but the move was so sudden that Keres was surprised. Zanna's blade came down hard, hitting Keres directly on the shoulder. The sound was loud, metal clanging against metal. It jarred Zanna and threw her off balance. Keres rounded on her, flipping her over her shoulder.

Keres' sword tip was inches from her throat. Both of them

were breathing heavily.

"That was stupid," Keres gritted her teeth.

"I bet that shoulder stings," Zanna smiled.

"You gave me your neck so you could get in one feeble blow?" Keres growled.

Zanna shrugged her shoulders and then winced. She knew her body would be sore if she didn't go see the healers.

"Keres, lower your weapon," Dorthran said.

"I should give just a tiny cut," Keres sneered. "To teach her a lesson."

"Keres!" their mother gasped.

Zanna didn't like it when she came. Eira, her mother, had always been a beauty and was treated as such. Her long blonde hair was nearly as white as her skin. She was delicate and fair, like all of her daughters, except Zanna.

Zanna was tall, and beautiful in her own way, but she was not an elf. Where the elves were fair skin, she had a natural golden-brown color, where their hair was blonde, hers was red like fire, and where their eyes were either blue or sea green, she had eyes like a night's sky. They were deep and dark, but the light seemed to always find them as if it reflected every star in the universe.

All of her sisters, all five of them, including Keres, looked like their mother. The only difference was Keres' body was lean and powerful from the extensive training. She didn't have to do the extra classes, but she chose to. She wanted to be in the king's guard. If she succeeded, she would be the first she-elf to make it.

Zanna couldn't fault her for her ambition. She knew what it was like wanting something that others said you could never have. In their world, she-elves were great warriors. Still, none of them had been allowed to enter the king's guard. Even if she hated to admit it, Zanna knew that if anyone could make it, it would be Keres.

Keres glared at her, but then lowered her blade and walked

away. Zanna lay there for just a moment longer and stood to her feet, brushing the dirt from her pants.

The arena was rather full today. She glanced around and noticed how Keres' friends were congratulating her. They made sure to look back at Zanna and sneer.

"You must control your emotions, Zanna," her father came to her side. "You will never master the sword if you never master yourself."

"I don't know why you make me do this," Zanna sheathed her blade. "You know that I am no match for Keres."

"Zanna," her father took her face in his hands, making her meet his eyes. "I am well aware that you are human, but you are still my daughter, the daughter that I chose. You may not have our strength or our magical inclinations, but you have something all your own, and that is passion, it is your heart. That is one thing that I admire about humans. You must work so much harder for the things you want in life. Once you obtain those goals, it means something. Do not let these things be considered your weakness, for they are your greatest strength. What will be your downfall is not harnessing the abilities you do possess."

"Yes, Father," Zanna told him.

"I love you, my daughter," he kissed her gently on the forehead.

"I love you," she suddenly wrapped her arms tightly around his waist.

She could feel him chuckle and then embrace her in return.

"Zanna," her mother glided to her side. "It is time for you to travel. You have much to study in your time away."

Zanna groaned internally. She enjoyed her lessons at Vaelkesh Academy, but the Instructors required that their students wear constricting attire. The girls had to cover their entire bodies and wear fabric on their heads, the males, it was nearly the same, and no one could enter the library with a weapon.

"Yes, mother," Zanna said, releasing her father.

"Go clean up," Eira told her. "Keres, you as well, take your younger sisters with you."

"Yes, mother," Keres came forward, and her sisters followed.

Zanna hesitated for only a moment and then followed the line of girls like a good little gosling.

Vaelkesh Academy was of great magnificence. It wasn't just a place of knowledge for children. Elves from all over came to study from its many books and learn from its highly trained teachers. It held every book ever written in any language. It was levels upon levels of knowledge. It was a castle, a fortress of immense power if you knew what you were looking for.

Each year Zanna and her sisters would spend the fall and winter months there working on their studies. Children from all of the upper-class Elven families were sent there as well.

Soon, all five young ladies were cleaned, dressed, and leaving in the family carriage to the school. Zanna sat beside her youngest sister, Esin, who had just turned eight. She was spirited and Zanna loved her deeply.

"You did well at your match today, Zanna," Esin said to her.

"Thank you, Esin," Zanna patted her head.

"Oh, stop that," Esin said, swatting her hand away. "I'm not a little girl anymore."

"Sure you are," Zanna tickled her and the young girl laughed.

"She only got in a hit because Keres got overconfident and Zanna cheated," Cielle, the middle sister, chided.

"I did not cheat," Zanna rolled her eyes.

"I am not overconfident!" Keres defended herself.

"I think your skills are increasing at an exponential rate," Siofra added, she was the second to youngest and one of the brightest elves in all of Vaelkesh. "It is very interesting. Only a month ago, your swing was wide and a bit wavering. Today, it was more focused and targeted, you had better control as if the weight of the blade didn't affect you as much. Very impressive."

"It was not impressive," Keres laughed. "She got lucky. It won't happen again."

"I'm telling you she cheated!" Cielle said again.

"She did not cheat!" Esin argued.

This went on for a while, but Zanna decided not to join in. She didn't care if they thought she cheated. She also didn't care if Keres thought she got lucky. What made her sit and ponder was what Siofra had said. Her skills were increasing. Of course, she had trained for years, but her level of abilities paled in comparison to Keres'. It was unlikely that she would have become that much better in just a month's time. What could have changed since then?

Upon their arrival, Zanna's younger sisters were escorted away by their teachers. Keres would be finished with her studies at the end of term, so she had her own class as well. Zanna had another year which meant she had to venture to the fifth level.

The fifth level was dedicated to the study of Vaelkesh History. There were bits of history taught to them in levels 1 through 4, but the 5th level left nothing out.

Zanna took her seat at her study table and opened the history book to the place she had marked the previous day. Her Instructor, Avra, was at the front of the room, writing an assignment on the board.

"You're bleeding," someone said to her.

Zanna looked over at her best friend, Javaid. His twinkling blue eyes always had an air of mischief to them. She tried not to jump out of her seat and hug him in front of everyone. He had been gone the past year, recruited to the King's Guard early. Zanna didn't think they would let him return to finish his studies.

"You're back," she said.

"And you're still bleeding," he smiled.

She looked down at her hand. A scratch she thought had stopped bleeding was still a bit raw.

"It's just a scratch," she shrugged. "When did you return?"

"Last night," he said.

"And you didn't come to see me?" she felt slightly affronted.

Javaid meant so much to her, more than anyone in her life. There was a moment when she wanted that to mean something more, but she quickly pushed it away. He was an elf and she was human, after all.

"It was late," he laughed, the sound making her feel more at home. "I'm sure you would have been asleep."

"That's never stopped you before," she punched him.

Javaid waved across the room. Two girls from a ruling class giggled. One was a former fling of Javaid's, Enessa. Zanna tried not to let it bother her.

"Oh, I see," she said. "You were...busy."
"No, I..." He turned to her, but then Instructor Avra began the class, putting an end to their conversation.

Their assignment was a bit different today. They were actually leaving the classroom and searching the shelves.

"You must learn to use the library to its fullest potential," Instructor Avra told them. "Swords and bows can only help you so much. Your mind is your greatest weapon. We are using the library today."

Zanna and Javaid began looking through the shelves for their assigned books. The thing was, they didn't know which books they were assigned. Instructor Avra said when they found the books, they would know. She told them that the library had a way of guiding one to what they seek. At this moment, Zanna wanted her bed.

She was always exhausted after her lessons with Keres. Her sister pushed her to her limit. Keres, on the other hand, never seemed to be the least bit tired.

Zanna knew the difference was because she was human and Keres was elven. Elves had more stamina, more strength. She couldn't help but feel a bit resentful knowing she would never be able to outmatch her sister.

"What book is speaking to you, Zanna," Javaid laughed.

He clearly thought the assignment was silly. She rolled her eyes. Javaid had never taken his studies seriously. He was too busy practicing his bow and chasing after the fairer sex.

Zanna hated him up until they were in their second-level classes. After they were paired up for an assignment, they had been inseparable.

"I suppose you're too busy looking at Enessa to know which book is calling to you?" Zanna teased.

"You mean, she's looking at me," Javaid said slyly.

Zanna rolled her eyes just as Enessa walked over to them. She was beautiful, but not just in the way Elves were beautiful. It was more than that. She had an inner light, a delicate beauty, soft and warm.

It was something that Zanna could never obtain, even if she went to the fabled transfiguration masters. Enessa had something that could not be replicated.

"Good day, Javaid," she greeted him, saying nothing to Zanna as if she weren't even there.

"Good day, my lady," he said respectfully.

Enessa was, after all, a part of the royal family. She was very far down the line, but royal, nonetheless.

"Javaid, you can call me by my name," Enessa seemed to blush, with a slight giggle.

"Oh, I couldn't do that, my lady," he was laying it on thick and Zanna nearly burst out laughing but recovered by playing it off as a sneeze.

"It's awfully dusty in here, my lady," Zanna said when Enessa looked at her. "Excuse me."

"Yes, well, I haven't noticed," her smile was strained.

Zanna wasn't surprised. Elves didn't seem to be affected by mundane things the way she did. Every winter Zanna became ill and only her. She spent at least a week in bed with a high fever. And every Spring she would stay with a headache and sneezing for the first few days of the fresh blooms.

Enessa had turned to talk to Javaid again. Zanna wasn't really paying attention and moved her way down the rows of books. Soon, she found herself far away from her classmates and in a part of the library she had never been to before.

"Can I help you find something?" A voice said to her.

Zanna jumped and turned to face one of the library staff. She was a much, much older Elf. It was always hard to tell because once an Elf reached maturity their aging process slowed down. An Elf could be over a hundred and still look 35 in human years.

Still, she was clearly older, her face a map of lines and her blue eyes a bit hazy with age. She even walked a bit slow and with a slight limp. Zanna supposed this was proof that even Elves finally had to face the signs of time and age.

Still, there was a liveliness to her eyes. They were dark, not like the ice blue eyes she was used to seeing. It was welcoming and refreshing.

"No, thank you," Zanna finally said. "I'm supposed to, um, let the book find me."

"Oh, yes," the old elf smiled. "Instructor Avra enjoys this assignment. It gets you young elves out from under her for a moment."

She must have lost her good eyesight as well, Zanna thought.

"I am not an Elf," Zanna told her. "I'm human."

"Oh, my eyes are not what they once were, but I can normally tell one from the way they carry themselves," she told her. "If you are indeed him, then you are the daughter of Dorthran and Eira. I am pleased to meet you. I am Mavka."

"It's a pleasure, Instructor," I told her.

"Oh, we are both mistaken today, my dear," she smiled. "I am no Instructor, just an old lady who enjoys helping."

Zanna smiled. She liked Mavka. It was rare meeting an Elf who didn't gawk at her for being human. She also noticed that Mavka had called her the daughter of Dorthran and Eira; just "daughter," not "human daughter," not "adoptive daughter," just "daughter."

"It was nice to meet you, Zanna," Mavka told her. "I've always found this part of the library to be the one place that has what I'm looking for."

She sort of waved her hand to the row of shelves right down from them. Zanna smiled and then turned in that direction. Mavka, besides Javaid, was one of the only Elves she had ever met that made her feel welcome.

She was Dorthran's daughter so there was a sense of protection that came with that. However, there were those who didn't care who her father was and they let her know it. There had been many times she was denied entry to a shop or spat at as she passed someone in the street.

The Humans and Elves have a long history of bad blood. Zanna learned there really were no innocent parties involved in their feud, but it was universally known who had spilled the first drop of blood and it wasn't the Elves.

A long time ago, well before she was born, Humans came to the land of Mirstone. They sailed here on large ships from a distant land. They were hardened and cold beings who were determined to take up root wherever they chose. Unfortunately, they chose Vaelkesh. The Humans were accustomed to taking everything they pleased with little repercussions. They were not prepared for the power of the Elves.

Many of them were killed in a war that didn't last that long. After all, how could humans face off against the Elves of Vaelkesh? It was known as The War of Hours, for that's all that it lasted. When the human armies were decimated, their King surrendered to the Elven King of Vaelkesh. The Elves were benevolent beings even if they defended their land without mercy. They allowed the small group of humans that were left to stay and even gave them a small portion of their land.

Humans are prideful and vengeful, however. There have been times since that day that small bands of them have tried their hand at raiding Elven villages or stealing from their outposts. Sometimes they may make off with a few coins or trinkets, but for the most part, they are stopped, tried, and punished by Elven law.

However, for the most part, humans had made a thriving city in the land that was given to them. They have their own ruling class, schools, libraries, and more. They lived a quiet existence and often traded with the Elven and Dwarven communities.

There were towns and clans that had broken off from the main city of Halesford. Some were nomadic, living off the land and never letting go of their ancestors' tendencies of pillaging and taking what they wanted. Zanna's family was part of one of these tribes.

When the Clan moved close to the base of the dwarven mountains of Rachdale they thought they could sneak in and steal some of the jewels that had been mined. On their mission, they came across a band of Elven Riders who were in the midst of trading with the Dwarves. The human thought this must have been their lucky night. Not only could they steal from the Dwarves, but they could take the Elves's horses for there were no finer breeds in the land.

To their peril, they were wrong. Assuming they could raid the Elven party while they slept, slitting their throats as they were unconscious, they snuck in and were instantly caught. A fight broke out and the humans were killed. After the dust settled the only humans alive were a woman and a small child. She had been carrying the baby on her back. The woman was mortally wounded and so close to death, but she clung to her infant.

"Please," she had said to Dorthran. "She does not deserve to die out here. Take her. Help her."

Dorthran had told Zanna the story many times. He had told her that she was the most beautiful baby he had ever seen, with a head full of red hair and skin like the fertile soil.

That was what Dorthran had done. He and his wife Eira had

already had Keres when he brought Zanna into their home. Both of her parents loved her, but she had asked many times why they had not given her to the humans in Halesford.

"How could I?" her father had said. "I had already fallen in love with you."

She knew his words were true, but there was more to it than that. Having a human child living amongst them was somewhat of an advantage. The humans of Halesford knew of her existence. They knew she had been spared. It was the Elves' way of showing the humans that yes, they could end their lives in a blink of an eye, or they could spare them. In other words, the humans were at their mercy.

Zanna often wondered what her parents were like. Would she like them? Would she have been like them? If they had never raided that camp, would she have grown up a nomadic human and thief?

She continued to move along the aisle, running her fingers across the spines of the books as she walked. Suddenly, she felt a tingle in her arm. She stopped and looked at the book that had caught her attention. It was a large, green leather-bound book. There were gold letters that decorated its spine. She pulled it out of the shelf and a surge of electricity ran the length of her body.

The book was large, but she was surprised at the lightness. It was probably some magic the Elves used to make their job easier. She found a secluded corner and sat down on the dusty floor, the book in her lap.

There were no markings other than the letters on the spine. They were Elven letters, ones she didn't recognize, yet the book didn't look that old. Touching the spine, she sounded out the words. With that combination, the words slowly formed into something she could read.

"The Armor of Dusan," she read out loud.

Zanna opened the book and the strange letters began dancing around the pages at her. They seemed to be moving with some sort of energy. The movement made her eyes hurt as she struggled to focus on them. Whoever had written this book wanted to be sure that only the determined could read it. That made her highly suspicious and curious.

Closing her eyes, she steadied herself. Taking a deep breath, she held the book and willed herself to concentrate. If she could read the title, then she could read the rest of it. The title. That was bothering her. She had heard that name before, "Dusan," but where?

She searched her memory, but nothing came to mind. After a few more minutes, she opened her eyes, and to her surprise, and relief, the words were a bit calmer. They moved, but it was more of a vibration. As she began to read, the words slowly started to form and make sense to her.

By the time she was finished, Zanna couldn't breathe. She stood up, the book still clutched in her hands. There were footsteps in the distance and she faintly heard a voice, it was Javaid. He touched her shoulder and she bolted, running from him and what she had read. Javaid called after her, but she didn't stop.

Zanna ran and ran. She needed air. The problem was, she was on the 5th level and she either had to run down all of those stairs to the courtyard or go up, to try and reach the roof, which was just as many floors, if not more, up. Not wanting to pass her Instructor, she entered a place she was never supposed to go, the Librarian's offices.

"Zanna!" she heard a voice, but still didn't turn around.

She continued to run. The offices were empty. The Librarians were out on the floor, helping their students and patrons. She vaguely took in the fact that she was running down a long stone hallway with doors here and there. There was sunlight coming from the end of the hall and that was her goal. She didn't know if it were a window or if it would even open, but she needed to try. She had to breathe.

At last, she finally reached the source of light and realized it was a door. Bursting through she found herself on a terrace, a large balcony covered with all sorts of vegetation and small birds.

Finding a weeping willow in the center, she ran to the sturdy tree and clung to it, taking in large deep breaths.

"Zanna!" Javaid came to her side but didn't touch her. "You're scaring me. What is the matter?"

Zanna said nothing, but she handed him the book as she continued to try and control her breathing. Javaid gently took the large bound book from her and she couldn't help but think of all the trouble she had just gotten herself into. First, she had read a book from a section of the library she was not permitted to enter, then she took a book without permission, and now she was in a location she clearly wasn't allowed to be in.

"I don't understand," Javaid said. "Why has this book upset you? What language is this? I can't even read it."

She turned to face him, shocked, "You can't read it?"

"No," he said then looked at her. "Can you?"

"I can," she said, almost fearfully. "The book is called The Armor of Dusan."

"Who is Dusan?" Javaid looked at the book again.

"He is…" For the first time, Zanna could feel tears fall from her eyes.

Javaid finally got down on his knees in front of her and touched her face. He pulled her close to him, comforting her. What he didn't know was that there was nothing at that moment that could take away the pain and betrayal she felt.

"Zanna, please don't cry," he said, releasing her and wiping away her tears. "Tell me what is the matter."

"I have been lied to, Javaid," she told him, tears falling down her cheeks. "I have been betrayed."

"How? What happened?" he looked concerned.

"This book," she took it from him. "It tells the story of Dusan. He was an Elven Knight who was promised to the princess of Vaelkesh. To prove his worth, he was sent on a quest to slay the dragon of the Ash Mountains that was terrorizing a neighboring town. He slew the beast but was horribly wounded in the process. The village that was being terrorized was occupied by humans. A kind villager found him and took him to the village healer. There, the healer and the healer's daughter, Ianthe, nursed him back to health. During that time, Dusan fell in love with her. He wanted to marry her. When he healed, a local priest wed them. Afterward, he took her and a section of dragonhide, back to Vaelkesh. He expected his father to welcome him and his new bride. His father was furious. You see, if an Elf marries a human, if they decide to bond their lives with a human, they give up their immortality. He ordered Ianthe to be banished from the kingdom and the marriage annulled by the Elven wizards. When Dusan refused, his father ordered the execution of Ianthe. Seeing no other way, Dusan rescued her and fled across Mirstone, hoping to find shelter somewhere. For a few months, they did, hiding in The Feywilds. While there, Ianthe gave birth to a daughter. Their happiness was not to last for the King's Guards found them. Dusan was not going to give up his wife and child easily, he fought, begging for Ianthe to run. She tried but was struck down by none other than his own father. Dusan was mortally wounded and was thought dead after throwing himself off a cliff. His father returned to the fallen body of Ianthe and saw that the infant was still alive. He drew his sword because he could not allow a half-blooded child to live. Dusan's father, however, was turned to kindness when he saw her face and took her as his own. His father was Dorthran. That child was me."

"Zanna," Javaid didn't know what to say. "Are you...are you sure?"

"I am," she said. "It is all here. This book contains the history of my fath...Dorthran's house."

"But, why is this book here? How did you find it?" he wondered. "Why would your father lie to you about this? Who would leave a written account of what happened?"

"I don't know," she confessed. "It happened rather oddly. It read more like a legal account of what happened. I think it's a copy of that account. It looks as though it is royal documents, but they have been spelled so that not just anyone can read them. Someone wanted this account kept secret, but someone else also wanted it known."

She told him about the strange woman and the way the words didn't seem to want to focus for her. Javaid opened the book and looked at the words.

Finally, Zanna stood up and walked toward the stone railing of the terrace. She took in a deep shaky breath. There were many emotions fighting for dominance inside her. If she were being honest with herself, betrayal was winning. She had always known that Dorthran was not her father, but she never knew who he truly was to her.

"What happened to him?" Javaid skimmed through the pages. "What happened to Dusan? You said they thought he was dead."

"He made his way back to the town he had met Ianthe and found her father," Zanna told him. "Both were filled with such anger and pain that they sought out a witch. Dusan combined his remaining Elven powers and her magic and made a suit of armor from the dragon scales of the beast he had slain. The suit was to give Dusan unimaginable power."

"Was?" Javaid wondered.

"Yes," she continued. "The witch's magic was dark. In order for her spell to work, there had to be a blood sacrifice. Dusan had to kill the one person in the world he loved the most though he did not know this at the time. He put on the armor, marched back to Vaelkesh, determined to slay his father, and lay waste to the kingdom. After all, he believed his wife and child were dead. The person who he had loved the most was his father. However, upon fighting his way through an army of guards, he found his father with a child, a child he knew to be his and not because of her fiery red hair. It was because the armor wanted her life, her soul. The only way to complete the spell and gain the full power of the armor was to kill his infant daughter. He wanted to do it, but somehow he overpowered the armor and resisted. Pleading for help, his father had the mages of the city encase his son in magic in the Ash Mountains. According to that book, he's still there."

"He's still alive?" Javaid wondered.

"I don't know," she turned to him. "But I'm going to find out."

"Wait, what do you mean?" He followed after her as she pushed herself from the ledge and headed back to the door.

"I'm going to find him," she said.

"You're going to find the man who asked to be encased in magic so he wouldn't kill you?" Javaid stepped in front of her. "You do know how insane that sounds, right?"

"He is my father," Zanna told him. "I have to."

"No, you have to stay alive," he argued. "And how do you suppose you're going to find him? The Ash Mountains go for miles in every direction."

"Did you not see the map in the back?" she asked him, opening the book.

"No, I see only gibberish in that book," he looked frustrated at the thought.

"It says here that he is at the base of the Dragon's Eye," Zanna told him. "Isn't there a dragon statue there? One that we all call Dragon's Eye? That must be where he is. I must go. I have to."

"Or, you could stay here," he offered.

"Javaid," she sighed, rubbing her eyes. "You don't understand. How could you? You're just as strong, just as fast, just beautiful as the rest of them with your long life ahead of you. You don't know what it's like to be me. Eventually, once you reach of age, you will stop aging, probably marry Enessa, and find a place amongst the royals. You will forget me."

"Zanna," he grabbed her shoulders. "I will never, never forget you. You must know what you mean to me."

"It won't matter when I'm old or dead and you still look like this," she gestured to him. "Javaid, you are my friend, I adore you, but in reality, one day we will not be together. If I can find my father, then maybe I can help him and I won't be alone."

She could tell Javaid wanted to say something, but she walked away, leaving the words unspoken. Hearing his footsteps behind her, they entered the library. Now that she was a bit calmer, she realized exactly where they were, and her nerves started to eat at her.

They snuck down the hall, trying their best to be as quiet as possible. For Javaid, it was second nature to be stealthy. For her, she had to try with her all might. She couldn't help but wonder why that was. If her father was an Elf from a talented family and was also a King's Guard, how had she not inherited his abilities?

Was it possible she had? Her sister believed her skills had increased in a way that wasn't humanly possible. Zanna was almost sure that with a bit more practice, she could finally beat Keres. She would be of age soon, even before Javaid.

She explained her thoughts to him, and he seemed to think she might be onto something. Besides, if Siofra had noticed a difference, perhaps it was true.

As they finally made it back to the library stacks, Zanna relaxed slightly. Not enough though. Her stomach was still in knots. Her shoulders felt tense and a headache was forming at the base of her neck. She knew that she would never truly feel the same again. She had to find her father.

With that thought she raised her skirt hem until she reached the tight white undergarment she was made to wear. Javaid's face went red and he turned around.

"What are you thinking?" Javaid whispered.

"I have to hide this book," she told him.

He peeked back around and saw that she had slipped the tights off and was now using them to strap the book to her inner thigh.

"You have gone mad," he told her.

"Perhaps," she said, not really paying attention to what he was saying. "Keep a look out for me, will you?"

He turned and looked down the aisle and when it seemed like she was done, he turned back to face her.

"I love you, Zanna," he told her.

"I love you, too," she told him. "You know that. You are my best friend. That is why I need you to understand why I am doing this. Put yourself in my place, Javaid. If he can be saved, I have to try."

He looked at her for a moment. There was something in his eyes, something in the way he clenched his jaw. For a moment, it made her feel uncomfortable. They had been friends for so long, but he had never looked at her like that.

"I am going with you," he said at last. "You are not to argue with me. You said to put myself in your place, and I am. I understand. Now put yourself in mine. Would you let me go alone?"

"No," she admitted.

"Besides," he told her. "I know ways in and out of here that you do not. We can leave this evening."

"How you do you...never mind," Zanna rolled her eyes. "All of your rendezvous, right?"

"You think so little of me," he smiled down at her.

"I know you," she said.

"I wonder about that sometimes." He looked serious again and once more she saw that look in his sky-blue eyes. "Come, we must at least pretend that we're not going to sneak out after nightfall and go on a quest that will kill us both."

Zanna sat at dinner that night, her legs bouncing up and down in anticipation. Male and Female students were separated at every opportunity, which included meals. She sat a little down from her classmates, but close to Enessa and her friends. Every once in a while, she would look up and catch eyes with Javaid. He would give her a reassuring nod.

"Where have you been?" Keres sat down in front of her just as she was about to get up and clean her area.

"Excuse me?" Zanna looked at her, confused.

Keres never spoke to her while they were at the academy. She was sure that Keres pretended she didn't exist for the most part, especially in public.

"Your Instructor said you were missing for half of the class," Keres continued.

"I don't see how she could know that when all of her students were spread across the library on assignment," Zanna shrugged, but she suddenly felt suspicious. Had someone seen her?

"Were you off with Javaid?" Keres questioned rather forcefully.

"I was with him, yes," Zanna told her. "We're often together if you haven't noticed."

"It is forbidden to fraternize with a fellow student," Keres told her. "You could be expelled."

"Fraternize?" Zanna was confused for a moment and she couldn't help but notice that Enessa was listening. "You think Javaid and I are…"

"You're always together, as you said," Keres told her. "And you were missing this afternoon."

"Keres," Zanna laughed and then was suddenly angry. "Javaid and I are friends. Besides, is it not against the law for Humans and Elves to…fraternize?"

"Stranger things have happened," she said, eyeing Zanna. "Besides, I see the way he looks at you."

Zanna suddenly wondered if Keres knew anything about her father, her real father. Why else would she have said that to her? Perhaps that was why she hated her so much. It wasn't just that was human, it was because she was a half breed.

"Does that bother you that much you had to come say something to me?" Zanna felt her temper rising. "The thought that an Elf could look at a Human that way? Does it disgust you because Humans are so beneath you?"

"I only said…" Keres began.

"I know what you said." Zanna stood up, glaring at her sister, and stormed away.

As she did, she thought about that word, "sister." Keres was not her sister, she was her aunt. Though some might not think that much of a revelation, it was one to her. It meant that she and Keres actually did share blood. Would that change the way Keres treated her? Zanna doubted it. If anything, Keres would probably be appalled, revolted, that she had a half-human niece.

Zanna could feel the tears burning at the back of her eyes but refused to let them fall. She didn't have the capacity to even talk to Javaid. They had their plan laid out, there was no reason to discuss it further. Her focus was to get out of the dining hall and away from Keres.

She laid in her bed that night waiting for the Instructors to make their last rounds. There had never been an incident of a student trying to sneak out and being caught, that she was aware of. Javaid claimed to have done it plenty of times. The Instructors were so sure of their ability to keep the students in line that once they made their last round, they either went to bed or stayed in their offices.

When Zanna was sure that she would have the halls to herself, she made her way out of the door. She had packed a small bag of provisions to take on their journey. She would need more food and water than Javaid, but he would bring some as well.

The stone hallways were eerily quiet. The flames from the torches that lined the halls flickered in an unseen breeze that tickled at the back of her neck. Her boots only made soft tapping noises as she moved as silently as possible around the corners and across the floors.

Reaching the armory, she looked for Javaid, but couldn't find him anywhere. A sinking feeling filled her stomach. If he had decided not to accompany her, she wouldn't begrudge him. This was her quest, after all. In fact, she had planned to go alone from the start. It was him who insisted on coming with her.

"Your steps are so loud I heard you coming from your bedroom," Javaid whispered into her ear.

Zanna jumped, whirling around, facing Javaid in the dark. He was mere inches from her face. His white-blonde hair reflected the torchlight, the flames dancing in his eyes.

"You're a monster," she said, shoving him back.

"And you're loud," he snickered.

"I was quiet," she insisted.

"To human ears, perhaps," he handed her sword to her. "If you really are half-elf then we need to learn how to tap into that side of your abilities."

"Do you think that is possible?" she wondered seriously as she sheathed the blade.

"It could be," he shrugged. "Now, let's move before we're caught."

They moved through the massive school, taking staircases and hallways that Zanna had never seen. Javaid was right, he did know places in and out of the structure that not many were privy to. However, Zanna didn't think it was merely for his escapades with his fellow classmates. Finally, they were out of the building and running across the grounds. The grass was wet from recent rain, it clung to her boots and the dampness extended to the air. She breathed it in, not exactly hating it because she had to run with all her might to keep up with Javaid. By the time they reached the edge of the property, she was panting.

"Do I need to slow down?" he smirked at her.

"Shut up," she told him.

He smiled and quickly climbed the tree beside them and gracefully leaped over the high wall. Zanna looked up in shock. When he said he knew a way out of the academy, she didn't expect him to take her on an impossible route.

Eyeing the tree, she gauged she'd have to take a running leap to reach the lowest branch. That's if she could even jump that high. Then she'd have to pull herself up the tree, through very precarious-looking branches. After that, she would have to make a 6-foot leap to the gate wall.

If she did actually pull this off, she already envisioned the swift kick to the shin she was going to give Javaid once she caught her breath.

"Are you coming?" Javaid called down to her.

"You must be really enjoying yourself," she hissed at him.

"You are half-elf," he told her. "Perhaps, it is time to start acting like it."

"It's not as if I can just snap my fingers and become an elf," Zanna glared at him. "If I had these abilities, don't you think I would have been able to use them by now?"

"You're about to be of age," he told her. "You said yourself, you felt stronger in your fight against Keres. How else do you explain that you were actually able to get in a hit? Besides, you didn't become an Elf. You are an Elf."

Zanna, sighed, not really sure how to take his words. She backed up as far as she thought was needed, bent her knees, took a deep breath, and took off. She ran as fast as she could and jumped, pushing up from the ground with all of her might. And she missed.

Zanna landed, hard, on her feet and went into a roll. She managed to stop herself before she crashed into the wall. She lay on her back, staring up at the sky for a moment, trying to catch her breath. Her entire body was tired and ached. She told herself when she did make it up the wall, she was going to kill Javaid.

As she laid there, she noticed that the wall wasn't as smoothed as it seemed. There were pieces of missing brick and some of the stone jutted out from years of settling. Zanna grabbed some dirt and rubbed it on her hands, stood up, and grabbed the first stone. She made sure to secure her foot and then began climbing.

"What are you doing?" Javaid called down to her.

"What…does it look like?" she said, as she found another place to pull herself up.

"You're supposed to climb the tree," he said.

"We both know…that…isn't going to…happen," she said

through movements and breaths.

Finally, she reached the top and Javaid helped her to the ledge. She was winded, but not as much as she thought she would be. Perhaps she wasn't able to scale a tree and leap 6 feet across onto a wall, but she could admit to herself that she did feel a change in her abilities.

"Can I ask you something and I need you to be honest?" he questioned, as he turned her to look at him.

"Alright," she told him.

"Are you going to find your father or are you going to find the armor?" Javaid's ice-blue eyes burned into hers.

"I'm looking for my father, Javaid," she told him, unsure of what he meant by the question.

Javaid said nothing for a heartbeat. He merely gazed at her, squeezed her shoulders, and nodded his head. He turned and gracefully jumped from the ledge and landed on the ground below.

"Arrogant showoff." Zanna muttered under her breath but was sure he heard her based on the deep laugh she heard from below.

Zanna was thankful to find thick vines had grown on this side of the wall. She used them to work her way down and punched Javaid in the side when she approached him. He flinched, not expecting her jab, and laughed even harder.

They headed down a small, overgrown path, but it was indeed well-traveled at some point. Zanna suddenly felt Javaid grab her around the waist and pull her back just as an arrow whipped by her shoulder. She hit the ground like a bag of bricks. When she looked up. Javaid was already coming to blows with an unknown assailant.

"Javaid!" Zanna yelled as his sword clashed with the attacker's.

Zanna jumped to her feet, drawing her own blade. As she did so, another man came out of the shadows and then another man. They surrounded her, circling like predators.

"Where's the book?" one asked, he had on a green cloak, she was sure he was human.

"We don't want to hurt you," the other said, he was heavy set and broad. "But we will if we have to."

Zanna could feel herself shaking. She had trained for moments like this, but nothing could really prepare for fighting for your life. The men seemed to sense that she wasn't about to give up the book, so they moved in at once.

Zanna took in a deep breath, time seemed to slow down and then suddenly sped up. The men slashed at her with their blades. She clashed with the man on her right and narrowly missed a hit from the man on her left. Zanna brought up her leg and kicked the man in the green cloak in the knee. Screaming, he went down. Without hesitation, she jabbed her sword through his chest.

She tried not to think of the force she had to use, or the sound it made, or how it felt. The only thing she allowed to pass through her mind was her next move. Removing her sword swiftly, she brought the blood-stained blade back around in time to stop the fat man from cutting through her face.

He sneered at her but glanced at his fallen friend. Zanna could tell he was overcome with emotion. She had to use this to her advantage. She swung her sword, again and again. She was smaller than him, lighter, faster. He was too slow, but he was strong.

The man caught her with the back of his hand across her cheek. She hit the ground, her ears ringing. He came charging toward her, bringing his sword down. Zanna rolled out of the way just as the blade slammed into the dirt.

Seeing her opportunity, she brought her sword up quickly, swiping the blade up the man's inner thigh, knowing she hit the spot she intended because hot, thick blood spilled onto the ground. It took the man only a few seconds to fall down and bleed out.

Zanna stood up just as Javaid came to her side. He helped her to her feet and they both took off at a high speed. They didn't have time to stop. The men were dead, and they didn't want to wait around to find out if anyone else was there to try and stop them.

They continued to run for a bit longer until they reached a small farm. Javaid apparently knew the man, a human, and his daughter lived in the tiny home on the property. Javaid paid him for two horses and saddles. As they left, Zanna couldn't help but notice how the farmer's daughter watched longingly after Javaid. Despite all that had just happened, Zanna felt something form in the pit of her stomach; something ugly. She pushed it away and focused on their current situation.

They rode quickly for a few hours. Soon, they arrived at Halesford, a human town of Mirstone. It was a bustling place at all hours of the day, but especially at night. Zanna had been just a few times. As they approached the gate, people moving in and out freely, she pulled her cloak over her head.

Many knew of her flaming locks, but it would still shock people who were not accustomed to seeing it. She didn't realize how unusual her hair was until she was here with her father, with Dorthran, and a woman rushed to her and touched it. It was the only time she had felt special.

Dorthran had explained to her that her mother's people were the last known human clan to have that particular feature. When they were wiped out, Zanna became the last human to have it.

Javaid went ahead. He knew the place better than her, so she didn't mind. They stopped at a rickety-looking pub near the port. Without saying anything they entered the loud tavern and made their way to the bar. He ordered them two pints and they settled on the stools.

"What are we doing here?" she asked him, not drinking her mead, and looking around.

She held her hands in her laps, trying to stop them from shaking. She didn't want Javaid to see her falling apart. In all honesty, she didn't want to watch herself be so frail either.

"If we want to cross the sea to get to the Ash Mountains, we either have to book passage here or keep traveling and cross the bridge," he told her. "Booking passage will save us days of travel."

"Alright," she nodded. "How do we book passage?"

"We find ourselves a captain," he told her.

Zanna suddenly felt very grateful that she had let Javaid accompany her. There was so much about this world that she didn't know. There was only so much one could learn from books and study. Dorthran kept his daughters as sheltered as possible. She could feel anger well up inside her. She loved him, she knew she did, but by keeping them locked up at home or the academy had put her at such a disadvantage.

"Oy, Elf," an older man who smelled of smoke and drink came up to him.

"Yes?" Javaid tried to contain his anger.

"Ya lookin' for passage for yerself and the female?" he asked as a few other men joined him.

"Ay," Javaid nodded, but his nostrils flared. "We just need to cross the sea."

"Whatcha willin' to pay?" asked the man.

"What are you asking?" Javaid returned.

"50 silver," he said. "Got me a good ship, good crew. Won't be no funny busy with the female if yur worried 'bout that."

"I'm not worried," Javaid smiled, a look flashing in his eyes that Zanna had never seen before.

The man was silent for a moment. His crew exchanged glances with one another. He took a long drink of the ale in his hands and nodded.

"We be leavin' at first light in the mornin'," he said. "Name's Wislow. My ship is The Black Briar at the end of the dock. I expect half payment when we leave, half when we get there."

"Fair enough," said Javaid. "In the morning."

Wislow nodded and left them. Zanna reached out and touched Javaid's hand. His head whipped around and looked at her.

"You're holding the hilt of your sword," she whispered to him.

He looked down and then back at her. Slowly he moved his

hand to the bar. Zanna stared at him, for a moment, it was as if she didn't know him. He had looked so angry, so feral. Was this him when she wasn't around, when he was on one of his assignments? She supposed he had to be different in places like this. Perhaps, she needed to be as well.

Again, she felt that anger rise in her. If only Dorthran had let them out now and then, maybe she would know how to handle herself in situations like this. It's not that she didn't appreciate Javaid or want his help; she just wanted not to need it.

"Barkeep," Javaid said suddenly, and the old woman came huffing over.

She was a middle-aged woman with a round face and an even rounder bosom. She had curly blonde hair and rosy cheeks. The green of her eyes matched that of some of the brew she handed out to the patrons. Zanna did not want to know what that concoction was, just the smell made her stomach turn.

"Yes, dear?" the large woman greeted them.

"Is there a place nearby we can obtain shelter for the night?" he asked.

"Just so happens we have a room out back," she told him. "It isn't much, but it is clean and will keep you and the missus from the cold and rain that's coming in. Just 1 silver and it comes with breakfast in the morning."

"We'll take it," Javaid slipped the woman a coin and she gave him a key.

"Come, Missus," Javaid said, and Zanna saw the smirk on his face.

Zanna was tempted to punch him in the back of the head. It if weren't for the full tavern, she would have.

On their way out of the door, someone grabbed her wrist and whirled her around. A tall man with long, jet black hair pulled her toward him. She instinctively put up her hand and stopped their bodies from colliding.

"Where ya runnin' off to, girlie?" he asked, his breath laced with mead.

"Unhand me, sir," Zanna warned him.

"What proper talk," he laughed and so did his party of six. "Are ye a lady, then? High born, I bet. Why are ye here, then? Lookin' for a good time?"

"You're going to be looking for a new hand if you don't take yours off of me," Zanna felt anger rush through her.

"Oy, a feisty one, boys!" he laughed. "Let's see what's hidden underneath that hood."

He reached up and as he did Zanna brought up her knee, catching him in the groin. When he leaned over in pain, she brought her knee up once more, connecting with his nose. He fell back, blood sprouting from a clearly broken nose.

Another man went to grab her, a big burly man with a mop of white-blonde hair, but Javaid was there, grabbing his wrist and easily lifting him off the ground.

"We don't want trouble," he told him. "Your man put his hands where they were not wanted, and he paid the price. What's done is done."

The blonde man looked from Javaid to his friend on the floor. For a moment Zanna thought this fool was actually going to try and take on an Elf while he was drunk. Being drunk would be his only excuse.

"Fine," the blonde man said and raised his hands in surrender.

Javaid let him go and before he, or anyone else for that matter, could change their minds and go to blows. Zanna grabbed him by the hand and led him out of the door. They made their way out of the tavern and toward the one-room shack they were staying for the night. On the way, they grabbed their horses and tied them to the post outside of the thin wooden door.

Once they were inside, Zanna began lighting the lantern and then helped Javaid throw wood in the fireplace. It was cold in the small room, but she shivered from more than that.

They had only been gone from Vaelkesh for a few hours and they had already been nearly killed and now in a tavern brawl. Her nerves were shot, but she wasn't going to let that stop her from making it to the Ash Mountains, even though someone clearly didn't want her going.

Was it her father, Dorthran? Would he kill her in order to keep the secret of his son and her birth? Surely he loved her? He had always treated her like his own.

Once the fire was going well, Zanna sat at the small table and pulled out the book. She read through the account once more. It seemed like something from fables, but Zanna knew in her heart it had to be true. Her father must still be alive.

There was a knock at the door, they both tensed and quickly grabbed their weapons. Javaid went to one side and Zanna went to the other side.

"Yes?" Javaid said.

"It's Lila," a cheery voice said, "The barkeep. I thought you might like some hot soup I had left over."

Javaid opened the door slightly while Zanna was ready to back him up if needed. Once he was satisfied that no one was with her, he opened the door a bit wider.

"I thought you might be hungry," she smiled and walked in, putting a tray down on the table.

Zanna was there in a flash, grabbing the book from out of her reach. She had already had to kill someone for it, she didn't want to have to stab the cheery barkeep.

"My stars!" Lila said, looking at her. "Oh, forgive me, ma'am. It's just...I haven't seen a head full of hair like that since I was a little girl."

Zanna had forgotten she had removed her cloak. Her hands automatically went up to her hair and pushed it back.

"You must be...Oh, dear, I'm so sorry," Lila bowed, but Zanna stopped her.

"Please," Zanna said to her. "Don't do that. I am not royalty, that is my...my father."

"Lila," Javaid said gently to her. "We thank you for your hospitality, but we must ask that you not inform anyone of our presence here. It is of vital importance."

"I understand," she nodded. "I may be a lot of things, but a traitor is not one of them."

"Thank you," Zanna squeezed her hand. "And thank you for the food."

Lila bowed, even though Zanna had asked her not to, and left the shack. Zanna released a pent-up breath and looked at Javaid.

"Do we trust her?" she asked.

"I hope," he said. "As of now, your father doesn't know you're missing. Whoever wants that book isn't associated with him."

"How can you be so sure?" she asked, sitting down at the table.

"He loves you, Zanna," he turned to look at her. "He would never hurt you."

She didn't say anything for a moment. Instead, she listened to the wind blowing outside, thankful they had four walls and a fire burning to keep them sheltered. She chose to enjoy it because all she knew this might be their last night with these comforts.

"You should eat," he said, pouring some soup in a bowl and handing it to her.

"So should you," she told him.

"I don't require as much food as you," he reminded her.

"Be that as it may, take a hot meal when it is offered to you," she said. "Besides, when was the last time you and I had supper together? Sit down and have a meal with me."

She could see the edge of a smile creep into his mouth. He poured himself a bowl of the steaming soup and sat across from her. After a moment they had relaxed enough to talk and smiled a little. Zanna needed it. She needed to laugh. She needed to push away the face of the dying men. The men she had killed.

"Rest," Javaid said after a moment. "I'll take watch."

"What about you?" she asked as she yawned.

"I'm not tired," he told her.

"Well, if you do begin to tire, come to bed," she began and then realized what she had said. "What I meant was…"

"I know what you meant, Zanna," he stifled a laugh.

Zanna had never felt uncomfortable around Javaid. They had been friends for so long, and he had so many admirers that she had long removed any thoughts of them being anything more. They had slept in the same bed as recently as last year when they went out stargazing. When she'd awoke, he'd been asleep beside her and while she had enjoyed his beauty, she didn't feel like anything had changed.

Now, as she stared at him standing across the room from her, she was wondering if something had. After that evening, he had left for an entire year on a mission for the King. He had been through much in his travels, and now, he was a different elf. He had that same light smile she had always found comforting, but there was something dark that swam beneath the surface of those ice-blue eyes. She had a feeling tonight was not his first kill.

She managed to nod and removed her sword from her waist. Feeling the weight of it leave her body was both reassuring and frightening. She leaned it against the bed so she would be able to reach it quickly if needed.

Laying down, she watched Javaid blow out the lantern light and stand guard at the window. He didn't move for so long he almost looked like a statue. She watched him until her eyes grew heavy with sleep.

It seemed as though no time had passed when she was jolted awake by Javaid. His hand was over her mouth. She could imagine what her expression looked like, her eyes wide with fear. His face, on the other hand, was severe but collected.

He placed a finger to his lips. Then he pointed to the door.

Zanna looked as she raised up, her heart beating wildly in her chest. The knob was turning left and then right. It was slight. If you weren't paying attention, then you would hardly notice at all.

Zanna stood up as quietly as she could and put her sword sheath back on her waist, quickly, and then drew her sword. They both went and stood on either side of the door. She reached over and gently took the handle in her hands. When Javaid nodded, she yanked the door open.

The man on the other side was so surprised that he stumbled into the room and fell to the floor. Javaid was on him before he knew what was happening. Zanna scanned the outside and as soon as her head was out of the door, she caught a fist to her chin. Staggering back, she threw her sword in front of her.

Blackness crept at the edges of her vision, but she saw a figure move into the room.

"Hand over the book, girl," a voice said, and the way he said "girl" made anger swell inside her.

She shook her head, trying to clear her thoughts and her vision.

"Come and get it," she challenged.

As the man lunged forward, her sight came back into focus. She may not have been an Elf, but she had been trained with them her entire life. She knew things, combat moves, that this man only wished he had learned.

He was fast, but she was faster. His size and form worked against him as she darted past him. It took him a moment to whirl around and when he did, Zanna struck a blow to his chest. He wore a breastplate, so he didn't go down, but he was shocked that she had managed to hit him.

Her eyes momentarily darted to Javaid who was still fighting with his own assailant. She looked back at the man in black.

"Who sent you?" she asked him, circling around him.

"No one sent me, girl," he said. "We've been looking for that book for a long time."

"Why?" she questioned.

"You know why," he said, inching closer. "It will lead us to the armor and with it, great power. Anyone who wears it will be invincible. Not even your Elf King could stand in its way."

"It was stopped once before," Zanna told him. "It can be stopped again."

"That was because your Daddy didn't want to hurt you," he said. "That much of the story, I do know. What I need to know is where they have it hidden. You wouldn't want to tell me that, now would you? I might even let you live if you do."

"And what about my companion?" she asked. "Will you spare him as well?"

"Sure, I'm feeling generous," he smiled, his teeth stained yellow, and lowered his sword slightly.

Zanna took that moment to pick up the lantern on the table and throw it at his feet. In the next moment, she reached in the fire and pulled out a half-lit log and flung it toward him. It took him a moment to realize what was happening, but by then it was too late.

The bottom of his cloak caught fire and quickly crawled up his back. He screamed, fighting to remove the garment, but now the flames were attacking his boots. The man began to panic and batted this way and that. Now that he was completely distracted, and the flames began to singe his hair, Zanna stepped forward and swung her sword quick and hard, severing his head from his body.

In the next moment, Javaid's sword went through the other man's chest. It made a sickening wet sound as Javaid twisted it, ensuring death.

Without saying anything, they grabbed their belongings and hurried from the cabin. Quickly they mounted their horses and headed for the docks.

The captain, Wislow, was there already, ordering his men to load large barrels of what looked like mead onboard.

"You be early," he narrowed his eyes.

"I'll pay you double if you let us on now," Javaid offered.

"Fine," he muttered after a moment and gestured toward the ship. "There be a cabin I set aside for you. It's only the one, so hope ye both don't mind bunking together. We'll square away payment when I'm done here."

They left their horses at the stables. Zanna gave her's a quick kiss in thanks and rushed onto the ship with Javaid. When they found their cabin, they entered quickly and closed the door.

It was small and cramped. It only had room from a very tiny bed and a round table. Standing, they were practically nose to nose, so Zanna sat down on the bed. When she did it felt like the weight of what just transpired came crashing down her.

She swore she wouldn't give in to nerves like she had the first time. It was either him or her and she would always choose herself, always. She reached inside her shirt and found that the book was still there. Pulling it out, she studied the green leather, wondering if all of this was worth the secret inside.

"Are you…" Javaid started.

"I'm fine," she said harshly and instantly regretted it.

He was only being her friend, but she couldn't have him be sympathetic at the moment. She had killed a man, cut off his head. The last thing she needed or deserved was to be coddled.

"I'm fine," she said a bit softer. "Any idea when we're leaving?"

"The sun should rise in about an hour," he told her. "The captain said they were leaving at first light. We'll just have to wait until then."

Zanna nodded. She moved herself back to the head of the bed, drawing her knees up to her chest, waiting. As Javaid paced the room she read the story again and again. Her father had to still be alive. All of this had to be for a reason. There was a purpose in her finding this book and learning his story. Otherwise, why? Why was this happening? Why was she headed to the Ash Mountains with a trail of bodies in her wake?

There was a knock at the door. She jumped up from the bed. Both she and Javaid had their swords out.

"It's Wislow," the old man said. "We're bout to be sailing off. Come to collect me payment."

Javaid fished out the coins and opened the door. He handed the man the money. Wislow counted it and then looked at him and then at Zanna, his eyes growing large at the sight of her red hair.

"Breakfast be served in an hour," he told them. "It ain't much, but it will fill your bellies. I do suggest you wash up though. Ye both covered in blood. There's a water basin there on ye table, small mirror 'bove it."

With that, he left them. Zanna finally looked at Javaid and he looked at her. Blood had dried on his face, neck, and hands. There were spots all over his shirt as well. Luckily neither one of them had been wearing their cloaks at the time so they were clean. Zanna assumed she looked just as bad. When she looked at her hands, she realized they were flaking with dried blood.

She tried not to rush to the basin, but she wasn't sure how much she succeeded in that endeavor. Pouring water from the jug into the basin she nearly spilled it all over the floor. Javaid came to the side and grabbed the container.

"Slow down," he said soothingly.

She wasn't sure why, but this enraged her. She ignored him and poured the water faster and then slammed the jug down on the table. She took a cloth from the table and began scrubbing her hands vigorously, wishing she had her many soaps from home because even though the blood was gone, she didn't feel clean.

"Zanna," Javaid said, but she continued to ignore him.

There was just too much blood on her hands, on her arms, on the sleeves of her shirt. She ripped off her cloak and began washing her face and neck. She washed and washed, splashing water all over the wooden floor.

"Zanna, please," he said, but his voice sounded distant.

A large stain was on the hem of her shirt and it sent waves of nausea through her. She hurriedly pulled the shirt over her head and dunked it in the water, trying her best to wash it away. When the water was bloody, she threw it on the floor, filled the basin, and began washing her shirt again. The stain wasn't coming out and she was mad, enraged. She began beating the shirt against the wall.

Finally, Javaid grabbed her arm and turned her around to face him. His icy blue eyes were full of something she couldn't understand at the moment. He pulled her into his embrace.

"Stop!" she yelled, struggled against him. "Let go of me!"

He said nothing, just held her to his chest, wrapping his arms around her bare back, the wet shirt pressed between them.

"I said let go of me, Javaid, I mean it!" She hit his chest with her fists.

He held her until she didn't have the strength to hit him anymore. Zanna wanted to cry, but she wouldn't let the tears come. This was her journey, not his. She had to be stronger than this. She had been ridiculed and stigmatized most of her life. That took every ounce of her emotional capacity to survive. She could survive this.

"May I have my shirt?" she asked him as she stood taller, realizing she was standing in front of him practically naked with nothing more than her long hair shielding most of her flesh from his gazing eyes.

"It is drenched," he told her, staring hard into her eyes.

"It's fine," she took the soaking wet shirt from him and put it back on, though not easily.

The ship began to pull from the port and as it did so, Zanna stormed from the room. She needed fresh air. She needed this shirt to dry. It was once a soft teal, now it looked more like a muddy brown. On her way above deck, many of the sailors jumped out of her way in surprise. Surely they knew they had passengers, but they were not expecting the daughter of Dorthran.

When she made it to the top, she was glad to see that there was already some distance between them and the shore. The air was a bit cool, but she didn't complain. It felt nice on her skin. She brushed her hair out of her face and noticed she was getting stares from the crew.

She was tempted to turn and ask them if they had something to say, but she knew it would be unfair. None of them had done anything to her. It wasn't their fault she was being chased down by a group of people determined to find her father's armor.

That was when she noticed about five or so riders storm up the harbor. One of them dismounted their horse and ran the length of the dock. It was Keres. Her long white hair was tied back in a braid, but Zanna knew it was her. She wore her armor and her sword was unsheathed at her side. Even though there was quite a bit of distance between them, Zanna knew that Keres saw her with her keen eyes. Keres pointed her sword in the direction of their vessel and then regrouped with her companions.

Zanna wasn't sure how long she had stood out there, but eventually, her shirt dried and her stomach gnawed with hunger.

"Zanna," Javaid's voice sounded from behind her.

She turned and saw he was guarded, unsure of her reaction. Zanna didn't smile at him. She was tired of smiling. That's what her mother would always tell her, even when she didn't feel like it, "Smile, Zanna."

"Are you hungry?" he asked. "You missed breakfast, but I saved you some food."

"You didn't have to do that," she told him.

"I know," he responded and handed her a bowl of porridge.

She took the bowl and ate it. It was bland, but she finished it, knowing it would be hearty and keep her strength up.

"I can take that, Miss Zanna," a young crew member came forward and offered to get the bowl from her.

She saw it on his face and the way he said her name, he recognized her. It didn't surprise her, but it was annoying. It made her want to hide, to find somewhere that no one knew her or Dorthran.

"Thank you," she said to him.

She never knew what to expect from people. Sometimes it was this reaction, this groveling as if she has done something other than being born with red hair. Other times it was as if she had the audacity to be born at all. The humans, for the most part, adored her. There were those who thought she should be ashamed, living with Elves. Maybe it was jealousy, but it was also their fast-held beliefs that the two races should not mix.

Zanna caught Javaid staring at her. When she looked at him, he didn't look away. There was that look again. She recognized it. He was angry. She was shocked. Was he angry at her? For what exactly? She traced back in her memory, trying to recall a moment when she could have done something to warrant his hostility. Nothing came to mind.

She pushed past him and the boy and went below deck to their room. Surprisingly, she fell into a deep sleep. Her dreams were full of dark shadows and faces of people she had never met. Strong hands gripped her shoulders, calling her name. She fought, but still, they held on.

"Zanna! Wake up!" It was Javaid, he was shaking her.

"What is it?" she was disoriented, but jumped out of the bed, ready to fight.

"You're safe," he told her. "You were screaming in your sleep."

Zanna looked at him and then at her surroundings. They were still on the ship. She felt it rock back and forth. Even though she couldn't see outside, she knew many hours had passed since she had fallen asleep. Zanna moved out from under his grasp, her heart in her throat, the phantoms of her dreams still playing in her mind's eye. When she felt like she could talk, she looked at him.

"I... you missed dinner," he said to her. "I brought you some of the food."

"You don't have to take care of me!" she snapped. "I can feed myself!"

"I never said you couldn't, Zanna," he looked as if she had slapped him.

"I saw her," Zanna said finally. "Keres, she was on the dock when we departed. She's following us. Do you think she knows? Do you think my father...Dorthran sent her after me...to kill me?"

"They love you, Zanna," he said to her. He lingered for a moment and then opened the door to their tiny cabin.

With that, he left the room. She stood there, an uncontrollable anger rushing up to her chest. Without being able to stop herself, she punched the cabin wall. She felt her knuckles give, but more surprisingly, so did the wall, if only slightly. Zanna looked at her hand. It hurt, but it wasn't bloody or bruised. She was a bit shocked. Just a few months ago that one action would have surely broken her hand. Perhaps they were right, she was coming into her abilities.

The next few days were tense. The ship was heading for a storm and Javaid had barely spoken to her, except for when it was necessary. She finally decided to join the crew at mealtimes. None of them said a word about her hair or who she was, for which she was thankful. In fact, they treated her and Javaid as one of their own. It was mainly due to the fact that both of them had done their fair share of work around the ship.

Javaid helped heave in and lower sails while Zanna did other deckhand work. She had never worked so hard in her life. Her body was tired, but she felt better for it at the end of the day. It almost made her want to stay right on this ship, officially become a part of the crew, and forget her plans of finding her father who was more than likely dead.

The thought sent pain and longing shooting through her soul. While it might be exciting to escape into the role of a sailor for a few days, she knew that's all it was, an escape. They would reach the shores of an unknown land soon and she would have to focus on the task at hand.

She couldn't help but wonder if Javaid would continue on the journey with her. Zanna knew she had given him no reason to want to stay. They would have to get over this rift and soon and the thought made her angry once again. She didn't even know why he was upset with her. Sure, recently she had been cold, but he was mad before then.

That night she laid awake in her cot while he sat at the table, the ship swaying back and forth. She could feel the storm brewing outside, but it was nothing compared to one inside her heart. Javaid worked on a piece of leather with his knife. The constant scraping seemed to seep into her mind, pouring into her marrow.

"If you do not speak on why you are angry with me, I may just take that piece of leather and strangle you with it!" Zanna jumped up from the bed.

Javaid looked genuinely shocked. He slowly put the knife back in the sheath at his ankle and the leather strap back in the small purse at his waist. He leaned back in the chair and crossed his arms behind his head.

"Sorry if I disturbed you," he said, closing his eyes and propping his feet on the table.

"Are you a child?" she knocked his feet down, nearly causing him to fall.

He stood up angrily and picked his chair back up, "I could ask you the same," he growled.

"Why will you not tell me what is bothering you?" she asked, moving closer to him. "We will reach shore in the morning and I am wondering where your mind is."

"Where my mind is?" he gruffed, inching closer to her. "Where else could it be? Right here and a thousand miles forward in the Ash Mountains, wondering what the hell we're getting ourselves into exactly."

"I never asked you to come, Javaid," she said to him angrily. "So if your sour attitude is because I took you away from your privileged life and latest conquests then by all means, when we disembark tomorrow, you don't have to come with me. I am accustomed to being on my own."

"There, right there," he put his finger in her face. "That's it, right there. Those words."

"What are you raving about?" she swatted at him. "Get your gigantic finger out of my face, Javaid."

"Or what?" he challenged.

Zanna didn't even think about what she was doing. One moment she was glaring at him and the next she had grabbed his finger, bent it, and then twisted his arm behind his back. He called out in surprise but quickly gathered his thoughts because she was suddenly on her back on the bed.

She punched him in the gut, causing him to bend over, gasping for breath. Zanna kicked up and wrapped her legs around his head, using his hair to pull herself up, and then wrapped her entire body around his head and neck, squeezing. Using her elbow, she delivered several blows to the top of his head.

Javaid turned and bit her inner thigh. She screamed and tried pulling away from him, which gave him enough room to grab her legs, pull her off of him and slam her against the wall. He pinned her there, using his weight to hold her place.

"Enough," he said to her.

"Get off me!" she spat at him.

"Not until you listen to me, you selfish brat!" he yelled back.

Those words seemed to douse the fire burning insider her. She looked up at him and that light that had been fading in out of his eyes seemed to be aflame.

"You have always acted like you were alone," he said, his voice trembling with emotion. "And I understand why. I will not pretend to know what you have felt all these years growing up as an outsider wherever you go and then finding out the truth of your lineage. That is something I cannot touch. But, Zanna," his voice was tense, yet tender, "You have never, never been alone. I...I have been there, right by your side...waiting for you to notice. I would follow you to the ends of Mirstone if you asked me. I am and you didn't even have to and you never stopped to ask yourself why? I do not care about my riches or my conquests, as you put them, they mean nothing to me. You, Zanna, you have and you will always mean everything to me. I told you standing in the library beside those old dusty books, I love you."

He let her go then and stood back, looking at her. If she weren't mistaken, there were tears in his eyes. Javaid said nothing more and climbed into the bed, rolling over on his side. Zanna stood there for a moment, just staring at him. Slowly, she made her way over and slid into the bed beside him. She wrapped her arms around him, holding him tightly. Javaid turned to face her, Zanna wiped the tears that stained his cheeks. He kissed her gently on the forehead and pulled her closer.

*

They spent that night in each other's arms, feeling safe there in the rocking ship, not knowing what lay on the other side of the sea.

*

After departing Wislow's ship, Zanna and Javaid spent only enough time in the tiny port village to purchase a few supplies and horses.

It was dingy, and smelled damp, despite being baked by bright sunlight. Perhaps it was because it was so close to the sea.

Children with dirty faces and no shoes crowded the harbor, asking the sailors about treats and their adventures. Zanna wondered where their parents might be but then thought maybe some of them might be the sailors themselves.

They were warned by some merchants that crossing the desert was certain doom, but none of the village folk seemed sad to see them leave.

While they clearly wanted a clear conscience, they didn't want an Elf residing in their town for long. Zanna had made sure to pull her under her cloak, despite the overwhelming heat.

She wasn't certain if she would be recognized beyond the Blackridge Sea, but she didn't want to take any chances. Ensuring her identity was secret would make it harder for Keres to track her.

170

As they mounted their horses, which were surprisingly well taken care of and healthy, Zanna couldn't help but wonder how far behind Keres might be. Perhaps it was days, or merely hours. With that thought, she was glad they were continuing their journey without delay.

The desert was harsh and unforgiving, as were most places designed to be wild and free. Still, there was something dangerously beautiful about the poisonous reptiles and hellish sun. It made sense to her. There was a purpose to their existence when she couldn't find one for her own.

Their first two days of travel were relatively uneventful. They traveled at the early hours of the morning until they could no longer take the heat, retreating into the heavy canvas tent they purchased at the port village.

Neither one had spoken about the night on the ship when they had taken comfort and refuge in each other's embrace. There were moments Zanna felt as though he were about to say something to her, she could feel the tension rolling from his body, but instead he would say he would take first watch or ask her if she were hungry.

Zanna thought it was for the best. Her future was unknown at this point. Perhaps, if their moment had happened at another point in time, there could have been further discussion. Now, it just seemed pointless. That didn't stop her heart from aching, or her body longing for his touch.

They had reached the edge of the desert city. Lights could be seen from the distance, but the desert sand muted any noise. It was like looking at a beautiful painting doused in all the colors of a deep red and golden sunset.

Their supplies were diminishing so Javaid made a quick trip early the next morning. He was in and out of the city before the sun rose and then they moved forward. Soon they could see the Ash Mountains in the distance. Zanna felt like a fire had been set aflame inside her. She wanted to keep moving, but it would be another full day before they would even reach the base and they needed rest.

The closer to the mountains, the darker the sky became. It was an eerie setting with dead and dried vegetation scattered here and there. The horses seemed hesitant to venture forward and it took much coercion to guide them toward the mountain. They, too, felt the heaviness that seemed to thicken the air.

After their meal of dried meat and fresh bread from the city, it was time to rest. However, Zanna was unable to beckon sleep to her tired mind. It was racing with thoughts of what they might find tomorrow. They would reach the mountain by dawn if they set out in a few hours.

She tossed around on her cot in the canvas tent. It was hot, so she moved the heavy blanket from her body. She stayed fully dressed at all times in case they needed to move quickly. It made her miss her thin and cool night dresses from home. She doubted she would ever have those comforts again. Things had changed beyond recognition. She had killed. Her sister was hunting her. Who knew what her father, what Dorthran would do with her once he found her.

"You're not asleep?" Javaid asked, coming into the tent. A brief stream of moonlight filtered in behind him before they were doused in darkness once more.

"Is it my watch?" She asked.

"It is, but a storm cloud is moving in," he told her. "There will be nothing visible for a while."

Zanna could just make out his form in the dark as he sat down in his cot. At that moment she heard thunder in the distance.

"I spotted a cliff not far from here," he said. "It looks as though there might be a cave. We should head that way. I'm afraid where we are might be dangerous for us and the horses."

"Alright," she told him.

They quickly packed up the tent and moved toward the cliff. Javaid was right, there was a small cave in the rocks. It didn't go back into the stone very far, but it was enough to put a considerable distance between themselves and the coming storm. The horses, unfortunately, would have to withstand the onslaught, but at least they wouldn't be in danger of getting washed away.

The rain came quickly and fiercely. Thunder bombed and the lightning lit up the night's sky. The horses were terrified and Zanna felt terrible there was nothing that she could do for them.

"They're fine," Javaid told her for the hundredth time.

"Do you think this will pass by the morning?" she wondered, wanting to leave as soon as they could.

"I'm not sure," he told her. "From what I saw, the storm cloud was large and moving in our direction. If it keeps up with this speed and doesn't slow down, we should be able to."

Zanna nodded and stoked the small fire they had set. The rain had brought with it a chill and she was eager to rid it of her skin. She wound the blanket on her shoulders a bit more tightly. The thunder seemed to be louder and the rain picked up speed. This was doing nothing for the anxiety building in her chest.

Javaid came and sat next to her, warming his pale hands and she couldn't help but stare at his perfect skin. Then she noticed, the closer she looked the more she saw the fine lines of scars that danced along his knuckles. She looked up at him and could make out just the slightest imperfection of his nose where it had been broken a few times. A thin scar, not visible to most humans lined his jaw down to his neck. She had never seen him like this before now.

They were clearly onto something. The closer she got to her 21st year of birth, the more her elven abilities seemed to enhance. Her stomach lurched when she realized her day of birth was only two days away. What would happen when she actually reached her full potential? Was this why Dorthran had wanted her to train just like her sister? Because he knew one day she would grow into her true self?

And how she was seeing Javaid, this had to be proof that she was indeed an Elf. And he had loved her before knowing that. He had risked everything, his own life, to come on this quest based solely on what she had told him. He couldn't read the book. He just trusted her.

"Why are you looking at me like that?" he asked her when he noticed her staring.

Zanna leaned over and kissed him. She wasn't sure what had come over her. Perhaps she needed somewhere to focus her emotions, or perhaps she just wanted to feel his lips on hers. She pulled away and Javaid stared hard at her for a moment. Even though her eyes were seeing things differently for the first time, it didn't change the vibrant blue of his eyes. They were still as beautiful, still as marvelous.

Javaid grabbed her face in his hands and kissed her, deeply, pulling her to him. The night on the ship had been amazing. She had found peace in his embrace. Still, that was all it was. He had held her as she drifted off to sleep and when they awoke, it was as if that moment had only been a dream.

This was different. This was the first time they had truly expressed how they felt. This was the first time that she felt his lips on hers and it opened up feelings she had long ago repressed.

Javaid kissed her as if he might never get the chance to do it again. In the back of her mind, she wondered if that were true. With that thought she kissed him harder, pulling him closer until she was wrapped around him. They needed no words. It only took a look to know what each of them thought, what they felt. At that moment, the storm outside could have destroyed the world and they would have been none the wiser. In truth, they would have never even cared.

Early the next morning, Javaid awoke her with a kiss on her shoulder. She rolled over and wrapped her arms around him, nuzzling into his chest and breathing in the fresh scent of his long, white hair. For just a moment, she lay there, listening to the rain that was still falling, tracing her finger across his bare skin, and accepting every kiss he offered.

For a minute more, she could see herself letting go of this quest to find the armor. If he would ask her, she would turn away from it all and go. Then, a cold gust of wind washed over them, and that moment was gone. She still laid there, taking in his beauty, but knew that they had to leave. She kissed him once more and then stood to get dressed.

"I love you," he said to her as she put on her shirt.

Zanna froze. What had happened between them had a name, but she wasn't sure she was ready to give it one. Javaid came up behind her and wrapped his arms around her. He kissed the top of her head, hugging her to him.

"I love you, Zanna," he told her again. "I just want you to know that."

He let go and got dressed himself. She didn't say anything to him as they packed up their belongings and headed out of the cave. The storm had passed, but there was still a steady rain. Their horses were soaked but in good condition. Zanna felt bad having to put her mare through another journey, but they had to keep moving.

For hours they made slow progress through the rain and mud. When Javaid asked if she was hungry and wanted to rest, she told him to keep going. There really wasn't anywhere to take refuge from the downpour and even though she did feel a bit of hunger gnaw at her stomach, she didn't think she could eat.

The mountain formation was so close. If they kept this pace they would be there by dusk. Although it seemed nightfall was eons away. Just when Zanna didn't think they would ever make it there, the ground became a little less muddy and when she fought the rain to see and looked up the mountains were there looming over her.

They dismounted and tied their horses to a scraggly tree. They would have to climb, and it was far too steep for the horses.

"And the map says we climb until we see the Dragon's Eye?" Javaid asked.

"That's what the book says," she told him. "I've been thinking and I don't think it's literal. I don't think it's the statue, that seems far too obvious. I think it means the volcano."

"You want to climb the volcano?" he asked.

"I really think that's what it meant," she told him.

"There is a perfectly good dragon statue right up there with a ruby eye that's sure to be some kind of magic," he told her as the rain beat down on them. "Are you sure?"

"I am," she nodded.

"Alright, up the volcano we go," he shrugged and they turned in the direction of the fiery rock.

Zanna could feel the anticipation build inside her. She wanted to run up that volcano. She wanted to burst through it and find her father. She would free him from the armor that encased him, and they would leave, start a new life somewhere else.

She thought for a moment. Is that what she really wanted? She knew she had to free him. He had been encased for so long. And she would do all that was within her power to help him accumulate to his new life. But now that she was coming into her own abilities, she wasn't sure if she wanted to spend them stationary. She needed to move, to breathe, to be free of the rules that had kept her bound to the walls of her home for so long.

As they reached the base of the volcano the air became thicker, heavier, and the rain seemed to leave dark stains upon their skin. The volcano had been sleeping for over a thousand years. Still, there would be reports that it rumbled from time to time. Zanna prayed to the gods that it remained a sleeping giant.

Up and up they climbed as the rain beat down upon their shoulders. Zanna was sure they would drown before they would reach the top, if they ever did. She wasn't sure how long it would take them.

The incline became steeper and the rocks were slick with rain and mud. Still, Zanna found her footing was sure and was able to stay on her feet. She wasn't as fast as Javaid, but this was another sign that her father was indeed Elf and she was reaching her abilities quickly. If they had taken this path a year before, the trek up the volcano would have been nearly impossible for her.

"Zanna, look!" Javaid called.

He was pointing behind him and when she turned her head, her eyes finding where he pointed, her heart gave a quick pang. Four figures were headed in their direction. They were several hours behind, but even in the rain, she knew who they were. Elves from Vaelkesh. Keres was amongst them, she had to be.

"We have to hurry," she turned and quickened her pace.

"Maybe if we just talk to her," Javaid offered.

"No," Zanna said. "Dorthran sent assassins after us. What makes you think Keres isn't another one."

"Because she is your family," he said to her. "And she loves you."

"Loves me?" Zanna couldn't help but laugh. "She doesn't love me, Javaid. She did everything in her power to make me miserable, every day of my life. If she had an excuse to kill me, believe me, she'll use it."

"But, you love her," he said to her.

"What?" Zanna stopped walking and turned to him.

"You love her," he told her. "She is your sister. And despite your differences, and how much you fight, you love her and she loves you. I see it."

"You can stay and talk to her if you want," Zanna felt that same sudden rush of rage. "I'm going."

Zanna turned and continued up the volcano. It wasn't long before Javaid was beside her. Occasionally she would turn to see that Keres and the other soldiers had made great progress. She wondered if they would make it to the top before they reached them. And when her resolve seemed to almost give in, she saw it, the plateau. It stretched further than she thought possible. The volcano was indeed sleeping, but there was a large cavernous drop a bit further ahead of them. They walked to it, peering over the side. It was too far down for even Javaid to see the bottom.

Zanna looked around and saw that there was no life here. There were no plants, no birds, it was barren and felt as though a creeping pressure were building up from somewhere, pressing down on them.

"What now?" Javaid asked.

"I...I'm not sure," she looked around again and suddenly a woman was standing a few feet from them.

They both drew their swords, backing away. She was tall, with long flowing black hair and pale skin. She wore a form-fitting gray dress with a black cloak to protect her from the rain. She stared at them with eyes like coal. She was so still that Zanna wasn't sure if she was breathing. That's when she recognized her.

"You're from the library," Zanna said. "You showed me the book. How do you look so young? Mavka."

Javaid looked from Zanna to the mysterious woman. He brought his sword up a bit higher, clearly not trusting her.

"I did," she said, her voice was crisp and ringing, even over the rain.

"Why?" she asked.

"Is that what you really want to ask me?" the woman took a step forward and Javaid did as well, but acted as though she didn't even notice.

"Where is my father?" Zanna asked.

The woman glanced at the crater and Zanna's heart dropped.

"Down there?" she asked.

"It was the only way to seal him properly," Mavka told her.

"Who are you?" Zanna didn't trust her.

"Your sister is nearly upon you," she told Zanna. "Do you really want to waste time on useless questions?"

"I don't trust you," Zanna narrowed her eyes at the woman. "Now answer me. Why are you helping me?"

"He came to me so long ago, broken in so many ways." She began walking toward the edge. "He had lost his family at the hands of someone he thought he could trust. He was angry. I helped him because he saved my village from dragon fire. Now, I am trying to help you. Your father, your true father, is at the bottom of this chasm and only you can free him.”

“If only I can save him then why have there been so many people trying to find him first?” she asked.

“They could take the armor, but it would kill him,” the woman said to her. “And do you think they would care? Only you care enough to save him.”

“And you care? That’s why you helped?” Zanna said incredulously.

“Like I said, he saved my life,” Mavka told her. “And I do not want to see that armor in the hands of just anyone. The armor he wears is unbreakable, unbendable, and holds a power none other has held before in all of our history.”

“And you helped him make it,” Zanna said.

“I did,” she admitted.

“You’re a witch,” Javaid sneered at her.

“I am far more than that, boy,” the woman spat at him. “I was here when this rock was formed and your people were created from dirt and dust.”

“Are you a goddess?” Zanna wondered.

“I have been reviled and revolted, child,” she told her. “I have been known by many names, but for the past thousand years your people have called me Mavka.”

“Mavka of the Forest,” Javaid said. “You are a witch then.”

Mavka sneered at him but said nothing.

“Why are you helping me?” Zanna asked again. “It’s more than what you’re saying.”

“She needs something from you,” Javaid sneered. “Something you have to willingly give.”

“I don’t like you,” the woman said to him.

“I’ll give it,” Zanna told her.

“Zanna!” Javaid rounded on her. “You don’t know what you’re

even agreeing to."

"I'll give it, if you can give me my father," she told the woman.

"Oh, sweet, innocent child," the woman smiled sweetly at her. "I cannot give you your father. You must take him, but in order to do so, without harm coming to him, must be done carefully. You see, the magic that created the armor was blood magic, the strongest known in every realm. If someone else were to take the armor, it would work, but not like it would for someone in the same bloodline. It was also blood magic that bound him to his tomb. He gave up his soul to be bound to that armor. Your grandfather gave a piece of himself to bind him to it, to save his son, and to save you. If you want to free your father…"

"I have to be willing to give up a part of myself as well," Zanna finished.

"Zanna, no, you…" Javaid seemed to freeze, his body went rigid and his eyes went wide with fear.

"I've grown weary of you, boy," Mavka said. "It's time for just us girls to talk."

"Don't hurt him," Zanna stood in front of Javaid.

"He's not in pain," she said and seemed a bit disappointed at the thought. "He just can't interrupt anymore. Now, where were we? Ah, yes, the price you're willing to pay to save your father. What are you willing to give the magic in return for him?"

"What does it want?" Zanna asked, feeling the weight of this decision as if she were holding the volcano up herself.

"Blood magic is strange, indeed," Mavka said, walking toward her. "You never know what is asked of you until you have offered yourself."

"That hardly seems fair," Zanna narrowed her eyes at the woman, if that is what she truly was.

"Is life really fair, Zanna?" Mavka offered.

Zanna watched as the woman moved closer to her. Her dark eyes seemed so lifeless, her form so rigid as if she hadn't moved her body in such a long time that she had forgotten how. Or, maybe it was because this wasn't her true form at all. She wondered what she might actually look like under the facade of beauty that covered her.

She looked behind her and saw that Keres and the other soldiers were making good progress up the volcano. It wouldn't be long before they reached her. As if her sister knew what she was about to do, she called out to her, "Zanna! Wait!"

"I offer the magic what it wants in exchange for my father's freedom," Zanna finally said.

She made a point not to look at Javaid. She knew that if he could move or if he could speak, he would be doing so. He would do anything to try and stop her. But this is what she wanted. She had come so far to find him, to free him. After all, she had been through, there was no turning back now. Besides, if she did not free him, who would?

"Very well," Mavka smiled.

She placed her hand on Zanna's chest. She wasn't sure what to expect. Perhaps she thought it would be a spell, or maybe something else, but instead, Mavka used unimaginable force and shoved her backward. Zanna didn't even have time to think before she fell over the side of the volcano.

She wanted to scream, but her voice was caught in her throat. Her arms flung wildly, trying to find something to grab on to, but of course, there was nothing. She was too far from the sides and the hole was just that, a dark chasm ready to swallow anything that came too close.

She felt like such a fool. Mavka must indeed be a witch and Zanna must be her sacrifice. If she could have stopped and shot back up to the surface like a bird of prey, she would have ripped Mavka's heart out with her bare hands.

Zanna fell and fell until there was only darkness. Even the dimmed sunlight was gone. It was so pitch black that she couldn't see her hand in front of her face or any of her surroundings. It was true darkness. Suddenly, Zanna hit something, hard and painfully.

She waited for death to follow, but it didn't come.

Instead, she rolled over on her side, in pain, but otherwise unhurt. It didn't make sense. She had fallen from a great height. No one should have been able to survive that fall. The only thing she could think of was that magic was at play.

She was afraid to move. The darkness pressed in around her, suffocating her, making her feel as if it were a coffin. Still, she couldn't just stand here. Moving her arms out in front of her and shuffling her feet, she slowly moved forward. She had only been moving for a few seconds when a voice boomed out.

"You have come for the armor," it echoed off the walls, bouncing back to her.

"I have come for my father," Zanna called back, loudly.

A bright light flooded over her causing her to shield her eyes in pain.

"No," it said. "You seek your father. You have come for the armor."

"No!" Zanna said to the voice, her eyes still closed. "I have come to free my father of the armor."

"Your father is not here, child," it told her.

"But, the book said he was imprisoned here," she felt panic rise in her chest. She wanted to see who she was talking to. "Who are you? Show yourself!"

"Very well," it said, the light becoming something she could withstand.

Zanna cried out and fell backward. A dragon with a hide as red as fire loomed above her. Its long body curled on the bottom of the volcano floor. Its body was covered in large scales and sharp horns. It was terrifyingly beautiful.

"You are here for the armor," it said to her again.

"I...I am here..." Zanna was finding it difficult to find her voice. "For my father. The book..."

"I know nothing of books," the dragon told her.

"And Mavka," Zanna started.

"I do know of that witch," the dragon rumbled. "She helped your father make the armor with her blood magic. The armor you have come for."

"I've already told you, I am not here for the armor," Zanna said. "I just want my father."

"He is not here," the dragon said.

"Where is he?" Zanna asked. "I have come a long way to find him."

"It is," the dragon told her.

"Then if it is here, how is he not?" she wondered.

"Your father left not long ago," the dragon said.

"Where did he go?" Zanna was starting to feel afraid.

"He passed on to the next world," it said and Zanna fell to her knees. "Just days ago."

"How?" she asked. "The magic, the armor was supposed to protect him."

"It would have," it said, "forever perhaps, but those were not his wishes. Do you know what your father used to make his armor? Dragon scales. The scales of my mate, the dragon he killed. Do you know what can easily pierce a dragon's hide? Other dragon claws or diamond weapons. Your father used a sword made from diamond, something beautiful, to murder my companion."

"I am so sorry," Zanna didn't know what else to say.

"When your father was sealed in this prison, I was the only one to keep him company," the dragon said. "I came to kill him, but first to torture him, knowing he had a long life to live. Instead, he became my friend. He knew the mistakes he made when this armor was made. He lived with regret for a long time. Eventually, I didn't want to see my friend in pain any longer. So, I asked him if he wanted me to help him pass. He said yes because he knew that one day his daughter would come to find him and he didn't want to ever be in a position to hurt her."

Zanna hung her head, letting the tears fall, her chest heaving up and down. He had sacrificed himself again, to protect her. She had come so far for nothing. She just wanted to know him. To return the favor of loving her, of saving her.

"But I could not do it," he said to her.

Zanna looked up at him.

"What do you mean?" she asked.

"He was my friend," the dragon said. "I wanted to save him. I tried to convince him to hold on. That perhaps you or someone else could find a way to free him from his prison. I finally convinced him. I sought out the witch who had made the armor and asked her to find you. I told her that if she found you and you were able to reverse the blood magic and free your father, I would give her something in return."

"What were you willing to give?" Zanna wondered.

"My heart," he said.

"Why?" she was shocked.

"A dragon's heart is very powerful," he told her. "And I am old and lonely. I want to be with my mate. My time in this world is over. I would do that for my friend and his daughter."

"What happened to my father?" she asked him. "If there were these plans, then why is he...why has he passed?"

"I was too late to save him," the dragon lowered his head sadly. "I leave from time to time, to hunt or be with my own kind. I left one day in search of food and when I returned...I saw him leave and your father was dead. He had been run through with a diamond blade."

"Who?" Zanna felt anger coarse through her body.

"His father," the dragon said. "Dorthran."

Zanna wanted to scream. She wanted to punch the ground and

break it open. If she could reach through time and space and grab hold of Dorthran, she would and she would hurt him. Why? How could a man who claimed to love her, and her father, kill his own son.

"I have offered myself to the blood magic to free him," Zanna said suddenly. "Now I offer myself to avenge him. Will you, dragon, show me the armor?"

The dragon unfurled its large red wings and a suit of armor, frightening and beautiful, stood before her. Zanna walked toward the armor, unsure of how to go about what she wanted to do, but her mind was made up.

"I understand your mate was slain for this armor," she said to the dragon. "It was wrong and vile. But I ask that you not hold it against me to use it to avenge not only her death, but the death of your friend. For there is one nation of people responsible for both."

The dragon nodded its head. Zanna reached out and placed her hand on the cold metal. She closed her eyes and in her mind she said,

Take what you need of me. Give me the power of The Armor of Dusan.

The armor seemed to start to melt. She stepped back and watched it whirl and puddle at her feet. Without really understanding how, she knew she had to step into the inky blackness. As she did so, the pool of hot metal began to creep up her boots and onto her legs. Zanna felt searing pain as if it burned through her clothes and melded with her skin, forming to her body.

It inched up her chest, covering her neck and face. The pain was unbearable, but she didn't scream, not until it poured into her mouth and eyes. That was when everything went dark.

When she regained consciousness, Zanna opened her eyes. She was still in the chasm with the dragon. Her sight was clear, sharp, and focused. Her body was light, freeing, despite the fact she had just been melded to magical armor. In fact, everything about her felt alive. She felt strong, powerful, more in control than she ever had in her life. She turned to look at the dragon.

She could see him, all of him, even looking through his scales to his beating heart. The armor had given her abilities that no one in Mirstone could even dream possible. She looked down at her feet and her hands. Every last inch of her was covered in hard, black metal.

She touched her face and it was as if she wore a horned helm atop her head. The armor fit her perfectly, aligned to her shape, and moved fluidly with her. She saw that her sword had been covered in the armor as well. She pulled it from its sheath and held it in her armored hands. It was magnificent. She was ready.

"I thank you for this gift," she said to the dragon. "Now I must ask you for one more favor."

"Anything," he said.

"Take me to Vaelkesh," she said.

Zanna climbed onto the dragon's back. It beat its mighty wings and shot up through the chasm with fire and a loud roar. They burst into the night's sky just as Keres and her men reached the top. The group stared up in fear as they landed next to them.

"Zanna?" Javaid looked at her, terrified at what he saw. "Why?"

Zanna stepped from the dragon's back and walked toward them. She looked at each one in turn, seeing them, truly seeing them for the first time.

"Did you know?" she asked Keres.

"Zanna, I…" her sister began.

"Did you know?" she yelled, and power rolled from her voice.

"Father told me when he learned that you found out," Keres answered. "And I was angry, Zanna. I was angry at him for what he had done. I didn't know I had a brother. I didn't know any of this. He sent me after you…"

"To kill me," she finished.

"Of course not!" she said. "To bring you home. To talk. To explain."

"To explain why just mere days ago my father, your brother, was still alive," she said and Keres looked shocked. "To explain why he returned here and murdered him? Was that what he wanted to explain? I don't need an explanation. I know and it is time Father answered for what he's done."

"Zanna tread lightly," Keres warned.

"Or what?" Zanna laughed.

"Zanna," Javaid walked slowly toward her. "I know you're angry. It's understandable."

"Don't try to reason with my humanity, Javaid," Zanna glared at him. "It's gone."

"Zanna," Keres said.

"Enough!" she threw her hands out and everyone around her fell to the ground by an unseen force.

Zanna looked at her hands, unsure of how she had conjured up something without thinking about it. For a moment, it scared her. It frightened the girl she once was, but it was fleeting.

"You are very powerful now," Mavka said from beside her.

Zanna had nearly forgotten about the witch. She looked at her and couldn't believe she had once thought she was powerful and beautiful. Zanna could see past all that now.

"I know that," Zanna snapped, keeping everyone penned to where they were.

"But you have yet to unlock the armor's true potential," Mavka said. "Remember, it is blood magic. It requires a sacrifice of heart and soul. You have given it a soul, yours. But you still need a heart."

"I could just take yours," Zanna threatened.

"It's not so literal," Mavka sneered. "You must sacrifice the one thing you love the most, or person, to complete the spell. Then, you truly will be unstoppable."

"I haven't forgotten, witch," Zanna spat.

"Then why do you hesitate?" she asked.

"It isn't easy," Zanna said. "I know what I must do, and I will, but it doesn't make it easy."

"Yes, matters of the heart never are," Mavka told her. "But you will live a long life, you'll get used to it. I have. So, are you off to kill dear old dad?"

"No," she said, walking toward the group. "I love him, but I don't love him more than anyone else."

"Oh, your lover then?" Mavka smiled. "This is interesting."

Zanna looked down at Javaid. He was terrified. Any other time she would have felt sorry for him. Now, he just seemed pathetic. He disgusted her.

"I do love him," Zanna said. "I always have. Maybe I always will. I'm not sure. But I do not love him most."

"Then who is it?" Mavka asked.

"The one person whose approval I have sought from childhood," Zanna said. "The one I looked up to. The one I wanted to be. The one who I followed after but didn't love me in return. My sister."

She looked down at Keres. Her sister was struggling against the power that held her to the ground. Zanna's heart broke. How she adored her sister, how she loved her. It took until this moment to realize that she loved Keres above all others.

"Zanna, please," Keres said, crying. "Don't do this. This isn't you."

Zanna knelt beside her. She took her hard, armored hand and caressed her sister's face. Zanna felt herself cry. She wondered if Keres knew that tears were falling behind the armor on her face.

"I love you, sister," Zanna said to her. "I always have."

"I love y….," Keres didn't get to finish.

Zanna shoved her hand into her sister's chest, seizing her heart. She pulled it out in one quick movement. Blood splatter her face and arms, but it was hard to see against the black of the armor that covered her body.

"Zanna! No!" Javaid screamed. "No!"

Zanna felt the magic swell inside her as the spell was completed. Power washed over her, more power than she had ever felt. She smiled though only she knew it. Zanna threw Keres' heart down and walked away. She climbed onto the back of the dragon without a backward glance. As they flew away, she saw Javaid scramble to Keres. She laughed, thinking his actions pointless and futile. Her sister was dead.

Riding the back of the dragon to Vaelkesh took hours instead of days. She knew that the guards would see their approach, but she didn't care. She wanted them to know they were coming. She wanted her father to be afraid. When they were only minutes from the palace, a large spear went flying by the dragon's head.

"We've been spotted," Zanna said. "Let's put on a show."

The dragon began flying in erratic spirals and spins. Any arrow or spear they shot at them didn't come close. When they were close enough, the dragon released a volley of fire on the palace. They burned through guards and terraces. The palace was not expecting an attack from a dragon. There hadn't been one in over a thousand years. The element of surprise was on their side and they took advantage of it.

"This is where we part ways," Zanna told the dragon. "I must go find Dorthran. Do your best."

"And you," the dragon bowed its head, and Zanna dropped to a palace terrace.

This was her home, she knew her father would be here, waiting for her. He had killed her real father, surely he knew she would come for him. She walked in as the dragon continued to reign terror outside.

Her mother screamed as she entered the living space. She was clinging to her father. Her sisters must still be at the school. Zanna was a bit disappointed in that. She wanted to take them all out at one time.

"Mother, don't scream, it's just me," Zanna laughed.

"Zanna, what have you done?" Dorthran asked.

"What have you done, Grandfather?" she hissed. "What have you done?"

"Please, Zanna," her mother said. "You must understand. We did it to protect you. If they knew you were half-human, you would have been put to death."

Zanna didn't want to hear her "mother" anymore. Her grating voice, giving excuses as to why her parents were even killed to begin with. In her mind, she imagined pulling a piece of her armor and forming it a jagged blade. The magic seemed to be guiding her on how to use it.

She hovered her hands over each other and the armor obeyed her movements. Zanna smiled as small pointed blades formed in her hands.

"Zanna, if you will just give us a chance to explain," her mother was still saying.

Zanna flung the blade at her mother, hitting her in the chest and neck. She went flying backward, hitting the wall with a loud thud. Dorthran stood up, shock and anger on his face, as he watched his wife dying.

"Where is your sister?" Dorthran asked her, his voice solemn.

"How do you think I have this much power?" Zanna asked. "Don't you think I love my sister more than even you?"

"Zanna," Dorthran seemed to crumble then, but he still stood.

"Don't worry," she said. "I'll send all of you on your journeys soon. You'll all be together, but not before I make you suffer."

"I am not proud of what I have done," he said. "But I did it for you and my son."

"You did it for yourself!" she yelled at him, sending black blades through both of his legs.

Dorthran screamed, falling to his knees. He looked up at her.

"You didn't want your king to know your son has produced a halfbreed!" she yelled again.

"Are you listening to yourself, Zanna?" Dorthran cried out. "The armor has warped your mind. I am willing to be held accountable for what I have done, for your mother, but I tried to do right by you and your father. I made my mistakes, horrible, terrible mistakes. My prejudices made me blind, but I loved your father. I love you! I knew it the moment I saw you. I have spent my whole life trying to make it right."

"Then why?" she asked. "Why did you kill him?"

"Kill who?" He looked confused.

"My father!" she flung more blades, hitting him in the thighs.

"I didn't!" he cried. "He was encased in the armor. He was supposed to be in slumber until I found a way to release him. Do you not think I have tried? I have! I have searched this world high and low for a solution. Please, you must believe me, Zanna. Please!"

"The dragon saw you," she told him. "He saw you kill him! He told me!"

"It wasn't me, Zanna!" he was holding his legs, crying in pain. "I haven't been there in years. I haven't been there. I couldn't face him unless I could find a way to release him!"

"You're lying!" she yelled. "He saw you!"

"He saw me," Mavka came walking forward.

Zanna turned and looked at her. She looked even more lively, more comfortable in her form than she had before.

"Witch!" Dorthran spat.

"Hush you," she laughed.

"You killed him?" Zanna began to advance on her.

"Slow down," Mavka put up her hands and Zanna stopped. "Surprise, I'm the bad one here. Look, Zanna, your father made a powerful blood oath with me and reneged on it. That doesn't sit well with me. I need my blood magic to work. That's how I get my power. Your grandfather was getting too close to breaking that spell entirely, so I had to get things moving. I tricked you with the book, tricked the dragon with my cloaking charm to look like Dorthran so he would tell you who your father's killer was, all that. It was all me."

"I'm going to kill you," Zanna threatened.

"That's sweet," Mavka said. "But you can't hurt me. That's one of the caveats in my spells."

"Why are you telling me this?" Zanna asked her.

"Because I want you to know your place," Mavka said. "I also want you to realize something. Even if he didn't kill your father, he did, in so many ways, kill your entire family. I mean, if it weren't for him, you'd have loving parents. So, either way, we're still here. You're still getting your revenge. And I'm getting my souls because every time you end someone's life, I get a taste of that magic. It feeds me and I thrive. I like it. I see this as a partnership. Just think, you can rid this world of all the prejudices that killed your parents. You can reshape it, start over, rebuild it how you see fit. Just wage a few wars, kill a few people, and there you go. What do you say? Do you want to remake Mirstone with me?"

Zanna looked at the witch. She was partly angry at her audacity. More than anything she wanted to kill her for tricking her and a number of other reasons. Mavka was a manipulator and Zanna didn't trust her with anything, but she was powerful. She had given Zanna great power of her own. Together they could reshape Mirstone. Zanna could build a world that was big enough for people like her mother and father. She would allow the witch to think Zanna was her puppet, her soul collector. And when Mavka was fat and comfortable, stuffed full of sacrifices, Zanna would get rid of her as well.

At that moment, with the moon highest in the sky and sounds of screams in the air, Zanna felt another rush of power wash over her. She looked toward the open window and could see smoke and flames. It was her day of birth, she was now of age. The age when, as an Elf, all her magical abilities came to fruition. She took in a deep breath, reveling in the magic, in her power, for just a moment.

Zanna pulled her sword from her sheath and severed the head from her grandfather's body. She turned to look at the witch, "What are you waiting for?"

THE END

The Ring of the Feywilds
Selah J Tay-Song

A long, cobble-paved road stretched out before Roul. Far distant in the thick blue haze of morning, he could see the fires and gas-lights of El Tal. The light of dawn caressed the city, waking people bleary-eyed from last night's festivities, all busy now as they began to pursue their fortunes for another day.

Beyond the city, a deep valley ran up a narrow gorge, still saturated by shadow. A small, surviving piece of the Feywilds. Roul shivered at the thought of what strange and wondrous creatures might be lurking in the deep woods.

Roul rubbed the sleep out of his eyes and picked the straw out of his thick black hair as he tapped time on the cobblestones. He didn't want the goldsmiths of El Tal to think him a hayseed bumpkin when he arrived, which should surely be by the time the stars were twinkling tonight.

"Tomorrow morn, I'll be awakin' to pursue my own fortune," he said to the cows beside the road. He would spend the night enjoying the sights, then rise and seek out the best goldsmith in El Tal, and apply as an apprentice. No more tapping out rough iron pans for the village wives, no more countless shoes to pry off the hoof, straighten out, and nail back on, getting kicked and shat on. No, in El Tal he would make items of intricate beauty for the noblest of women. He would ply his talents as a smith on more deserving arts.

At high noon, the road began to shimmer ahead, and about an hour on, the cobble-stones on which he walked glinted with tiny flecks of gold. Roul counted it a good sign that he was getting closer, though the city never looked any bigger to his eyes, and picked up his pace. At the same time, he lamented the waste of the gold to a goat as he paused to feed it a hank of grass. "Seems a shame to be walkin' on it instead of wearin' it."

Another set of rolling hills passed and he heard a sound coming up behind. He looked over his shoulder, but couldn't see anything but hills. As the sound grew louder, he made out the rhythm of hoofs cloppity-clopping along, and a creak heralding a wagon or carriage of some girth. He stopped to the side of the road, startling some chickens into the hedge, and waited.

Minutes later a contraption came round the bend, an odder juggernaut than he had ever seen. It was a house on huge iron wheels, larger than the cottage he was born in. It was painted in panels of every color he could imagine, from the brightest song-bird yellow to the deepest night-time blues. A blue-skinned boy of maybe ten years sat all the way up on top of it, a little cap holding down a mop of blonde curls, driving the team of six mismatched horses with a long pair of reins.

As Roul watched, the boy slapped the reigns and yelled at the horses, and the creaky house came to a halt. The horses reacted poorly to the stop, bunching up and bumping into each other. One nipped the other and it pulled away, nearly dragging the whole contraption off the road before the boy got them under control again.

Roul watched in awe. Not even to the city yet, and already he'd seen at least ten things he'd never seen before in his life: a house on wheels, hair like gold, a team of six horses, and—

A door that he'd mistaken for a square of orange paint opened on the side of the house, and a woman peered out. At least, he figured she was a woman, but he couldn't tell her race, because she was swathed in veils. She made an "eeep!" sound and jerked the door closed again. The door opened again, and people began to pour down the steps of the house and onto the cobblestones. One side of the wagon came down, creating a little stage where the people gathered.

Roul had never seen such people in his life. They were varied in race and costume; including a teifling with rich dark skin like spring soil, and a silver-scaled fish-headed man pale as the moon in a blue sky. Those were the strangest races; the rest were a mix of dwarves, elves, gnomes, and humans. Some were swathed in veils and robes like the first lady, others wore next to nothing.

Roul could not help but stare at the bare skin of the red-haired elf who wore only scraps of velvet over her breasts and long, silky pants that revealed the shape of her legs, but he stared in equal fascination at the barrel-chested gnome wearing nothing but a loin-cloth.

He realized his mouth was open and he closed it. What a

hayseed bumpkin he must appear to these sophisticated city folk. He wore his feast-day shirt with vines his mother had painstakingly embroidered on the sleeves, but his trousers were simple, workaday trousers with holes about to wear through the knees. He felt humbled by their beauty and ashamed of his own lack.

A man with an air of authority, a tall human with blessedly familiar features, dark hair and the simple white robes of a pilgrim, approached him.

"Ho, fellow traveler! Are you going to El Tal or have you come from there?"

He wanted to ask what they were all doing together in that house on wheels—there had to be at least twenty of them, wandering over the road now, some relieving themselves in the hedge, others sitting on the road and breaking apart a loaf of bread amongst themselves—but he didn't want to seem uneducated, so he said, "I'm goin' to the city."

"Like a ride? We've room for one more if you'd like to reach it a bit sooner. All we ask in return is that you be an extra in our entertainments at the inn tonight."

"Won't I reach it today afoot?" Roul asked, forgetting to pretend he knew what he was doing.

"Ah, no, by foot you'd have about another two day's travel. We can take you far as the Crossroads Inn, and shave off half a day."

That sobered Roul because he'd eaten the last of his traveling bread the eve before, and he was sorely hungry and counting on a charity meal in the city tonight.

"I don't know anything about acting. But I'll check your horses' shoes if you'll sell me a loaf," he said to the player.

"I'm afraid we'll need all of our food for the Feywilds," the man said. "Can't eat nor drink there. But you'll reach the Crossroad's Inn by day's end. They'll likely let you wash dishes for a meal and a stall."

Roul tipped his hat and kept walking while the players packed their house back up. Not twenty minutes later, they passed him again. The boy driving the horses waved, but all the rest of them were hidden away.

The flecks of gold in the cobblestones were nearly blinding by the time he reached the crossroads, late in the afternoon. The inn was a tall, white-washed house with a weathered timber frame, the only thing to announce its hospitality was a small sign over the door with three letters pressed in the wood and embossed in gold. Roul couldn't read, but he admired the letters all the same.

The traveling house was parked before the Inn, all its garish color a contrast to the stark white wall. The boy and the horses were nowhere to be found, but a blue girl a few years older than the boy sat on the steps, surrounded by pots, pans, and washtubs, haggling with a dusty farmer over some sacks of grain.

The inn was full of music and people, but as he looked around the common room, Roul realized that most of them were peculiar players. The teilfing stood by the bar, in earnest conversation with another traveler. The others occupied tables and stools, but none of them were drinking. They were all engaged in conversation, even the veiled women.

At the end of the room, the beautiful elf lady in red pants and not much else stood, singing, and the gnome in the loincloth played a dulcimer to her tune.

"An extra, an extra, we truly need this
Extra . . . We asked him, we asked him—"
She pointed straight at Roul here, and he felt all the eyes in the room swivel to face him—
"But he'd rather be the star
In his own play,
Oh, won't you, won't you, won't you . . .
Be . . . Our . . . Extraaaaaaa . . ."
She hit a high note and kept going. Reddened, Roul tried to be casual as he approached the proprietor at the bar, a safe distance from the teifling.

"I need a meal and a stall or a loft for the night, if you have it," Roul said, loud enough to be heard over her song. He could have slept in a haystack again, but he wanted to look his best when he reached El Tal. "I've no coin, but I'm good for fixin' things. If you've pots and pans you need mending or horses you need shod."

"No coin, eh?" The innkeeper was a portly man with stains up and down a once-white apron. He tapped out a pipe on the counter and brushed the ash down to the floor. He tamped the pipe and stuck it in his jaw unlit. "Dunno about no coin. I've brand new pots and all. Smithy came last week to shoe my horse."

"Well, I can wash-up, or haul anything heavy you've got. Please, Sir? I meant to reach the city today, and I ate the last of my bread."

The innkeeper glared down his nose at Roul. A big boil was on the end of it, and Roul wanted nothing so much as to pop it. "Alright. You can haul up the wash water tonight for a loaf of bread. There's no room for you here, though. You'll have to sleep in the hedge tonight."

Roul wanted to haggle, but the teifling was approaching and he did not desire a conversation with him. "Alright, Goodman. I'll get started right away. Which way to the pump?"

Before the innkeeper could speak, the teifling reached them and clapped Roul on the back in a friendly way. Roul suppressed a shiver of dread. Up close, the teifling was big. His horns looked sharp.

But his tone was pleasant when he said, "The name's Lajic, my friend. I've a tip for you. Be our extra tonight, and the troop might cut you into a sweet little profit. Want to know what draws us to the Feywilds?"

Roul was suddenly curious, but he stifled it with a shrug.

"Legend has it there's a ring, hidden deep in the Feywilds, which endows its wearer with the power to smith gold from any metal. We plan to distract the Fey Court with an outrageous performance, while one of us sneaks away and steals the ring. Extra for us in the Feywilds and a percentage of a great profit could be yours."

The allure of a ring that would make all metals gold tugged at Roul, but caution stayed him. Bad enough that he was face to face with a teifling. The Feywilds teemed with all manner of creatures, many benign, others far more dreaded than demon-descent.

"I'm for El Tal," Roul said firmly. "Surely one of these other wayward souls will extra for you?"

"Lanise has had no luck yet," Lajic replied. "It will really be a shame if we show up in the Feywilds without our extra. We might have to use our driver, Ghen, but he's all wrong for the part."

One of the barmaids came then with buckets and showed Roul to the yard, where he pumped the buckets full. He spent the next few hours hauling water up and filling the ten copper tubs in the men's bathroom, while the stable boy brought wood for heating them. The room turned smoky and steamy. On the stairs, he passed a girl in buck-hide trousers hauling buckets up to the women's. She gave him an impish grin as he stared at her strained shoulders. The third time they crossed paths, she with empty buckets coming down, she spoke.

"Off to 'prentice in El Tal, are ya?"

"Goldsmithy," Roul grunted. The buckets were damn heavy. "You?"

"Tailor, can'tcha tell?" She giggled all the way down.

"You workin' off your bread and board too?" She asked on the next pass, surprisingly chatty with the weight of the buckets on her shoulders. "I'm savin' every coin for my 'prentice fees."

Roul said nothing to that. Tailors must be a strange folk if they charged willing workers to learn. On the next pass, he mentioned it to her. Curtly.

"Oh, all the Crafters in El Tal are like that. You think we're the only bumpkins to come to the great city to learn? Do you mean to say you've nothing laid by at all?"

On the next pass, she said nothing, only looked at him strangely, and after that, she said in a softer tone, "I don't mean to be discouraging. But you'll have a hard time of it if you show up in El Tal asking after all the smithies without a 'prentice fee to show. Go home, farmer, and save up some coin. Sell extra tomatoes or eggs in the market or something. I hunted deer and tanned and sold hides for three years before I had the coin I needed."

He tried not to pay her heed, but her words troubled him, and while he was eating the meal he'd earned—a surprisingly generous portion of roast chicken with bread, sardines, and olives—he asked a couple of other travelers to confirm her story. The players still dominated the common room, but they had either found an extra or given it up because they were subdued as they ate their evening meal. The couple on the stage had been replaced by the fish-headed man, wearing baggy trousers and playing a washtub bass.

The would-be tailor's story was confirmed by no less than five other travelers, some going toward their own apprenticeships, others heading out from El Tal to start their careers. None had worked with goldsmiths, but one, a handsome man in a silk waistcoat, said with a haughty air that the apprentice fee charged by his master, a jeweler, had been worth the price of a mid-sized farm.

By the time he'd buttered his last piece of bread and choked it down, Roul was completely disheartened. And just around that time, Lajic clapped him on the back again and set down two ales in front of him, pulling up the chair to his side, nearly knocking down the haughty man's tankard.

"A gift for you, my friend," Lajic said, a little slurred. "Just to prove to you there are no hard feelings. I drink to your health."

"Did you find an extra, then?"

"No. The driver-boy will play the extra, leaving his own part unfilled. A hole in the play may arouse suspicion, but we will take the risk."

"You're certain this ring is there? That you can find it, and make it work?"

"We are certain. My friend, you cannot imagine the riches! We will have enough money to build a theatre in the heart of El Tal if we succeed in this. A permanent theatre, with a stage as large as a throne room! With ropes and cranes and trapdoors and the most beautiful, red-and-gold velvet seats you can possibly imagine! Balconies and chandeliers and damask wallpaper! We will have it all if we can please the rulers of the Feywilds . . ."

"I'll do it," Roul found himself saying, swept up in Lajic's description of the theatre. Surely a mere fraction of that wealth would pay for his apprentice fees and more. And if they allowed him to use the ring himself . . . Beyond the wealth, the allure of working huge bars of iron into gold tugged at Roul. "I'll be your extra."

" . . . Riches beyond your wildest dreams, farmboy! Your percentage would be a tiny fraction of the wealth, but you could buy your mother five farms and the slaves to work them if only you would—"

"I said I'll do it," Roul said louder, taking the first sip of his ale. It was stronger than the stuff the brewer in his village made. "I'll be your extra."

The clap on his back nearly made him choke, and he almost regretted consenting when Lajic burst out in loud, jubilant song, "He'll be our extra, our extra, he'll really be our extra . . ." And all the other players joined in.

When the noise finally died down, Roul asked the questions he should have asked first. They would only be in the Feywilds a fortnight, Lajic assured him. Their appointment was to perform for three nights, but time in the Feywilds worked differently, so they'd be coming out in a fortnight. And the players would be coming directly to El Tal after they left the Feywilds. His share would be a generous twentieth of some vague sum of riches that Roul could not quite pin him down on.

"Will you pay for my lodging for the night?"

"Lodging?" Lajic swallowed his ale and laughed. "You'll sleep on the pageant wagon tonight, my friend. We set off at sunset. You can only approach the Feywilds at certain times, and tonight is one of those rare times. Under a full spring moon, as the constellation Riazonid is rising on the eastern horizon, when it hasn't rained in exactly four and a half days, and when a two-headed calf has been born within six leagues of the Feywilds. Only tonight are the signs all correct."

So it was, without a decent night's sleep to call his own, Roul found himself sitting atop the wagon, yawning while the girl in buckskins yelled at the horses.

"You!" Roul said in surprise.

"I have a name. Katrice." She rolled her eyes. "Ghen fell ill and has to stay behind, so they hired me on to drive. I'll have a chance to sew costumes, too. Besides, I couldn't pass up a chance to see the Feywilds."

A scarlet sky framed the shoulders of the deep, dark valley where the Feywilds lurked. When the inn had disappeared completely, Lajic's horned head appeared beside Roul, startling him, from a hidden window in the wagon house. "Any metal on ya, extra?"

"My name is Roul. I've a pocket knife."

"Chuck it in the ditch, my friend. We'll pick it up on the way back. Can't take metal into the Feywilds."

He disappeared into the wagon again. Roul hesitated, then considered the girl selling pots by the inn, and threw his knife into the bushes. He had no coin, and his belt was woven linen without a buckle.

"What are the horses shod in?"

"Pure ivory," Katrice said with a grin. Roul did not know if she was making fun or not.

The sky faded to a deep cerulean and the stars came out, followed by the moon, a pale, featureless head on the shoulders of the Feywilds. Swaths of farmland gave way to dense forest. The night grew chill. The road grew narrow, and the cobblestones turned to bare earth, moss growing in the center between the ruts. The horses slowed as the grade steepened up the valley. Roul thought he could see lights far away between the trees, and moonlit shapes moving beside the road.

Presently, a distant lantern drew closer, illuminating the road ahead with a bright orange glow, warm and welcoming. Katrice slowed the horses, finally pulling them to a stop where the road leveled out.

They were close enough that Roul could see the lantern casing casting shadows over the peculiar procession that followed it. The woman who held the light wore a long dress of white silk, the perfect backdrop for the shadows. Did Roul imagine it, or did wings like a butterfly's grace her shoulders? She wore a crown of forget-me-nots on her brow. Behind her came a train of Fey folk so long that it disappeared behind the bend of the road. More winged ladies like her were in it, and strange little elves with hats made of leaves and bramble, and a young boy leading a unicorn, several small folk riding foxes, and even a girl on a wildcat.

Those were the creatures he could see clearly in the light of the lantern. In the shadows, even stranger creatures lurked. Roul squinted to make out concubus, hags, bark-skinned Kapre, and mouthless, whispy marunae. All around them, sprites and fairies fluttered and glimmered like little stars catching the light.

While Roul was staring agog at this strange procession, the beautiful winged lady had stopped beside the foremost horse of the pageant wagon, stroking its nose, and the wagon door had opened. Roul half expected the stage to open again, and the play for the Fey Court to begin, but only Lajic stepped out.

The teifling made an elaborate leg before the lady with the lantern and spoke quietly to her. Roul could not hear the words he uttered, but her reply was projected to carry.

"I am sorry you have come all this way, but the Feywilds are closed to mortals at this time."

Her voice was like a clear, tinkling brook, enchanting Roul. He began to question his decision to seek his fortune in the city. Might not it be better simply to live in the Feywilds forever, merely to hear that voice again?

Un-enchanted, Lajic argued. "But we have a show, a spectacular show, and we've been rehearsing for months and months to offer this entertainment to the Fey court. Is there nothing you can do, my friend?"

"The border is closed for your safety, player. There is an infestation of blights about. Come no further down this road; only death and despair await."

"We have come far, and it is quite late. Can we at least camp here for the night?"

"Of course. The blights will not stray past the border. Rest, teifling, and turn around tomorrow."

The door opened again, and players poured out of the wagon. They soon had a fire lit, horses unharnessed, pallets set up beside the road. The Fey watched them for a while with apparent fascination, but eventually, they lost interest and melted back into the shadows.

As soon as the wildcat's moonlit tail disappeared into the night, Lajic whispered, "break stage!" In seconds, the horses were harnessed again, the fire doused, the bedding stowed.

"How did they do that so fast?" Roul asked Katrice as she whipped the horses forward again. "It should have taken at least twenty minutes to set and break camp."

"They're players," the girl said in a tone that made Roul feel ignorant. "That's what players do. They didn't actually unharness the horses, silly."

Roul thought about that and realized that he had seen a flurry of activity around the horses and assumed they were being unharnessed, but they hadn't broken from their places in front of the wagon.

"But we're continuing? Even after that warning?" Whatever the blight were, Roul had no desire to meet them.

"Of course. This is our only chance to enter the Feywilds. The blight'll prolly just try to scare us." She sounded nervous, though.

The road continued through thicker and thicker forest. The night grew darker and colder. A shadow fell across the moonlit road ahead. A wide, dark shadow, black as tar, surrounded by strange, twiggy shrubs.

The horses in the front shied at the sight and tried to veer from the road. Katrice whipped the reins across the backs of the horses nearest the wagon, and they plunged forward, pushing the front pair into the shadow.

The front horses fell to their knees and screamed, a sound that ripped across Roul's heart like a piece of broken glass. The twiggy shrubs rose, surrounded by shadow, to pull them forward and down. The other horses fought the pull, but it looked like the whole wagon would be consumed by the shadow mire in seconds. Windows and doors opened and the heads of several players popped out, but the wagon was lurching with the motion of the horses, and in the darkness, Roul knew they could not see clearly what he knew was there.

"Cut the harness!" Roul shouted, leaping from his seat atop the wagon house. He searched his belt for his knife and found it missing; cringed when he recalled chucking it into the roadside. Katrice leaped down beside him and worked the fastenings; together, they freed the bulk of the team from the foremost struggling, screaming horses just as they disappeared completely into shadow.

The second the hind four horses were free, they turned alongside the blighty darkness. In their haste to be away from the terror, they reared and plunged, and the entire house tipped on its side, straight into the shadow mire.

Roul watched in stunned disbelief as the shadow swallowed up the gleaming wagon house. He caught a shadowy glimpse of veiled figures trying to flee out the side windows, but the shadows pulled them back into the mire. The remaining horses were screaming and trying to break free. For a moment that stretched to eternity, Roul and Katrice were too shocked and horrified to do anything.

Katrice came out of her shock first and managed to get one of the horses free of its harness while Roul watched dumbly. Roul thought she would free the others, but instead, she climbed the horse like a tree and slapped its rump. The horse was happy to comply; the two disappeared back down the road toward El Tal.

Then the twig blights came out of the shadow. Roul took a stunned step backward when several dark tree shapes rose from the mire and took on demonesque forms. He shivered in terror, afraid to move. They paid him absolutely no heed, but instead lifted the sides of the shadow mire like a blanket and carried it away into the dark depths of the forests—horses, house, players and all.

They left behind an eerie silence, and Roul just stared at the road where the mire had been, too shocked and horrified to move. The coldness dug into his bones and he played the scene over and over in his mind, wondering if he could have saved them somehow.

Presently, he heard a quiet singing above, rich and deep. He looked up to see a vague outline of an elven woman's huge, pale face in the starry sky. Her arms rested on the shoulders of the valley, and as she sang, she reached down toward Roul. Frozen in place, he did not resist her touch, and her arms folded around his shoulders, soothing him. He grew warmer, and after a moment he realized that a creature of flesh was holding him in her arms. He stepped away and saw a mature elf in a cerulean, star-studded dress standing before him. Her hair was pitch black, and her face glowed softly like the moon.

"Who are you?" He whispered, forgetting the malaise of the shadow mire in his awe.

"I am the spirit of the night," she said in a voice like wind through the trees. "Nycteria is my name. I saw what the blight did to your friends down here. It's such a shame."

"They ignored the warning," Roul said. "Lajic should have listened to what the butterfly lady said. We should never have come."

"Why did you come? What was so important?"

"Just a play and a promise of riches," Roul said. Now that his shock was wearing off, he was starting to see his predicament. He was sorry for Lajic and the rest, but here he was, stranded in the Feywilds, farther away from El Tal and apprenticeship than ever, and nothing to show for it. He didn't blame Lajic exactly, nor Katrice, but his magnanimity didn't change his situation. Still, the horror of being swallowed up by shadow played over in his mind. He said as much to Nycteria. "Is there nothing we can do for them?"

"Once the blight have someone, they don't let go easily. They have run off to the caves, where even I can't find them. But there may still be hope for you."

"For me?" Suddenly self-conscious, Roul glanced down and

noticed that his hands and forearms were shrouded in shadow. Even the light from Nycteria's gleaming face didn't touch it. "What is it?"

"Didn't you know? Though you didn't get stuck in the mire, some of the shadow blight touched you. Your death will be slower than that of your friends, but it will come."

She said it with sadness, but also matter-of-factly. What were trivial matters of life and death to the night? Already the players must be new stars on her mantle. As Roul would soon be. He felt heavy like he could hardly take a step. The shadow weighed on him. Eventually, it would crush him.

"Save me," he gasped, and found that he could scarcely move his lips, the shadow had him so much in its grasp. "Please. I don't want to die."

"Shhh. I will take you to the Fey Court. There may be something they can do."

The night gathered him up in her arms, unafraid of the darkness coating his soul. She carried him from glade to moonlight-dappled glade. Cringing from the bright stars on her arms, the shadow retreated a little, and he was able to breathe easier.

They soon came to a glade far vaster and brighter than the rest. Toadstools scattered over its mossy ground, each one occupied by a different fairy. At one edge, cradled in the roots of a giant, ancient cypress, sat the queen of the Feywilds. She was taller than all the other fairies in the glade, of a height with Roul. Her robe was made of millions of tiny forget-me-not petals, sewn overlapping like scales. Her crown was a trumpet vine, the rich red of the flowers contrasting her pale dress. She held a scepter, a flowering olive branch, in her right hand. A band of very small elves, each one about as tall as Roul's hand was long, capered before her. She laughed at them as they somersaulted and cartwheeled and tumbled over the moss.

The glade went silent, and the capering stopped when Nycteria swept in and set Roul down at the Queen's feet.

"Ewww," was the first sound out of the Royal Mouth. "He smells like the mire, Sister Night. What is it? Some new form of blight?"

"One of their victims," Nycteria said, drawing near. "He escaped the pull of the mire. His companions weren't so lucky.

Can you help him, Fey?"

"Is that what happened to the night's entertainment? I was beginning to wonder if I would have to watch the faerie elves tumble all night. They are very funny, but it's a rather low humor."

"What's this about blight? Someone got caught in the mire?" A man stepped around the huge trunk of the cypress, and weak and uncomfortable as he was, Roul recognized him immediately as the Fey King and was awed by his presence. He was slightly taller than the Queen, and antlers grew from his forehead, making him appear even taller. His robe was a simple deerskin, draped on his shoulders, that the lowliest forest hermit might wear, tanned with the fur still on it so that he might be mistaken for a deer himself, crouching down in the right light.

"Didn't the warning troupe I sent out get through? Blight didn't get them, did they?"

"We—were—warned, Majesty," Roul gasped out. He felt the shadows creeping across his skin, pressing down on his chest. "Lajic didn't want to miss the show. He ordered us to press on. He—paid—dearly—for failing to heed."

He went silent, trying to get a full breath in. The shadow weighed so heavily on his heart that speaking just a few words had taxed him considerably. He wondered how much longer he had to live.

"Please—don't want to die. Save me, if you can."

"What a shame," the Queen said. "They were supposed to be the best troupe in the country. I was really looking forward to their show."

"He-elp . . ." Roul managed to squeeze out before his voice gave out completely as the shadow smothered his mouth. The whole assembly gasped as one.

"He won't last much longer," Nycteria put in. "Can't you save him?"

"Of course." The Queen stood and stepped closer. She appeared dim to Roul through the darkness shrouding his eyes. "But we must have his consent. Human, do you give us your consent to bring you back to the living? You will become part of the Fey if we do. You will keep your body and appearance, but you will gain our immortality and all the qualities that make us Fey. All of our powers and our limitations. If you consent, raise your fist from the shadow and open it."

Roul had no hesitation, but his body would not cooperate. He clenched his muscles and fought against the pressure of the shadow to raise his fist.

"The alternative is a horrible death if you don't," the King put in helpfully as if he thought Roul was dithering. "You think it's bad now, but the blight has just begun. Once your body is smothered completely in shadow, your soul will be theirs. They will eat it slowly, at their leisure, under the earth."

Roul threw everything he had into wrenching his fist up, out of the mire he had become, and spreading his fingers.

A bright light appeared above him. It was faint at first, through the shadow, but grew brighter and brighter. It settled on his chest, then sank into his body. His whole body glowed outward from the light. Then a pressure rose in his chest, and the light pushed against his skin until he thought he would burst. He stood up suddenly, and feeling weightless, leaped into the air and floated above the glade. Shadow and light shot from his skin, scattering all over the glade, both hitting the assembled Fey.

He drifted down to the glade again to stand beside Nycteria and the King and Queen. The shadow was gone completely, and in its place was a gentle golden glow on his skin. He felt vibrant and alive and terribly hungry.

"All welcome the newest citizen of the Feywilds!" the King said, lifting Roul's hand high in his. The glade erupted with cheers. Food was brought, and Roul feasted. While he ate, he thought about Lajic and the ring. Was it here in this very Court? Did he dare to inquire about it? How had Lajic planned to steal it?

"Your Court is very beautiful," Roul said after he had eaten his fill of fresh venison and sweet berries and drunk a whole thimble-full of moss wine. "But I don't see any gold here. Don't you like gold?"

A hush fell in the glade, and the Queen and Nycteria exchanged a glance.

"We can tell him," the King said decisively. "He is one of us, now."

Roul shivered a little at those words. He was grateful to be alive, but the realization that he was now bound in some profound way to the Feywilds was just settling on his shoulders. He felt oppressed, almost as the shadow had oppressed him.

"Very well. Tell him." The Queen wet her lips with elderberry wine. She sounded uncertain.

The King shrugged. "Centuries ago, a ring was given into the care of the Fey Court. The ring has the power to turn simple iron into luscious gold. The races of Mirestone were fighting over the ring, on the verge of complete destruction. A secret council was formed to hide the ring, and they hid it in the Feywilds. The Feywilds are difficult for mortals to enter, even more difficult to leave, and protected by powerful guardians—such as the blight your party encountered."

Roul's heart went cold in his chest. "They were protecting the ring."

The King nodded. "We got word that Lajic and his party had a scheme to enter the Feywilds under the guise of giving us a show. One of the party would sneak off during the show and steal the ring. They even planned to plant a dummy ring on some dupe they brought along, in the event that their theft was discovered. We tried to turn them back, to warn them away, but they heeded not our messenger."

The coldness in Roul's chest spread through his limbs, paralyzing him. The blight had not been some independent wild Fey acting alone. The Fey Court—the very Fey whom Roul was dining with—had ordered the deaths of Lajic and the others—including Roul. And as for the troupe—Roul had been nothing more than a dupe to them, a scapegoat should they be discovered.

"Why save me?" he asked. "Why not let the blight finish me?"

The Queen rested her ancient eyes on him, capturing him with her gaze. "Because it costs us little to let you live among the Fey," she said softly. "And if you should return to mortal lands someday, you will serve as a warning to those who try to steal the ring again."

Roul finished his wine in silence and contemplation. He should have guessed something was strange about Lajic's offer. He thought the revelation that he was nothing more than a dupe to the players should have made him feel better about their deaths, but it did not.

After that, he lost track of the time he spent in Faerie. The nighttime feasts and frolics kept him happy and content. During the day, there were both wild hunts and long naps in cool glades with Nycteria's brother, Photo. Roul came to know all the people and places of the Feywilds, both gentle and sinister.

His joy was tempered with sorrow for the players. He trekked one day up to the shadow caves and found the skeletons of five horses scattered among the shale beneath them, along with bits of bright wood. He wondered often what had become of Katrice, the buckskin girl. Had she been afflicted like Roul? Had she died by the side of the road on the way back to the inn?

After an unknowable time had passed, he grew bored. There was little new to do in the Feywilds. All of the smaller creatures made the clothes and food and shelters. Everything was simple. There was no craftwork. Roul missed the feeling of metal in his hands. As time drifted past, he slowly recalled his dream to visit El Tal and apprentice himself to a goldsmith. He thought of the magic ring, and his deep desire to possess it, to work with unlimited quantities of gold.

There was no metalwork in the Feywilds. If he wanted to achieve his dream, he would have to return to mortal lands. And if he was going to return to mortal lands, why not take the ring? It was doing no one any good here. He had a right to it, for he was Fey now. And he would keep it safe, use it only to create works of beautiful art.

Shortly after Roul convinced himself that stealing the ring was a good idea, but before he cultivated any real plan, he had a stroke of fortune. He was sitting by a stream at noon, resting after the hunt, when he overheard two water dryads talking about a lake deep within the Feywilds.

"The lake of the golden ring?" said one dryad.

"The very same," the other agreed.

Roul knew at once they were speaking of what he had come to think of as *his* ring. The next day, he packed some supplies and a bedroll. He started from the stream of the dryads and followed it to a larger creek, then a wide river, then up and up into the mountains until the river forked into many different headwaters.

After many days of travel, long after his rations were gone and he was living off berries and dew, he came to a tiny blue jewel of a lake, nestled in a mountain valley. The water was clear as sapphire. Roul stripped off his clothes and dove into the depths.

At the very bottom, farther down than he could have imagined, sat a wooden chest. Roul wrenched it open. On the floor of the chest was a ring of finely woven thin crystalline threads. As his fingers closed on it, Roul felt a surge of power emanating through his body.

He kicked upward and thrashed to the surface, gasping for air, choking on water. The light of Photo beamed down on him, and he kept the ring carefully hidden in his palm, knowing the eyes of the Fey were everywhere.

Once he dried and dressed again, he stowed the ring in a hidden pocket inside his breeches. He ached to try its powers, but he dared not arouse a glimmer of suspicion. Besides, there was no iron here in the Feywilds to convert to gold.

Back in the Fey Court, he asked the King and Queen for their leave to return to the world of mortals. He told them he missed his own kind. They warned him that much time might have passed since he'd seen the mortal world, but gave their blessing.

"Follow the constellation Riazonid east whenever you wish to return," Nycteria said, shedding a soft mist of tears on the glade at his parting.

No one mentioned the ring. No alarm was given that it had been stolen. Roul marveled at the ease of it all. He left the Feywilds with a leather satchel stitched from a deer the King himself had brought down, filled with a small feast and fine Fey wares, worth a mortal king's ransom in their own right. And of course, the magic ring, burning hot as coal in his hidden pocket.

He walked the better part of the day through dense forest, on a dirt road with grass growing between the ruts. As night settled, the forest thinned out to fields with few trees growing between them. For the first night in a long while, Nycteria did not visit him when the stars came out. He was beyond her reach. He felt emboldened to take out the ring and place it on his finger. He sensed its desire for gold, as strongly as his own.

"Soon," he whispered to it in the dark. He thought of the Inn, with all the metal left there by travelers preparing to enter the Feywilds. "Soon, we will feed your hunger."

He slept that night in a hedge. He expected to reach the inn the next day, but instead, he came upon a humble little house beside the road. A beautiful old woman sat on a rocker on the porch, mending some clothes. Her hair was fine silver, and her face, though crinkled with age, still held a spark of vitality.

"Hello," Roul said. "I've been traveling, and wondered if I could trade a bit of work for a meal."

The woman yelled something incomprehensible, and Roul thought for a moment she was yelling at him to leave, but then a shuffling sounded within the house, and a patter of footsteps approached the door.

"Ma!" the door swung on its hinges, and the speaker, a tall, gangly blue girl with a mop of curly blonde hair corralled under a linen bonnet, hove into view. "Come out to the porch, Ma! Got a visitor!"

Roul's suspicions were confirmed when a second face peeped out of the door frame, a younger boy with the same unique hair. He looked from the children to the old woman and said hesitantly, "Katrice? You married the boy who drove the wagon?"

The old woman tapped her chest with a hollow thump. "Katrice," she confirmed weakly. She didn't say anything else. Roul wondered if she recognized him. He thought she was too senile, perhaps, to understand, even if she did.

Roul got a meal of bread and stew from Katrice's daughter-in-law, while her grandchildren stared at Roul like he was—well, Fey. Roul wondered what he looked like in their eyes. He offered to do all sorts of work in return, but the mother wouldn't hear of it. In truth, Roul thought she wanted him gone quickly. Katrice's son was "off hunting, back any minute now," she said several times. Roul yearned for a mirror.

As he was leaving, Roul tipped his hat to Katrice, who was still rocking away in the shade, picking at her mending. Roul recalled that she wanted to be a tailor, and wondered if she had returned to El Tal and realized her dream before marrying Ghen.

"Sorry," Katrice said.

"What's that?" Roul asked.

"Sorry I ran off with the horse. I always regretted it, you know. Leaving you to your death."

"I always wondered if you'd made it," Roul replied. "I'm glad to know you did. As you can see, death worked out pretty well for me."

On an impulse, he pulled out the ring and held it up for her to see.

"I found the ring. I'm headed to El Tal to make my fortune, and I won't be needing apprentice fees. Not with this."

Katrice's eyes shone hungrily as she looked upon the beautiful, sparkling ring. Then she threw back her head and laughed, a high, eerie cackle that chilled Roul's soul.

"You fool," she gasped out when she had finally caught her breath. "Oh, you poor fool."

She said no more, just laughed and laughed, and finally, Roul left, trying to ignore the anxiety her laughter had planted in him.

The next day, Roul reached the inn. The going had been much faster by wagon. Roul missed the mossy bowers of the Feywilds, the carefree days, the pleasant feasts. Still, it was nice to be among mortals once again. And always, the power of the ring tugged him toward the city and the iron it held.

The inn stood in the same place, white and pristine. The chimney was new, with fresh red bricks giving the place a homey air. Roul intended to pay for the finest room, then hire a horse to take him the rest of the way to El Tal.

As he walked toward the crossroads, something inside of him began to burn. He doubled over in pain. Ahead, a pile of washtubs and pots and pans, a heap of iron, beckoned him. The closer he got to the iron, the greater the pain grew. He took a step back, and it lessened.

Still, he was sweating and heaving. He saw a clean chamber pot sitting out by the roadside, drying in the sun, and he leaned over to retch in it.

When his hands touched the rim, they burned with agony. He pulled them away and a wisp of smoke rose from his palms. He retched on the bare cobblestones.

He fled, running back up the road as fast as he could. Finally, when the inn was the size of a crate in the distance, he stopped. The pain was gone. He felt hollow and sore and his throat burned, but no worse than that. Even that was fading as his Fey nature healed his ills.

He sat on the road looking toward the inn and realized his error. He had seen it all along, but never thought to question why metal wasn't allowed in the Feywilds or to guess that as one of the Fey, he would have an aversion to iron.

Roul stared at the ring in his palm and heard Katrice's laughter echoing in his mind. After gazing at the ring for a long time, he turned and began the trek back to the Feywilds.

THE END

ABOUT THE AUTHORS

Alison Reeger Cook (A.R. Cook) is the author of THE SCHOLAR AND THE SPHINX young adult fantasy novels, THE SCALE SEEKERS high fantasy series, and short stories found in CHRONICLES OF MIRSTONE (Dragonfire Press), WOMEN OF THE WOODS (Fabled Collective), WILLOW WEEP NO MORE and SHADOWS OF THE OAK (Tenebris Books), and THE KRESS PROJECT (Georgia Museum of Art).

Her theater plays have been performed and work-shopped at the University of Iowa in Iowa City; Western Springs, Illinois; and Atlanta, Georgia. She has placed as a finalist in various screenwriting competitions, including the Austin Film Festival, Screencraft, The Script Lab, and The Launch Pad. She resides near Chicago, IL, with her husband Dave and their furry diva, Daisy May.

Visit her at www.scholarandsphinx.wix.com/arcook, or visit her on Facebook (www.facebook.com/ARCookAuthor) and Twitter (@arcookauthor).

—

Richard Fierce is the author of over 20 fantasy and sci-fi books, including his bestselling series Dragon Riders of Osnen. A recovering retail worker, he now works in the tech industry when he's not busy writing.

He's married with 3 stepdaughters (pray for him!), three dogs (huskies!), three cats, two ferrets, and a hamster. Basically, he has a zoo.

His love affair with fantasy was born in high school when a friend's mother gave him a copy of *Dragons of Spring Dawning* by

Margaret Weis and Tracy Hickman.

You can check out all of his books at www.richardfierce.com

Follow him on Facebook, Twitter, or Bookbub.

—

Jeremy Hicks is an archaeologist, author, and the co-founder of Broke Guys Productions. Alongside long-time friend Barry Hayes, he co-authored *Finders Keepers* and *Sands of Sorrow*, the initial installments of the *Cycle of Ages Saga*, first as screenplays and then novelizations. *Delve Deep*, the third installment, is Jeremy's first novel as a solo author. He has published a number of short stories in various anthologies, including the Amazon #1 best-seller *The C.A.M. Charity Anthology – Horror & Science Fiction.*

You can visit Jeremy's website at https://jjeremyhicks.com/

—

David Alan Jones is a veteran of the United States Air Force where he served as an Arabic linguist. A 2016 Writers of the Future silver honorable mention recipient, David's writing spans the science fiction, military sci-fi, fantasy, and urban fantasy genres. He is an author, a husband, and a father of three. David's day job involves programming computers for Uncle Sam.

You can find out more about David's writing, including his current projects, at his website: davidalanjones.net

—

pdmac spent a career in the US Army before transitioning to education as a university Academic Dean. He transitioned again and now writes fulltime. He has a MA in Creative Writing and a Ph.D. in Theology. He is a member of the Blue Ridge Writers Guild, the Steampunk Writers and Artists Guild, and the Georgia Writers Association. A diverse author, writer, and editor, he has also edited a Literature anthology, served as managing editor of an archaeology magazine, ghost-written an autobiography, and has had poems, short stories, articles, and editorials published in various literary journals, magazines and newspapers. His most recent short stories appear in the *Short Story America* anthologies III and IV, *Poets in Hell*, *The Mulberry Fork Review*, and the Fantasy Anthology *Chronicles of Mirstone*. He has also sung back-up for Broadway plays, provided voice for radio plays, and acted and directed theater stage productions. In his off time, he and his wife enjoy cycling, kayaking, and occasionally backpacking sections of the Appalachian Trail. Additionally, he and his wife love to travel, their favorite place so far being Crete, Greece.

You can visit pd's website at
http://www.pdmac-author.com/

—

A.G. Porter is the author of The Darkness Trilogy, a YA Paranormal Thriller, and two poetry collections, Pieces of My Heart and Pieces of My Soul. She is currently writing a spin-off of her The Darkness Trilogy characters, as well as a new YA Paranormal series, The Sacrifice of Ava Black, and her next poetry book. When she isn't writing, she's either busy being the coolest mom on the planet, crafting, or reading. Mrs. Porter lives in Alabama with her husband, Billy, and her amazing boys, Brenton, William, and Garrett.

You can check out her website here:
https://agporterbooks.wixsite.com/author/n

—

Selah J Tay-Song is living proof that if you persevere, you'll catch your dreams. She decided to be an author at the age of six. Today she is the author of the Dreams of QaiMaj series, an epic fantasy series described as magical, poetic and engrossing. When she's not writing, she's stalking the urban river otters that live less than a mile from her home in the Pacific Northwest.

You can check out her website here: www.selahjtaysong.com

As always, thank you for supporting the writing community!